The Gold Trail

A Western Trio

Also by Max Brand
in Large Print:

Sixteen in Nome
Outlaws All: A Western Trio
The Lightning Warrior
The Wolf Strain: A Western Trio
The Stone that Shines
Men Beyond the Law: A Western Trio
Beyond the Outposts
The Fugitive's Mission: A Western Trio
In the Hills of Monterey
The Lost Valley: A Western Trio
Chinook
The Gauntlet: A Western Trio
The Survival of Juan Oro
Stolen Gold: A Western Trio

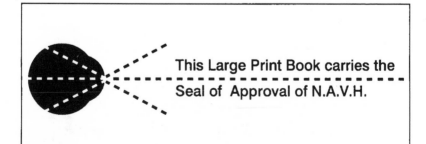

This Large Print Book carries the
Seal of Approval of N.A.V.H.

MAX BRAND™

The Gold Trail

A Western Trio

Thorndike Press • Thorndike, Maine

Additional copyright information may be found on page 360.

Published in 2000 in conjunction with
Golden West Literary Agency.

The name Max Brand™ is a registered trademark with the
United States Patent and Trademark Office and cannot be used
for any purpose without express written permission.

Thorndike Press Large Print Western Series.

The text of this Large Print edition is unabridged.
Other aspects of the book may vary from the original edition.

Set in 16 pt. Plantin by Al Chase.

Printed in the United States on permanent paper.

Library of Congress Cataloging-in-Publication Data
Brand, Max, 1892–1944.
    The gold trail : a western trio / Max Brand.
      p.   cm.
    Contents: Without a penny in the world — Phil, the
fiddler — The gold trail : a Reata story.
    ISBN 0-7862-1587-9 (lg. print : hc : alk. paper)
    1. Western stories. 2. Large type books. I. Title.
PS3511.A87 G65 2000
813′.52—dc21
                                         00-034370

Table Of Contents

Without a Penny in the World

For Frederick Faust 1922 was a year of prodigious output with eleven serials and twenty-nine short stories published — the majority in Street and Smith's *Western Story Magazine*, but in *Argosy/All-Story* and *Country Gentleman* as well. "Without a Penny in the World" was among them, appearing under the John Frederick byline in the October 21, 1922 issue of *Western Story Magazine*. The tale illustrates how the pursuit of wealth can blind people to such a degree that they no longer see the obvious in front of them, as in the case of this story's three main characters — Steve Borrow, Jess Fanning, and his daughter, Jessica.

I
"CONTRASTS"

The consciousness of a good bargain made ran in the veins of Steve Borrow like the warmth of old wine. There needed only one thing to raise the sensation to an ecstasy: that was to have made the bargain for himself. However, every dollar he made for Fanning was in reality a dollar made for himself. When he married the rancher's daughter, he would be heir to the whole estate.

Now and again it would come into his mind, as he reflected upon the deal, that it was hardly fair to have pushed it through while the purchaser was under the influence of liquor. But he shrugged away that weight of conscience. If a man chose to drink moonshine in defiance of the laws of the land and, also, of the laws of common sense, he was not to be pitied, if he made bad business deals. To be sure Steve was a little bit sorry that it should have been an old acquaintance like Harry Cushing who was the unfortunate party to the affair. But Steve believed that business was one thing, and friendship was quite another. He never mixed the two. Where the one began, the other left off.

What he had done was to sell to Harry Cushing, who was the purchasing agent, a great herd of Jess Fanning's beef cattle at an aggregate sum of ten thousand dollars more than a good market price for them. It was the greater triumph because it was the first time that Steve had been sent away with the cattle to make the sale on his own responsibility. It was the crowning act of trust on the part of Fanning, who had advanced Steve — in the process of the past eight years — from common cowpuncher to foreman.

Now he was to advance still further. Every jerk and sway of the train was carrying him closer to the ranch, and on the ranch he would appear as the man who was to marry Jessica Fanning within the month. After that marriage he would be the junior partner. The next step would be the retirement of Jess Fanning, leaving Steve to control the destinies of the ranch.

Once that happened, Steve could expand to greater and greater length. He wanted more land. He wanted to breed up the cattle to a better grade. In ten years he would double the percentage of return. A mist of pleasure dimmed his eyes, as he calculated the sum.

Then, and not until then, he would let Jessica have what she wanted and what she talked of getting at once — a new, well-built, modernized house, with a garage full of automobiles. She might talk as she pleased, but, when he had the reins in his hands, he would drive in a different direction — straight ahead for a rigid régime of ten years' economy. In that time, he would treble the capital, and the income would soar to the skies — and he could afford to give her what she wanted. In the meantime, if she were discontented, she could go sulk in Paris for all he cared. He would not greatly miss her.

At the thought a grim smile twisted his lips and disappeared at once. His face was not one of the kind which smiles readily. It was like the rest of his body, lean, hard, big of bone, iron-like in muscle. Habitually he looked downward, his mouth a straight line, his teeth set, a knot of muscle flexing in and out at each base of his jaw, as if he were preparing himself for some hardy effort. His life had been full of such efforts. He had started as a foundling, with father and mother unknown. He had graduated from waifdom in the streets of San Antonio, drifted farther West, learned that dollars may be added to dollars out of monthly pay envelopes, and formed the good habit of keeping his money so secure that, by the middle of the month, when the other men on a ranch were broke, he had money to lend. If he loaned ten dollars, it was on the consideration that he should get back twelve. Now and then he did not get any money at all, as the guilty party decamped for parts unknown. But when such a thing happened, Steve Borrow, like an up-to-date corporation, raised his rates of interest until the lost money was regained, and then he kept the rates up.

By such means he put by a not inconsiderable sum. He was twenty-one when he started to work for Jess Fanning. Even then he had that unknown thing among cowpunchers, a bank account, and was able to take Jess himself out of a bad hole in the very first year of his work, with a loan of a hundred dollars. It was the only loan for which Steve did not charge interest. He believed that he might get the extra coin in a different way, and he was right. Fanning never forgot. Impulsive, reckless, spendthrift to a degree, Fanning kept that good turn in his mind.

He heard his other cowpunchers complain of the usury of Steve, but he gave them no attention. At the end of the third year Steve, at the absurdly early age of twenty-five, was made foreman. The following year he was given a corner of the ranch and a few cattle to run on the side in his own interest. And he had managed to do the two things — keep the big ranch prospering and manage his own place so that it throve at the same time.

In a region where men usually do not begin to do things until they have reached the age of thirty-five or more years, Steve was something of a boy wonder. At twenty-five it had been predicted that he would "blow up." But here he was, four years later, the most successful ranch manager in that district. By rare good luck, patience, and endless labor he had wiped out a mortgage of thirty thousand dollars for Jess Fanning and piled up a fat account in the bank for his master and himself.

Was it any wonder, then, that Steve could hardly keep from smiling on his way back to the ranch? Yet, he allowed only an occasional twitch at the corners of his lips.

He dismounted at the little dusty station, and the fierce sun that burned through the shoulders of his coat and seared the backs of his sweating hands was welcome to Steve. Yonder came Jess Fanning and his daughter, Jessica, to greet him. For the moment his heart leaped at the sight of the rancher.

Big, fat, brown-faced Jess Fanning advanced with shouts of welcome that brought scores of faces to the windows of the train; and every face was still watching and grinning, when the train pulled out again. For they had seen Fanning grasp the hand and then beat the back of his tall foreman. There was something so infectious in his pleasure that half the passengers in the train were chuckling for no good reason.

"The best li'l ol' foreman in Texas!" Fanning thundered to the world at large. "By guns, I'm glad to see you, son!"

"Father," protested Jessica, "you're swearing in public again!"

"Damn the public!" roared Fanning. "Ain't your sweetheart just come home?"

Jessica flushed a little and said no more. In appearance she was less like the daughter of Fanning than the sister of Steve Borrow. Like him she was tall and lean, with a long, lean face and blue eyes that seemed as sun-faded as her hair. She affected a rather mannish costume, with heavy gauntlet gloves, divided riding skirts, a man's heavy sombrero, a tan pongee shirt, and even a neckerchief, although this was the color of her skirt and not the brilliant bandanna which was generally worn by the cowpunchers. Her manner of showing pleasure at the return of her fiancé was distinctly different from her father's. She greeted Steve Borrow with a single firm handclasp and a single smile, but she had not spoken a word. Only, as they walked toward the waiting automobile, her eyes wandered once up and down the tall form of her lover, and there was a secret flash of approval in them.

When they proceeded to get into the machine, there was a dispute between father and daughter. They could agree about nothing, it seemed. Fanning would have taken the wheel.

"So that you and Steve can sit back there and grin at one another and get some of the foolishness out of your systems," he explained.

"No," said Jessica. "Let Steve drive. You know he's better with the car. Besides, you and he will want to talk business. You sit up there together."

"Talk business? I'll see business damned first," exploded her angered father. "I never seen a girl like you, Jessie. Here comes your lover you ain't seen for three weeks, the man you're going to marry in ten days, and you get enthusiastic like this. Good Lord, Jessie, you been so cold to your father all your life that I sure been thinking you was saving up all the warmth for your husband. But I'm beginning to see that you ain't got any in you. Then what you marrying him for? Just because you can't think of anything better to do?"

Jessica was not the type of a woman who flushes when she grows angry. Instead, a pale spot appeared on either cheek, and her eyes fixed gloomily upon her father.

"Do you think this is the proper place to discuss my affairs of the heart?" she asked.

"Heart!" exclaimed her father. "You ain't got one, looks to me. But tumble into the car, Steve, and do what she wants you to do . . . take the wheel. It ain't hard to see who'll wear the pants in your house!"

Fanning's rough jest pleased him so much that he burst into a tremendous laughter which continued until his eyes were dim with satisfaction, and the lurch of the starting car took his breath. He had been so blinded that he had not noticed the faint half smile with which Steve had heard the remark. Jess Fanning might have doubts about who would control the Borrow household, but Steve himself, it was apparent, had none at all. But even at that moment he had managed to turn in the seat and cast back at Jessica a look which was meant to convey silent compassion for her position, silent sympathy, a silent promise that her time of liberty was not far away.

Steve now sent the machine ahead. It passed through intermediate to a whining high speed, as it shot up the long slope from the station. Presently they were swerving around hillsides, thrusting higher and deeper among the mountains. As the singing of the engine was beginning to throb in his ears, Steve was raised to the seventh heaven.

"Steve," said his employer, "you cleared about ten thousand more than I thought I'd get on those cows."

"Thanks," said Steve. "I guess it was a tolerable fair price, right enough."

"I got an idea that about half of that ought to go to you, Steve. It'll give you a flying start on that little ranch of yours, eh?"

It would, indeed, give him a flying start. With five thousand he could make the last of his payments on the land itself. If the sum were six thousand, he would be able to clear off his last obligation, which was the price of a small herd of cows he had just purchased.

"There's only one thing that bothers me," said Jess Fanning. "I just got a letter from Joe Cushing. He says that the lot he bought in from me looks good enough, but that the price was too steep . . . and he goes on to say that the reason you got Harry to agree to such a price was because you'd got Harry drunk first and sold the cows to him afterward."

II
"BLIND EYES"

For a moment Steve Borrow considered, and then he shrugged his shoulders and said nothing. Such a remark was best unanswered.

"Of course," went on Fanning, "I know that there ain't anything to it. Harry was mad, when he figured that he'd been stung a little on the price. You sure must have talked up the cows to him, and he had to tell something to his father. So he made up that poor yarn about you getting him to do business when he was drunk."

He looked expectantly, but half apologetically, toward Steve, as though by no means willing to believe anything against his foreman, but still feeling that an assurance of some sort would be most welcome.

"You know Harry," said Steve. "He's fond of his whiskey. He puts away a shot of red-eye, when he can get it. I suppose he'd had a few drinks that day. Can I be blamed for that?"

"You sure can't," said Fanning heartily.

"But the yarn that Joe Cushing got from Harry was that you'd taken him into a moonshine dive and stayed there with him until the booze got to working on Harry's head. Then you talked him into buying the cows at your own price."

Steve Borrow moistened his lips to speak, for they had become suddenly dry. On the day of the purchase everything had seemed natural enough. Now, as he looked back, the highlights were heightened strangely, and the shadows were just as strangely deepened. It might even be considered a dastardly thing that he had done. At least, people who did not understand that business was not a matter of sentiment might be tempted to judge him in that fashion. As for men of good, hard sense, they, of course, could not but think exactly as he himself thought.

The car in the meantime had dived over the crest of a rise, and he cut away the flow of gas and let it dip smoothly and silently onto the downslope.

"After all," said the dry voice of Jessica close behind him, "it was just exactly what he deserved. A man who can do no better than lose control of himself and debase his brain with poison. . . ."

"Heh!" roared her father. "Stop right

there! I like a drink as well as the next man, and I guess that I ain't debased. Leastwise, I ain't going to sit still and listen to my own daughter tell me that I am."

"You've formed the habit of never listening to me about anything."

Steve Borrow detached himself from his own problem and listened in an abstracted manner to her. Would she speak in just such a voice to him a year hence? He promised himself that he would find a manner just as repellent.

"Now," continued Fanning, swinging backward toward Steve, "just tell me fair and square . . . did you, or didn't you, do business with Cushing after you'd let him get half soused?"

"What a word!" cried Jessica. "Soused!"

"Will you be quiet?" thundered her irate father. "I'm asking a plain question."

"You're simply insulting Steve, it seems to me."

"Let Steve fight for himself, will you?"

The good nature of Fanning was being turned to acid under her attacks, and Steve, put bluntly against the wall, hesitated. In that course of pure living which he had clung to since his childhood and which he had resolutely cherished, the more he was surrounded by careless men of wild habits, he had not yet told a lie about an important thing. It was one of the things upon which he based his complacency. Even when he had been talking to Harry Cushing about the good qualities of the Fanning cows, he had not told an actual falsehood.

But what could he say to blunt Jess Fanning in this emergency? It would mean an explosion, if Fanning heard the truth. Perhaps he would even disavow the sale and offer the excess money back to Cushing. In that case the bonus would be lost to Steve. Besides, he said to himself, a life of virtue made a single lie forgivable.

"The fact is," he said, "that I didn't drink a drop that day."

But Fanning would have no evasion. "I know you, Steve. You never drink. It might be worse for your head, but I think it might be a little better for your heart, if you did. But tell me . . . did you know Harry Cushing was half drunk when you made that sale to him?"

"Certainly not!" said Steve.

The lie was told, but how could he have avoided it? And who was there to bear witness to the manner in which he had encouraged Cushing's drinking? He had even gone to the extent of pretending to drink with him, while he secretly tossed the contents of his glass away. If a man did not know his capacity in liquor, it was not Steve Borrow's duty to tell him the facts of the case. His mind flashed back to the places where he had been with Harry Cushing during that dizzy little whirl on the trail of moonshine. No, he had certainly not seen a face that was familiar, no one who would be apt to come into this far-off corner of Texas afterward and bear witness against him.

"I'm glad to hear it," said the rancher, breathing hard. "I never doubted you for a minute, Steve. I knew that you'd play fair and square, but it's a weight off my mind to hear you say it. Now I can sit down and write to Joe Cushing. I'll tell him the straight of it."

Just then the car slid into a series of twists and elbow turns, so that Steve Borrow was excusably silent as he worked at the wheel. He needed that silence and the swerving road, so that the flush, which had stolen unbidden to his face, should pass unnoticed. When they reached the bottom of the decline, and he went into second to climb the farther slope, the roar of the engine made conversation almost impossible. By the time they had reached the next crest all was well, for now they swerved out into full view of the ranch. They looked down from the height and could see every detail of the ranch buildings, none left out — all simply reduced in scale by the great distance though which the eye fell.

Here Fanning's good nature at once reasserted itself. He was in view of the home which he loved and had made. Moreover, he was riding beside the man who had made that ranch prosperous — who had brought him his first steady stretch of good luck. He could not resist the combination, and the great car rushed down the long incline with Fanning thundering out a mighty song and beating time to it by clapping his driver on the shoulder.

They reached the ranch house in a truly festive spirit, but, as they started into the house, Jessica found an opportunity to fall back beside her fiancé and whisper to him: "Steve, was it really true?"

He strove to face her, and he strove to answer in assumed sincerity. "Of course, it was true," he whispered back.

But in spite of himself the color crept into his face, and his glance wavered from her searching eyes. He saw her smile a little, as she seemed to estimate him anew. Her smile apparently was the outcome of her discovery.

"Don't be an idiot, Steve," she said.

"Brace up, and see that father doesn't find out. He looks on whiskey as a sort of natural son, and he hates to see anyone abuse it."

She laughed silently at her jest, and then they passed on into the house. Just inside the door she twitched at his sleeve again. "Doesn't it mean five thousand to us, Steve?" she asked. "Is it really wrong to give a drunkard some good reason to regret his drinking?"

There was enough in what she said and her manner of saying it to give Steve a new glimpse of her. All that he saw, he recoiled from. She actually seemed to like him the better for what he had done on that day in Chicago. It gave her more assurance that he would get on in the world and make a comfortable place for her. However, the revelation staggered Steve, and it was a sad-hearted young man who sat down to the supper table that night. Yet, who could be sad for long, when he was hardly ten days from a marriage which made him a prospective millionaire. Before ten minutes passed he was looking at Jessica, and his eyes saw not the actual flesh, but the mist of dollars with which she was surrounded by his thoughts.

III
"INSPECTION"

The week went smoothly, smoothly to Steve Borrow and his bride to be. They spent their spare moments planning the future. As for Jessica, she was very deep in her schemes for the house with which she was to startle the eyes of the natives. As for Steve, he was secretly smiling at the plan and laying deeper ones of his own in which no house at all figured. The old building in which they now lived was good enough for him. Besides, he preferred to please himself with a growing bank account rather than to make a display before the eyes of the neighbors.

"I'd rather have one banker approve of me," said Steve habitually, "than a thousand of the folks who drive past a house and give a gape at it."

Jessica had never heard him say this. If she had, she would not have grieved greatly. In her mind there was no doubt about who should be the dominant factor in the home of Borrow-Fanning. In fact the two were heading as fast as they could for a crash, soon after the wedding. But like most other people, the wedding itself loomed so large that they could not consider themselves in the light of the future which lay over the hill.

So they came to the Monday before the Thursday on which the ceremony was to take place, and the evening of that day found Steve in the midst of his weekly inspection of the bunkhouse. The cowpunchers lounged in front of the bunkhouse, rolling cigarettes and smoking them in gloomy silence. Steve, in the meanwhile, went from bunk to bunk, looking carefully at the blankets, noting the manner in which things were arranged, and making notes. Jessica accompanied him. She felt that it showed a touching interest in his work, an interest which she did not in the least intend to exhibit after their marriage. Steve felt that it was well to let her come and go as she pleased, which was a thing he did not at all intend to tolerate after that all-important Thursday.

From time to time Steve made jottings upon a pad of paper. And she read carelessly over his shoulder: "Mullins . . . dirty blankets. Loftus . . . cigarette butts under bunk. Pipe and dice under pillow."

"I should think," she said, "that they'd hate you for prying into their affairs like this."

"They do hate me," admitted Steve, and he went on to the next bunk.

"But in a country full of men who love free and easy ways," she said, "I should think that you'd find it hard to keep enough men. Don't you, Steve?"

"I don't suppose you've noticed," he answered dryly. "You keep your head in the clouds and pay mighty little attention to the way things go on the ranch. Maybe you've noticed that your father brings out a new man about once in two weeks."

"I don't see how you can keep them at all . . . or do anything with them!" exclaimed Jessica.

"You don't understand," said Steve, and he smiled.

There was something about that faint smile of his that stopped Jessica, as though she had heard a bullet whiz by her ear. In dismay, she stared at him. "I think you're actually glad because they hate you," she said.

"One way or the other," said Steve Borrow, "it makes no difference to me."

"But how can you get them to do anything for you?"

"How does an officer in the Army get men to work for him?"

"But they have to sign papers when they

enlist in the Army."

"I have a better way," replied Steve. "I keep them owing the ranch money. It doesn't take much. I keep hunting until I get regular pay-day men who scoop up their coin on payday and go to some place to spend it, if they can. At first I used to try to keep them away from town. But soon I saw the other way of doing. And now, maybe you've noticed, I dump 'em all into a machine on the first of the month and run 'em into town. They can take a day, or even two days. At the end of that time they may have a new bandanna or two in the crowd, and maybe some fancy clothes, but all of their hard cash is gone. Then I take 'em back out to the ranch and keep 'em here . . . when they get hard up for coin, I let them have a little. It ain't money out of their pay, understand. It ain't anything, but a little private loan on which they pay interest. The beauty of it is that it anchors 'em here. The minute that loan gets bigger than a whole month's pay, they're lost. They'll never be able to pay it back . . . and then I can keep 'em here as long as I please. That's why I keep my men longer than most foremen. Once in a long time one of 'em gets enough to pay off his old debt. And occasionally one of 'em runs away without paying. But most of 'em stay . . . and the reason that we keep a string of new boys coming out is because we're adding to the list as we expand, and I keep on looking 'em over and looking 'em over until I find the ones that are strongest in the back and weakest in the head, the ones that know most about what's best for cows and least about what's best for men. The minute I find a man like that, I buckle onto him and start in advancing him money, and that anchors him here forever. After that he's got to toe the mark and do what I tell him to do. I don't run no loafer's bunkhouse here. I keep a barracks, same as the Army!"

He had continued in his talk without noting Jessica. He had been too full of enthusiasm about his scheme to look closely at her. Now he considered her more particularly, and he saw that she was only beginning to smile.

"No wonder," said Jessica, "if they should hate you."

"They hate me, right enough," chuckled Steve. "I'd rather have 'em that way. I don't pretend to take 'em on here as foster brothers. I take 'em on here as men that got to work for me, and the minute that they let up, I begin to rub 'em hard."

"Yet, I never hear of them trying to fight with you," mused Jessica. "What on earth can be the way you manage that?"

"Men fight their equals, not their superiors," said Steve.

Somewhere he had read that, and he loved to quote it. Again Jessica flashed a sharp glance at him. She was deciding that there were phases of him of which she had hitherto remained in absolute ignorance, for the simple reason that she had never seen him in intimate contact with his work, and in his work was his real life. Although she saw that there was more mental muscle to him than she had suspected, she still felt that, with some effort on her part, she would prove herself his superior. One who was able to exact discipline from others was generally more easily disciplined himself. At least she understood that to be the case.

"For another thing," said Steve, "I've let 'em all know that I would *not* fight 'em. Once or twice, when payday came, a couple of them have tried to make trouble, but I always tell 'em that we've got a sheriff in this county, and that that sheriff is a law-enforcing man."

"But doesn't that make them think that you're a coward?" asked Jessica.

"I don't care what they think," said Steve, and shrugged his shoulders.

A little thrill of wonder and admiration

ran through Jessica. She herself cared but little about the opinion of her fellows, but she had never been able to attain to such a sublime indifference as this. She admired Steve profoundly for it, and she began to dread him a little. A chill of fear ran through her, and it was the first time in her life that she had ever felt fear of anything. Perhaps, at the same instant, the first spark of what might have grown into love flashed in her dry and hard nature.

"You watch me with the new man your father is bringing out tonight," said Steve. "I'll pour him through a sieve and get exactly what I want to know. They'll be here any minute now."

Presently they went out to the front of the bunkhouse. Steve raised the hand that carried the pad and cleared his voice. Instantly cigarettes were lowered. Glancing around the semi-circle of hardy faces, Jessica was interested to see that they were all intensely expectant, intensely worried. One or two managed to summon half sneers to their lips, but none of the sneers was really firm. They were all angry, but they were all a trifle frightened, with the exception of a youngster at the extreme left. The lad yawned in a real indifference, and Jessica was willing to wager that this was the man who was due to be discharged in favor of the newcomer of that evening.

"Rhodes!" said Steve in the sharp manner of one calling a roll.

The youngster whom she had just noticed jerked up his head a little.

"There are three things wrong with the way you've kept your bunk," said Steve. He glanced at Rhodes who shrugged his shoulders and was about to snarl a retort, but Steve quickly cut off his opportunity. "But I guess there's no use dwelling on them. You won't be troubled to stay here much longer. There's no use in my doing the dirty work, getting you ready for some other man's bunkhouse. Mullins!"

Jessica admired the manner in which he skipped on to the next man before Rhodes could muster his anger in words.

"Mullins," went on the foreman, "this is the second time that I've warned you about dirty blankets. I'm mighty careless about the way this crowd gets on with its blankets. I ain't been half as hard on 'em as I used to be on the old crew. But still, you can't keep things up. Have you got anything to say?"

Flushing deeply, Mullins cast a glance around the semicircle. Had there been a single glance raised to meet his own, a single glance of expectant amusement, or scorn, that Mullins should submit to such a discipline, he would have flared into a fighting rage at the foreman. But no eye met his. Each man sat with his head a little bowed. All had been scored in the same fashion before this. All felt, rather, pity and sympathy for Mullins than scorn for him. So they studied the ground and silently hated the foreman who was about to lay on the whip.

"I washed my blankets when the rest washed theirs," said Mullins heavily. "I figured that was doing my job as good as any of the rest."

"I dunno how well you did that washing," said the foreman instantly, darting in at the first opening which was offered to him. "Maybe you washed them blankets just the same way that you broke that pinto hoss for me last month!"

In spite of themselves the men burst into a subdued chuckling. For all of them recalled the picture of Mullins, expert rider though he was, flying into the air out of the wild pinto's saddle. Now they looked up at the faintly smiling foreman. For the next picture that came to them was that of Steve Borrow himself, sitting firmly in the same saddle out of which Mullins had just been pitched, and they agreed, as they stared at him, that he was willing to do whatever he demanded from the hardest worker of them all.

Mullins had colored to the top of his brown forehead. He took off his hat, frowned down at it, and then replaced it, tugging it down so that the shadow from the wide brim fell thick and dark across his face. He said not a word, although Jessica, with her wise eye, could see that he was on the verge of a torrent of speech. But here, clever as ever, the foreman, having gone as far as was safe, refrained from further taunts.

"Loftus!" he said.

Here the roar of an automobile's exhaust, a crackling roar which told of an opened muffler, came close and clear to them, followed by the trailing echo, as the machine swept up the road in the face of the opposite cliff.

"It's Father," said Jessica. "He's come with the new man."

"I'll talk to you later," said the foreman, with a dark glance at Gus Loftus, and he turned with Jessica to meet the rancher.

"You can start talking out right now," broke out Loftus, and he rose suddenly from the sagging box on which he had been seated.

It was a sharp and unmistakable note of

revolt. Loftus, a wide-shouldered, thin-hipped, long-armed type, the perfect ideal of the horseman, glowered at the foreman, and then knocked his sombrero back with a blow of his left hand. His right, hopelessly crippled for the time by a bad rope burn that he had received the week before, hung swathed in bandages which Nell Parker, the good angel of the boys on the ranch, had bound around it. Perhaps it was well that the right hand of Loftus was crippled. At least the foreman took careful note of it. For Loftus was a famous and a deadly fighter. But now the revolver which never left him and which sagged far down on his right thigh was meaningless. He could do nothing with a gun wielded in his left hand alone, and yet he stared at the foreman, with the rage of a born battler.

Steve Borrow whirled sharply around upon him. He felt the crisis in all its far-reaching implications. For the first time, almost, he was being bearded. And here was Jessica to look on. All the long, striking muscles up and down his arms leaped into hard ridges. The hot desire to fight poured through him and misted his brain. All his life he had throttled and fought back that primitive instinct. Now it came upon him for the thousandth time, and it was as strong as it had been on the first day in his child-hood. In the vacant lots of San Antonio his name had spelled terror among small boys. But since those days of bloody fingers and skinned knuckles, he had kept the peace. For one thing he was a silent and grim-faced type that does not invite challenge. For another thing he kept himself steadily aloof. He never boasted, so as to draw comparisons, and he never went out of his way to find trouble. The result had been years of peace. He waited now until the red blur was gone from before his eyes, and until the cords of his wrist stopped trembling under the strain to which they were subjected.

"You've let everything slide," said Steve. "Your bunk is a mess."

"I've done as much work as any man ought to do with one hand," said the cowpuncher.

"Do you need more'n your left hand to pick up cigarette butts?" asked Steve, feeling the hot wave of anger pour into his brain again.

Immediately he felt that Jessica at the side was watching his face eagerly, anxiously taking notes, as it were, of him. He must not let her see too much, to be sure.

"I ain't heard any complaints about me in the bunkhouse," said Gus Loftus, "and it looks to me that what's good enough for the boys that got to live with me ought to be good enough for the foreman."

"The foreman will be the judge of that," said Steve. Then he raised his hand and pointed to Gus. "I'll be back here to talk this over with you later on. You can get anything you got to say ready for that time." Then he turned on his heel. Jessica was watching him intently.

"I'll let him simmer along for a while," said Steve. "When I come back, he'll be cooled down. Gus in the best man I got. I don't want to lose him because he happens to be foolish just now."

"But," said Jessica, "would a man be really foolish if he left this ranch?"

Steve Borrow turned with a faint smile to her. It was he, rather than Gus, who in reality needed time to cool down.

"Of course not," he said. "I work my men harder than any ranch in the mountains. Two men do the work of three for me. That's one reason that your father has got money in the bank."

Jessica smiled, but her smile was lifeless. *What,* she was saying to herself, *would be the attitude of such a man to his wife?*

Certainly it was a matter open to the very gravest doubts. But now they stepped on to the ranch house, just reaching the front verandah as the long, dusty car shot around the curve and came to a staggering halt before them with a scream of the brakes. Jess Fanning always drove an automobile as though it were a bucking horse. He jumped down to the ground.

"Hello, Jessie," he roared to his daughter, and to his foreman: "Hello, kid. Here's your new man. Come, clap an eye on him and tell him what's what. I couldn't even give him the layout of the ranch . . . it's been so long since you've let me do anything around the old place. Steve Borrow, meet Mike Grady. He's worked for the Judsons. He ought to suit even you."

But the foreman, fixing an intent and anxious gaze upon his new prospect, was troubled with a vague uneasiness. Somewhere before he had seen that face, and in disagreeable associations, but he could not recall the place or the instant.

IV
"DUST OF ASHES"

He was not left long in his doubt. Mike Grady had all the proverbial heartiness of his race on the tip of his tongue. A fine, red-faced fellow, he tumbled out of the automobile and, advancing upon the foreman, wrung his hand with a great paw that would be a handy tool at bull-dogging.

"Oh, hello," he cried. "Now ain't this queer! If you ain't one of them I seen in Chicago a couple of weeks back, I'll swear off red-eye! Why, Borrow, I seen you in that moonshine dive of Clancy's . . . you and a little gent with a scar down one side of his face."

"I'll bet that was Harry Cushing," cried Jess Fanning, and at once he bore down upon them. "You saw Borrow and Cushing drinking together?" he asked.

The sudden pallor of the foreman and his tensed lips warned Mike Grady that he had said too much. He attempted to back adroitly from the incriminating talk.

"Well, now that I have a good close look at him," he declared, "I guess that I was

40

wrong. The gent that I seen with him with the scar on his face wasn't within twenty pounds the weight of Borrow and. . . ."

"Nonsense," said the rancher. "You saw them together, and that was just about the time that you and Harry were doing business together. Ain't I right?"

"Come to think of it," said the wretched foreman, "I guess that you are right. Must have been along about that time that I was talking business with Harry."

"In a moonshine dive?" went on the rancher, whirling upon Mike Grady.

The latter cast an unhappy glance at the foreman, but he had no time in which to pick up hints. All he knew was that it would have been a thousand times better had he not introduced the hapless topic. He decided to cover up the issue.

"You see," he said, "the way I happened to be in Chicago was that I got plumb tired of working all my life for the Judsons. I figured that there is something in the world besides sand and bunch grass and cows. So I collected my back pay, sat in and won a stake from the boys at stud, and then blew north to Chicago. What I had with me lasted about two weeks, and then I started south underneath the trains that I'd rode the cushions of going north."

He laughed heartily, and Jess Fanning seemed to have forgotten his original question.

"You step over to the bunkhouse," he said. "Any of the boys will show you where you fit in. Fix yourself up, and, if you want anything to make you comfortable, come up to the house and make a holler."

This speech was most significant. For all of these were directions which Fanning in the ordinary course of events left for his foreman to give.

Mike Grady shambled back to the car, shouldered his roll of blankets, and started on for the bunkhouse, while the rancher turned back to his foreman.

"Steve," he said, with a rather affected carelessness, "suppose you come inside with me. I got a couple of little things that I'd sort of like to talk over with you."

"Father!" cried Jessica.

"Well?"

"You've got the old Nick in your eyes!"

"How come?" asked Fanning.

"You're going to quarrel with Steve?"

"Me? I should hope not!"

"But I can see that you are. And it's all because he told you a little fib a while ago."

"A lie?" asked her father. "He told me a lie?"

"I didn't say a lie," retorted the girl, wincing from the blunt truth. "But there's that nasty little cook spying on us. Let's go into the house."

Steve Borrow glanced up and saw, framed neatly in the kitchen window, the pale and tired face of Nell, looking out at them in fear, as though she had been disturbed by the violent tones of the rancher. Steve scowled at her. She would report all she had heard to the men in the bunkhouse, and that was gall and wormwood to his proud spirit.

"I didn't speak of an actual falsehood," went on Jessica. "But I said that there might have been a small fib."

"What's the difference?" asked the rancher.

They passed into the house and sought the seclusion of the library, that brand new, never-used library, whose precious morocco bindings had never felt the touch of a sympathetic hand. For Jessica was the only reader in the household, and her reading was largely confined to realistic fiction and the magazines of the day.

"A whole world of difference," said Jessica.

"I don't see it," snapped Fanning. "Besides, I can get along without you just now, Jessie. You run along, will you?"

"I'm not to be ordered out like a child," said Jessica. "I certainly have a right to stay right here where I am!"

"You're got a right to do what I tell you to do. Jessie, march!"

Fanning extended his heavy arm in the direction of the door. Jessica watched him for an instant with a thoughtful frown. Then, deciding that discretion was certainly the better part of valor, she suddenly ran to her father and threw her arms around his neck.

"Dad, dear, old Dad," she whispered in his ear, "you won't be too hard on him?"

Instantly Jess Fanning melted. "Sure, I won't," he grumbled. "But him and me have got to have a straight talk, that's all."

Jessica started to leave the room. At the door she glanced back to Steve and saw that he was nervously biting his lip. Then the two men were left to themselves. Now the heavy silence hung like a pall on the room, and every second it gathered a fresh import.

"Well, Steve?" asked Fanning at length. "Was Grady right?"

Steve waited a breathing space. "Yes," he said at length, as great beads of sweat suddenly broke out on his forehead.

Fanning whirled about and strode rapidly up and down the room. It was a silent tribute to the regard he had for his foreman.

Never before had Steve known him to hesitate in the speaking of his mind. At length the older man paused, breathing hard. "Steve," he said, "it's kind of late for us to be getting at the truth of this, ain't it?"

"Mister Fanning," began Steve, "I. . . ."

"Hell!" snapped the other in deep disgust. "Don't start mistering me. I'm plain Jess . . . plain all the way through . . . plain and honest, Steve. You know that. I take a man's word for things. I took your word that Harry Cushing was wrong in what he told his brother. And I've wrote back a letter to Joe Cushing, telling him what I think of him for trying to crawl out of a business deal like he done. Now d'you know what I got to do?"

Steve dropped his head.

"I got to write to him and apologize and tell him that I was wrong, and that I'm enclosing a check for ten thousand . . . because my foreman lied to me! That I'm enclosing a check for ten thousand dollars! Because I'm an honest man, and they're going to get every penny of it back."

He thundered all except the last sentence. Certainly those shrewd, sensitive ears of Nell in the kitchen must be hearing it all. The very soul of Steve Borrow quaked before him. He felt rage at the rancher, too.

Much of this was exaggerated. There was a great deal of injustice in it. Yet, he was determined to control his own rising anger. There was far too much hanging upon a good agreement with Jess Fanning. His whole future might be ruined by the wrath of the other. So he said not a word.

"You done exactly the thing that you swore to me you didn't do," groaned Fanning. "You got poor Harry Cushing drunk. Well, anybody that wanted to could always do that. I know the Cushing boys. They always been friends of mine. I've sold a terrible pile to 'em. And when they knew that you come from me, Harry just took you as being good as gold. Then you get him drunk and make a fool of him." His plump brown hand beat against his forehead. "My Lord, what Joe and Harry must be thinking of *me*, right now."

"Yes, I know," said Steve, "but it was this way, Jess. I tried to keep him from drinking. I sure wanted to get the business through. But he kept insisting on more booze. I didn't want to drink. I kept telling him that. But he had to have his own way. He kept on drinking, and I went the rounds with him, trying to pin him down to business."

"If it had been me," roared the rancher, "I'd've got drunk with him that night, and sold the cows to him, when we was both sober, the next morning. But sooner'n cheat him because he was a good fellow and wanted to buy the drinks. . . ."

Throwing up both arms, he let them fall and clap heavily against his thighs. A host of answers thronged into the throat of Steve. The old fighting rage was driving insults up against his teeth. But he kept them back. He kept saying to himself in a sort of chant: *I got to hold back . . . I got to hold back.*

He was a rich man, if he held his temper; he was a poor man, if he did not allow Fanning to speak his mind unhampered. That was what it amounted to. Having gone this far, Fanning could not do more than spend his anger in words.

"I'm sorry," said Steve humbly. "I'm sure sorry, Jess."

What he wanted to do was to jerk up his head and cry: "You infernal liar! I know how honest you are, now that your bank account is fat! But when you owed money, you were keen enough to drive as hard a bargain as the next one. But, because you were too stupid to get the best of another man, now you preach honesty." Still the words remained unspoken. The rage kept him trembling a little, but otherwise he gave no sign.

"Sorry!" retorted the rancher. "Little

good your sorrow does me now. I got to write that letter to Joe Cushing. I got to write out that check for the ten thousand that you're costing me. Will sorrow write a check for ten thousand?"

"No," said Steve, "I can see what you mean, right enough, and it makes me sick to think that you'll be losing your trust in me, Jess."

"For eight years," groaned Jess Fanning, "I been trusting you like a brother . . . like a son. Now this. . . ." He sighed heavily, then suddenly shrugged his shoulders. "Let it go, Steve. I'll figure it that you simply made that one bad slip. After all, it wasn't to put the money in *your* pocket. You didn't know that I was going to split the velvet fifty-fifty with you. You didn't know that. You were just trying to drive a hard bargain for *me!*"

"That's the way I looked at it," said Steve, still not daring to lift his fiery eyes from the floor, for fear they would reveal too much of what was in his heart.

"Well," went on the other, "I'll tell you what you do. You go out and take a walk, and, when you come back, you have a letter all framed up to write to Harry Cushing. Tell him that you're sorry for pushing that deal through. Will you do that?"

It was the dust of ashes in the mouth of

Steve, but he nodded slowly.

"Then step out," said the rancher. "I'll be waiting for you here."

V

"A FINE FURY"

There were only a few steps across the room and a dozen down the hall, but to Steve Borrow it seemed that there was a mile of agony between him and the outer door. He had been humble before in his life, but never as humble as this. Every word to which he had been forced to listen in silence now began to stab into his soul, as he remembered.

How brutally the rancher had berated him. And the men could hear. The men were sure to hear. They would greet him, when he saw them next, with smiles half masked from him, but patently open to one another. When he sat with them in the cook house during the roundup in the upper valley, they would have remarks to make, veiled remarks clearly intelligible to one another and turned upon the scene with the rancher.

Yes, it would be rare meat for them. Nell would be certain to have forgotten nothing, and what she said would be carefully improved upon. They would embroider the facts with extravagant lies. They would doubtless have him falling upon his knees and begging Fanning to forgive him and not to discharge him.

As he thought of this, he ground his knuckles against the wall, sick with self-contempt, wild with desire to turn and rush back into the presence of his employer, hurl Fanning's words into his teeth, and leave the house no longer the foreman of the great ranch, but a free spirit. Yet he controlled himself, reached the outer door, opened it, staggered out into the open, and dragged down a great breath of air. Then he saw that Jessica was confronting him.

He would rather have faced any other human being in the world. It was she, and she was greeting him with a smile of the most supercilious disdain. She had condescended to speak in his behalf to her father, but now that they were alone together she would make him pay the price of that concession.

"Well," she said, "I see that you're safe out of it, Steve."

Calmly he nodded as he closed the door softly behind him.

"For my part," said Jessica, "if I'd been through what you've been through, I guess there'd be a crime on my hands . . . if I were a man, I mean."

In silence he glared at her, but apparently she wanted to add her weight to that of her father and crush him, since he had been weakened by a first blow. That, indeed, was the cruel intent of Jessica. She had watched him with the men that evening and learned to dread his spirit. Now she saw an excellent opening to strike so effectually that he could never thereafter hold up his head to its full height in her presence. She would stamp her superiority upon him, while he was softened and ready for the impression. It would be of advantage later on.

Yes, in all the years of their married life, she would have reason to be glad that she had crushed him in the beginning. Never should he be allowed to forget that she knew how her father had humbled him.

Certainly it promised to be an easy victory. He merely stood with his head bowed. She was half ashamed to strike again. But there were instincts of the bully in Jessica. She set her teeth and raised her hand, metaphorically speaking.

"If it had been I," she went on, "I should have quit the house and left my father . . . yes, if he had ten times his money."

His head merely dropped a little farther.

To add a new sting, a subtle poison, she went on with a cleverly conceived lie. "I heard every word. I was listening at the door."

At that he started forward and jerked up his head. "Jessica," he said hoarsely, "you didn't do that!"

She merely smiled. In the first place, she was a little surprised to see that there was so much spirit in him. In the second place, she was a little worried to find that her heart ached a trifle because of his silent agony. For Jessica did not intend that her heart should ever rule her brain. She preferred to keep her likes and dislikes purely affairs of the intellect. Therefore, it was that she smiled daintily in his face.

"Of course, I did," she said.

"Was that honorable?" he asked.

"Honor!" cried Jessica. "Do you dare to speak of honor to me?"

It was a little more than she had intended — a bit more of the lash than she meant to apply to him.

"Look here," he said, "you can't rub in things too much. I've got some pride, Jessica."

"You showed your pride, when you were talking to Father," she said.

"Do you think that you can do the same

thing with me?" he asked.

"No," she answered, "because I remember that I am only a woman. However, you shall not bully me the way you bully your hired hands, Steve."

From one side came a faint laugh. Both of them turned — at the corner of the big house, leaning against the wall and blowing away a cloud of cigarette smoke as he laughed, was big Gus Loftus. A red haze poured across the brain of Steve.

"We'll go back into the house, if you don't mind," said Jessica.

"I prefer to stay out here," replied Steve.

Here the laughter of Gus Loftus became open mirth. To Steve that laughter was the mere forerunner, the pointing finger, to the mockery which was to be his portion thereafter on the ranch.

"Get out!" he exclaimed to Loftus. "Get out and go back to the bunkhouse where you belong!"

"D'you own the ground I'm standing on?" asked Gus Loftus. "If the lady wants me to go, I'll go. If she don't want me to go, I'll stay here where I am."

Steve Borrow gasped. "Jessica," he breathed, "tell him to go."

She turned her back on him with a shrug of the slender, thin shoulders.

"If you can't manage your hands," she said, "I'm sure that I don't care to have you coming to me for assistance."

Now Loftus had left the corner of the house and was sauntering forward, grinning.

"Loftus," cried Steve, "go back where you belong. D'you hear?"

But Loftus only laughed loudly, and that laughter snapped something in Steve's brain; or, rather, it was like a drop of acid that suddenly precipitates the solid hanging in the solution. The first note of it jarred through all his being and found a center of nerves and wild rage together. He whirled upon his heel. One thing in the world he could see clearly. That was the point of the jaw of Gus Loftus. All of his muscle, all of his weight shot into the effort. The blow crashed home. And Loftus, without a sound, lurched to the ground, and slid with a grating sound in the gravel, so terrific had been the impact which knocked him down.

There was a faint scream of horror from Jessica. "You brute . . . you beast of a bully!"

Steve Borrow's brain cleared, and he saw, as for the first time, Gus Loftus lying awkwardly upon his side. Presently Gus began to attempt to rise, although he was still blank of face from the blow. As he worked, he tried in vain to push himself up with a bandaged right hand. For the first time Steve remembered. He had struck down a helpless man! The whole horror came over him coldly. He could not move. Then a great hand slammed down on his shoulder and jerked around his nerveless body.

"By thunder," exclaimed Jess Fanning, "you yaller-livered hound! Go pick him up, and then get down on your knees in front of the world and beg his pardon. Why, you miserable. . . ."

The blood raced through the veins of Steve Borrow, and suddenly his brain was clear. Yes, he was able to see all things as he had never seen them before, since he did not pause at the surface, but pierced deep into the heart of them. He looked at Jessica and saw suddenly how withered and prematurely old she was in the face and in the callused heart. He looked to the rancher and saw how vain, how stupid, how outrageously worthless the fellow was. Then he struck away the hand that gripped his shoulder. Fanning gasped, caught his arm where the blow had fallen, and then thundered again: "Borrow, have you gone crazy?"

"Why, you poor, fat-faced fool," said Steve Borrow, and every syllable sent a thrill of the most exquisite pleasure through his whole body, "you blockhead, you yaller-hearted hound, what come into your head that you thought you could put a hand on me?"

He stepped back a little, sneering, and, yet, he felt nearer to laughter than to sneering. He saw that Gus Loftus, now back on his feet, was clear of eye and gaping of mouth. He seemed one walking in his sleep, as he stared at the rancher and the foreman. Jessica, too, had clasped her hands in childish wonder; and the rancher himself was the most amazed of the trio.

Then, making a nice calculation, making it with a perfect coolness and a perfect and perverse joy, Steve Borrow estimated that every word he had spoken had cost him a thousand heavy dollars. Yet money, millions of it, could not be balanced against the exquisite satisfaction. He was still drinking, like a famished man, the expressions of fear and wonder around him.

"I ain't through talking," he said. "But we better go inside to finish it."

Without a word the rancher turned and strode through the door.

VI
"A FREE MAN"

As for Jessica, she did not follow at once. She was not staying behind to comfort the injured cowpuncher. She had turned her back upon big Gus Loftus, whose brain was now totally cleared from the effects of the blow he had received. In fact, the cry of horror, with which she had noted the fall of the cowpuncher, had really not been from sympathy on seeing a helpless man struck down. The blow that struck down Gus Loftus, at the same time knocked her dreams literally into a cocked hat. For she saw, as she stared at Loftus, lying on the ground, that a man capable of doing that would not be a man whom a woman could rule.

It never occurred to her to analyze more carefully. She might have seen that the blow had been struck as the result of an unconscious reflex. She might have seen that she herself was to blame for it, since she had maddened the foreman with her upbraidings and her scorn. But she did not pierce as deeply as that into the causes of things. She merely felt that a man who would strike down a cripple would be capable of doing the same with his wife.

She did not respect Steve Borrow the less for what she had seen him do. Indeed, she respected him more. For she was incapable of respecting truly one whom she did not dread. She despised her father because he was gentle. She had scorned the foreman because he had been quiet in his manner toward her. But now a thrill of fear made her gaze after him with new eyes, and she saw a man whom she would never marry. No, not if the marriage ceremony had been set an hour hence, instead of three days away. Then a consuming curiosity to hear what would now pass between her father and Steve overtook her. So she hastened into the house.

Presently she located them in the library, and, passing on to the living room beyond, she was able to sit down in a chair from which she could look into a great mirror at the end of the room, and in the mirror see, in the reflection through the folded doors, all that passed in the center of the library.

She had missed nothing during her absence from the first part of the scene. The calm brow of Steve was now gathered in a frown, and the horror and amazement of her father had so far kept him silent. The two stood on opposite sides of the heavy library table, staring at one another.

"Borrow," said her father at length, "d'you know what you've done?"

"I've taken water from you," said Steve slowly. "And then I've thought it over and changed my mind about it. That's what I've done."

"You admitted that you'd done something wrong," said her father more quietly than before. "D'you call that taking water?"

"It was, the way you put things up to me."

There was a long pause.

"Have you got anything that you're sorry for?" asked Fanning finally.

Another pause, and then to her amazement, Steve answered: "I got nothing to say I'm sorry about . . . not a thing. I've told you the truth. I'll let it rest there."

"Steve," said the rancher, "don't it appear to you that it's going to be tolerable hard for you and me to get on peaceably together after what's passed?"

"I expect it is," said Steve.

"Don't it look to you like one of us had ought to give way."

"I expect that's what you want me to do . . . but I ain't going to give way, Fanning. I'm tired of taking water from anybody.

Right now is where I begin to be a free man."

The rancher shook his head. "You're wrong there. You can't get along without this ranch, Borrow. You got too much work and eight years of your life tied up here. You can't bluff me like that. I ain't that much of a fool, son."

"I can get along without the ranch better'n the ranch can get along without me," said Steve.

"What?" cried Fanning.

"I mean it."

"You think my hands are tied behind my back? Kid, I ran things before you ever was heard of."

"You were running broke," said Steve quietly. "That's how well you run things."

"You lie!" thundered Fanning, his voice roaring at full volume.

"Don't say that," responded Steve Borrow, and there was a little nasal quiver in his voice — a hard and ringing sound that shuddered home in Jessica and awakened a new fear. "Don't say that," he went on. "You've told me I lied before. You'll never tell me so again. About the ranch . . . I say it was going to the dogs, when I got hold of it. How many thousand have you got in the bank now? Add the two together, and you'll get some idea how much I've done for you."

"You've been working for yourself," said Fanning. "The minute you laid your eyes on my Jessie, you made up your mind that you'd marry her. But by Harry, Borrow, I won't have you for a son-in-law unless you change your attitude."

"It ain't any of your party," said Steve Borrow. "If she wanted me for a husband, she'd have me whether you were for me or against me. That's how much of a man you are, Fanning, and that's how much of a woman she is."

"Are you hunting for trouble, Borrow?" asked the rancher darkly.

Jessica sat up breathless in her chair. Among her faults, cowardice was not one. If it came to a crisis, she would rush in between her father and that terrible wolf of a man.

"I'm not hunting trouble, Fanning," said the foreman. "I'm merely talking facts to you. The truth is that she'll have her way. That's why she was willing to marry me. She figured that because I'd been a foreman for her father, she'd be able to handle me pretty easy."

"Why do you say she *was* willing?" asked Fanning. "D'you think that she's changed her mind?"

"She sure has," said Borrow quietly.

Jessica stiffened in her chair. She was overwhelmingly rejoiced that she had come to overhear this conversation. Her eyes were being opened wide.

"What makes you think that?" asked Fanning. "Has she told you so? So far as what's happened between you and me, there don't have to be no absolute break-up, Steve. You're young, and you've got a hot temper. I know that. We can smooth some things over and forget some of the rest."

Jessica strained her eyes at the reflection of the men in the mirror, and again she was astounded. For Steve Borrow had shaken his head.

"There ain't no way of forgetting," he said. "She's through with me, for one thing. I seen it in her face. I ain't tame enough for her. I don't stand under a tongue lashing well enough for her. She wants a man that'll stand without hitching. As for you, Fanning, I get a terrible bad feeling every time that I look at you and remember what you've said to me today. If I was to live a hundred years, I'd never forget a syllable of it. I ain't built that way."

How much truth there had been in the statement of Borrow that the ranch needed him as much as he needed the ranch, Jessica was now able to read in the face of her father. For he had turned a sickly gray. He moistened his lips. His eyes shifted from side to side. Apparently he was searching his mind for some good excuse for asking Borrow to stay. But he could find none, and Jessica stared in amazement. She had come to take their prosperity for granted. But now she remembered how pinched they had always been for money before the time of Steve's arrival; she could recall how coin had grown abundant, almost at once after the youngster's coming. Would it mean, when he left, that the ranch would run downhill again? Would her father, after living in retirement, so to speak, for five years, be able to take up the reins of management again on a moment's notice?

She began to feel that her late decision might have been taken too suddenly. Better, far better to be the rich wife of a dictatorial man than the poor wife of the most subservient spouse.

"What I want," said Steve, "is to be free. I've been a slave for eight years. For eight years I ain't been able to let my temper go. Today was the first time. But after today . . . why, Fanning, I'd tear you in two, if you was to start to say one tenth of the things that you said five minutes ago. I'm different. I feel different all through. I feel better. I'm stronger. I got no weight on my heart and my head. And it's all because I'm free."

Yes, Jessica thought to herself, *I was right the first time. It's better to die an old maid than to marry such a tyrant as he'd be.*

"You'll break Jessica's heart," said Fanning with a sigh.

But Steve laughed. "Look here," he said. "She's hard as flint, and I know it. The minute she found out I wasn't made of putty, she was through with me. Besides, I guess she knows that I was thinking of money all the time. I wasn't in love with her. I never really pretended that I was."

Fanning made a last attempt. "Steve," he said, "you can't cut loose and live on that little ranch of yours. Look here . . . I could make you easier terms on it, if you was to keep working as foreman. I could give you easier lines to work on, all along."

"I owe you five thousand for that land and another thousand for the stock that ain't been paid for. Well, Fanning," said the foreman, "I've never gambled in my life, but I'll roll dice with you . . . one throw for the whole slice of coin."

Jessica saw her father start. "One throw for six thousand dollars!" he cried. "Steve, are you crazy?"

Steve had stepped to one side on the room, and from a little cabinet he took a dice box and poured the ivories into it. "Aces wild," he said, and banged the dice box on the table, so that it gave out a strong, hollow sound, and the dice jingled and danced within.

"Six thousand dollars!" gasped Fanning, screwing his courage to the sticking point.

"One flop," said the foreman.

"Yes, one flop . . . razzle-dazzle . . . aces wild! Shoot it, Steve!"

Steve spun the dice out on the table. "There's an ace and three threes. That makes four treys for me. Here you are, Fanning." He swept up the dice, poured them into the box, and passed it to the rancher.

"Four of a kind," breathed her father, shaking the box and meditating upon the sound of the jouncing dice close to his ear. "That ain't so bad. I've seen that lose a pile of times."

Here someone called outside the house, and Steve Borrow turned his head toward the sound. As Borrow did so, Fanning made his cast, glanced over the dice, and, before the foreman could look again at the table, the hand of Fanning flew out, turned one of the dice, and he was stepping back with a forced smile, as the foreman faced him once more.

"Four kings," he said, "beat four treys, eh?"

Jessica, sick with scorn for the cowardly trick by which Steve had been beaten, turned her head. She could not watch the pale image of her father in the glass. Then a hot thrill of satisfaction ran through her. Afterward she would tell her father what she had seen, and for dread, lest she should repeat the story elsewhere, he would never dare to oppose her will thereafter.

"Four kings beat four treys all hollow," she heard the foreman saying. "You're six thousand dollars richer than you were a while back. Now what do you say, Fanning? You look sort of yaller around the gills. But have you got the nerve to roll them dice for the rest of what's on my ranch? Listen to me . . . the land and the cows and hosses I got are worth twenty thousand, if they're worth a cent. That's less than Thompson offered me for my share no longer ago than last week. Well, I've lost six thousand, and that leaves me fourteen. I'll shake the fourteen . . . one flop of the dice . . . against the eleven I owe you. Will you take me?"

"Take you," breathed her father suddenly. "There's the dice!"

The box was swept up by the foreman; the ivories tinkled softly on the table.

"Three tens," said the rancher. "Now watch!" There was no fear in him now. The gambling fever had him. He threw with a reckless certainty. The dice jounced out with the lights winking upon them.

"Four kings again . . . four naturals!" cried Fanning. "Son, you don't own no ranch!"

Jessica stared at the reflection of Steve Borrow's face. He was a little flushed, but no one could say that the glitter in his eyes told of a desperate despair on account of his losses.

He picked up his sombrero and jammed it hard upon his head. "Good bye," he said.

"Steve," asked Fanning, "are you leaving?"

"D'you think I'm staying?"

"But, Steve, you don't mean . . . you ain't going to leave me flat like this?"

"Look here," said Steve, "I've paid twenty thousand dollars just now to be free. Don't you figure for that price you can afford to let me go and hire another man?"

"But who else can handle the men that you've got together on the ranch?"

Steve raised his head, and his smile was hard to face. There was a cold and devilish pride in it. "That'll be a little hard, maybe," he said, "but it ain't a thing that I'm worrying about just now. Fanning, you been a rancher for a long time, and now you're twenty thousand dollars ahead of what you were a minute back. I'll tell you another thing." Leaning forward, he brought his unhandsome, strong face closer to the other. "Fanning, I wouldn't swear to it, but it seemed to me that on the first throw, when my head was turned, you flipped over one of the dice."

He waited an instant. There was no answer from Fanning. The older man stared upon his late foreman with a species of terrified horror.

"Well," said Steve suddenly, "I guess that'll be about all."

Then he began to back slowly for the door, stepping through the opening to the hall, and he was gone, leaving Jessica stunned with the realization that the foreman, in departing, had not dared to turn his back on her father — for the latter, shaking with shame and rage, would have been apt to fire upon the defenseless back of the foreman.

VII
"READY TO TALK"

We know little about those nearest and dearest to us, because, by the very reason that they are nearest and dearest, there is no crisis through which we pass with them. They go untested, but, if the test came, how many hearts would ache.

So it was with Jessica. Shrewd and cruel herself, she had always cherished the belief that her father was simply a great, whole-hearted, careless fellow, incapable of doing any living thing harm. But in that brief interview with the foreman, she had seen him suddenly develop all the signs of cruelty and treachery and cowardice.

It sickened her, and yet it made her heart go out to Steve Borrow. She slipped into the hall, and there she encountered Steve. He paused, stared at her, and then dragged off his hat. Somewhere behind him a door banged heavily. Her father was locking himself in, perhaps for fear the terrible enemy might return.

"Well?" asked Jessica.

"Well?" said Steve coldly.

"I've something to say to you," said Jessica.

"I can guess what it is."

"You can?"

"That you think we'd better not marry."

She started. "What put that into your mind, Steve?"

"But isn't it right?"

She hesitated.

"I can make a guess," said Steve, and he smiled in a singular fashion at her. "You were somewhere near, and you heard everything that I've just been saying to your father."

There was no need for her to answer. Her blush did that for her. But she was surprised again to see that he was not angered. He merely shrugged his shoulders. Did he despise her so completely, then, that her eavesdropping was no surprise to him?

"I'm sorry," said Steve Borrow. "I said a lot of things to him because I was hot under the collar. And there was a pile of them that I wouldn't have said about a lady. . . ."

"If you knew that a lady was listening," she could not help interpolating bitterly.

"If I hadn't been plumb wild with anger," he replied steadily. "I'll never forget myself that far again. I was getting something out

71

of my system. It'll never get back there again. For what you may have overheard, I'll tell you that I'm dog-gone sorry, Jessica. It'd do me a pile of good, if you was to shake hands with me and say that there's no hard feelings when I leave."

She looked on him in profoundest wonder. Truly this was a day of revelations to her. Never again would she ever profess that she knew a man's soul. There was a strange generosity and frankness about Steve she had never dreamed was in him.

"How much is left to you after your eight years of work?" she asked.

"This," he said, and drew the heavy Colt from its holster beside his right thigh.

It spun with a peculiar grace and ease in his fingers. She recalled having seen him practice with the weapon, but, although he had shown the very greatest skill with it, it had never seemed to her that there was great significance in his marksmanship. Now it was another matter. The heavy gun glided back into the worn, leather holster, and Jessica looked up with a gasp into his face.

"Your gun," she said, "and the horse you ride on? That's all that's left?"

"What horse?" he asked. "Nope, everything on my ranch is gone. It belongs to your father again. But that don't bother me none," he went on, as she caught her breath. "I got good legs for walking, and it won't be hard for me to do my walking along my own way, with nobody to bother me."

She stood back a little and studied him. It was true. There was nothing in the world that was actually necessary to him. He stood alone, utterly independent.

"Will you let me do one thing?" she asked.

"I suppose so," he said, "so long as it ain't to give me anything."

"It's only a horse. You've always liked that big roan. You can have that horse, Steve."

He shook his head. "I take it mighty kind of you," he said.

"But you must," she insisted. "You've got to take that horse and some money. You have a lot more than that coming to you . . . a whole lot more!"

He looked grimly at her, as though he were busy with conjecture as to whether or not she, too, guessed at the crooked work of her father in the dice game.

"Nobody hears a peep out of me," he declared. "But I can't take your money, or your hoss. The reason why? Well, the reason why is that you don't really own the hoss or the money. It's just something that your father gave you to make you happy. If it come to the point of law, it would turn out to be his. He pays the taxes on that hoss, buys its grub, and hires the gents that keep care of it for you. I'd be taking charity from him, and him and me don't mix that well. We don't get on together, Jessica."

"I think you're a little foolish," she replied stiffly, and feeling that she had certainly done her share.

"Maybe I am," he said. "Maybe I am. But it'll have to stay the way I want it."

"Very well," she said, suddenly eager to have him gone — he and all his knowledge of the shame which rested upon her father's head and hers. "Good bye and good luck!"

"Thanks," said Steve, and bowed so low that he seemed to overlook her extended hand.

Now he was gone down the hall and through the front door. As he stepped on into the outer light, she saw him clap his hat on his head with a sudden violence, and shake back his shoulders, as though he were well out of a disagreeable scene. The stinging truth darted home to her — he was, indeed, glad, very glad, to have stepped out of her life.

And so he was. For, when Steve Borrow closed the door behind him, it seemed to him that he had walked out of a shadow into a region of greater peace, greater brightness. His head jerked up, and his eye kindled, as it glanced away through tremendous space to the pale horizon. As men go, he had been rich five minutes before, and now he was a pauper. But he had a new form of wealth — that kind which a man can carry with him in his heart.

Slowly he walked around the house. First of all, he would go out to the bunkhouse and tell the boys he was going to say good bye to them. Also, he would tell Gus Loftus that, when the latter's hand was well and he wanted satisfaction, he, Steve Borrow, would be only too delighted to come any distance to give him all the satisfaction that was in his power. It would be pleasant to sit down and speak to those men — not as one aloof, but as a hard-handed equal, not too proud to fight.

Full of the joy of anticipation, he came to the rear of the house in time to hear the voice of strong Bud Mullins — a strong voice, too, even when he strove to keep it lowered, as he did now. It floated out clear and distinct through the kitchen window.

"Look here, Nell, it ain't likely that you couldn't hear. Why, that voice of the boss a gent could hear roaring clear out to the bunkhouse, except that the whole thing was over and done with when we come a-running. All we know is what Gus Loftus heard, and all he heard was that Steve Borrow and the boss had a falling out . . . but what it was all about he couldn't tell."

He waited for the girl's joyous laughter and then her story. But no laughter came, only a pause, and then: "I've told you the whole main truth about it. I didn't hear no more, boys. Honest, I didn't!"

"Why, look here, Nell, are you afraid that we'd go and tell him we'd found out from you?"

"Don't be so dog-gone mean, Nell. Loosen up and tell us, won't you?"

That was Gus Loftus entreating her, and Gus was known to be, if not her favorite, at least a very good friend. It was more the power of Nell than the money he owed to the ranch that had kept Loftus with them all these months.

Nell replied: "I don't see why I should tell, even if I knew."

"Why you should? Ain't he been downright mean to you all the time? Ain't it been him that kept Fanning from getting another cook to help you out here at the house? And wasn't it his damned iron face . . . asking your pardon, Nell . . . that said that there wasn't more work for one able-bodied person, and that, if you wasn't able-bodied, he'd get somebody that was able to do it, and glad to do it? Didn't he say that?"

Yes, Steve remembered with a flushed face. He had said that. It had seemed natural enough at the time. Why was it that in the memory it made his heart shrink and grow cold?

"I know that he said that," Nell was saying, "but he said it right before my face. That's why I'm not going to talk behind his back."

There was a groan from more than one throat. All the hands seemed to have crowded into the kitchen.

"Sure takes a lot of nerve," they said, "for a big man to bully a little girl."

"I . . . I'm not little!" cried Nell indignantly. "Leastwise, I'm as big as most."

A chuckle rolled in upon her, and the late foreman recalled that she had always been fighting to make people consider her older and larger. For she had supported herself with the drudgery of a woman's work since she was a child.

"You're big enough, honey," said the voice of Gus Loftus, lowered to a liquid smoothness of flattery.

Why should Gus be so flattering to her? Steve tried to summon up a picture of her against the blank of his mind. But all he could remember was that her hair was slicked back close along the top of her head. As for her features, they were a blur. In his life on the ranch she had simply been the machine that placed before him food to be consumed. He knew her hands far better than he knew her face.

"Don't call me honey, Gus Loftus," said the girl patiently.

"Why not?" asked the big man, while the others chuckled again.

"Because I don't like it," she said. "You know I don't like it. You can't say such things to me."

"God bless you, Nell," said Gus Loftus heartily. "I sure ain't going to talk to you no way but the way you want me to talk. You can lay to that."

There was a murmur of assent from the other men.

"Well," said Gus, "if you don't talk, we ain't got any way of making you talk. But I'd sure like to learn what come to that hound. Him and me, we got a settlement coming!"

"Gus!" cried the girl. "You ain't going to fight him?"

"I sure am going to have a talk with him, anyways," said Loftus.

Steve Borrow stepped out from the corner

of the house and strode up the steps to the open kitchen door. On the inside he saw every one of his men crowded around Nell.

"I'm glad to hear that," he said. "I'm here to tell you that I'm ready to talk to any of you."

VIII
"IN THE KITCHEN"

They spilled back from their closed circle, and all faced him, and he noted, with that new sharpness which had come to his eye, that every man made some sort of a subtle motion to reach his revolver. That was the way they regarded him then — almost as a deadly personal enemy.

"Well, boys," he said, smiling coldly upon them, "it sure ain't hard to make out that you don't lose no sleep worrying about my good."

"D'you expect that we should?" queried Gus Loftus. He stepped forward from the rest.

Nell ran to him and drew him back. "No, no, Gus! You're helpless, ain't you? Don't get him raging."

Steve turned white with self-disgust. "D'you think I'd do him a harm," he asked, "now that he's got a bad hand?"

Nell turned on him, trembling with her anger. "Didn't you hit him before?" she queried, her voice sharp. "Didn't you knock him down? Ain't the mark of it on his face right now?"

Steve moistened his lips. It was hard to face her, harder than anything he had ever done in his life. A singular panic was trembling in him. He wanted to back away through the door and take to his heels, for in this combat he had no weapons against her. "Nell," he said, "one reason that I come here was to tell Gus that I'm sorry for what I done."

"Then tell him," she said, stepping back. "Tell him and let him go. You've done him harm enough."

"Gus," said Steve, "you've heard me say it before. I say it again. I'm sorry I hit you. I sure apologize for it." It was the hardest thing he had ever done — harder even than it had been to face the girl in her passion of righteous indignation.

"I hear you talk," said Gus. "Talk is tolerable cheap, I figure."

On the faces of the other men Steve saw faint smiles of the most utter contempt. They believed, then, that he had come to apologize because he feared what Gus might do when his hand was recovered from its injury. He gasped down a great breath. All things went wrong on this cursed day.

"Gus," he said, "if you want trouble

81

about it later on, you and me can tangle whenever you get well enough to fight. Fight? Why, man, it'd do me a pile of good to have it out with you. But for what I done a while back, in hitting you . . . I got to tell you and the rest that I was pretty near crazy with a lot of things that had gone wrong. I owe you that much explanation, and there you have it. If you want any more, just send for me when you're ready." He turned a little from Gus and faced the others. "That goes for the rest of you," he said. "When I was the foreman of this outfit, I kept away from you. But now I'm neither the foreman of this ranch, nor the owner of a ranch of my own. I got nothing, boys. I'm poorer than the poorest of you. I'm cleaned out down to nothing. I ain't even got a hoss to ride. I've got nothing, but my boots and my gun. But, while I got that gun, I'm here ready to talk up to you, if you got any grudges for what I've done to you."

There was a sort of gasp from the others. Then each looked to the other, as though wondering how this could be true. Before a single man could answer, before even Gus Loftus could frame a retort, Nell stepped between.

She glided in between Steve Borrow and the others, with her hands dropped on her hips and her head high, color blazing in her cheeks. "There'll be no fighting in here," she said. "The whole lot of you get out of my kitchen."

"Nell," said Steve, "I don't aim to start no rumpus here."

"I don't care what you aim at," she said hotly. "What I know is that I'm the boss in my own kitchen. If Mister Fanning ain't man enough to bother me in here, you ain't man enough, neither, nor two like you, nor a hundred like the rest of you!" Suddenly she pivoted and whirled upon the others. "The whole lot of you get out," she cried. "I'm tired of your gabble. You get out and move quick."

"Aw, Nell . . . ," began big Loftus in protest.

"G'wan!" shrilled Nell. "This ain't the range . . . this is my kitchen. Start moving!"

Move they did, shamefacedly glancing aside to one another and then laughing without heart in their mirth. But Steve Borrow, as he moved on the heels of the others, was caught by the shoulder and waved back.

"You stay right inside here, and wait till the rest of 'em have scattered," said Nell. "I ain't going to have my doorstep all messed up. It's as bad as the kitchen floor, pretty near."

He backed into a corner as the others herded out, and Nell banged the door behind them. Then, although he was looking at her back, he saw a change come over her. She seemed to wilt and shrink. She sank into a chair as she turned back toward him, and there she lay inert, with her head fallen against the wall and drooping a little to the side, as though she had not the strength to hold it straight. The color had snapped out of her cheeks, the glitter out of her eyes.

"I'm glad that's done," she sighed wearily, as she looked up to Steve Borrow.

"I don't believe," he said thoughtfully, "that you were mad at all. It was just acting to get them out of the kitchen . . . get them out and save my hide."

"What do I care about whether you're saved or not?" asked Nell. But there was no life in the manner of her speech.

"Sure you don't," said Steve. "It was only for the sake of keeping a clean floor." He grinned broadly at her.

It was a new expression for Steve. He had not smiled so broadly in years, and the smile came from the tickling of something in the very heart of him. After the smile there was a welling of bright good nature, like sunshine pouring through his spirit.

As for Nell, she pushed herself into a more erect posture and blinked at the late foreman. "Well," she said, "you're a queer one. There's something to you, after all."

That remark wiped the smile from Steve's face. It implied so many things that he needed long moments of reflection. Most of all, it brought home to him a stunning truth — that the cook whom he had scarcely deigned to look at during his reign on the Fanning ranch had all the time been looking straight into him and seeing nothing worthwhile.

No sooner had she spoken than she clapped her hands over her mouth, as though to recapture words that were already flown. Over the edge of her hand her eyes grew great, as she stared in apprehension at him. "Oh!" she gasped at last. "I shouldn't have said that!"

Steve Borrow laughed, and he was amazed by his own laughter. An hour before, had such a thing been said to him by the cook, he would have gone straight to Fanning and demanded her instant discharge. For, as he had always said, men who did not respect him could not work for him. But now he found himself delighted by the very spirit which had scoffed at him.

"Now that you've said it," he replied, "let

it go. I suppose you've kept that bottled up for a long time, and it simply had to pop out."

"I suppose so," said Nell. "But now that I've said it, I see that I'm all wrong. I shouldn't have said it at all."

"Come, come," said Steve Borrow with a faint frown. "You can't absolutely bamboozle me, you know."

"But I mean it," said Nell. "I . . . I don't know what's happened to you, but you're changed."

"I've got an idea," said Steve, watching her narrowly, "that you know exactly what's happened to me."

A brilliant blush suffused her cheeks. She was wonderfully changeable, wonderfully impressionable. It seemed to Steve Borrow, as he watched her, that she must live thrice as hard as common people, since she put so much soul into every new shadow of emotion that crossed her path.

"About you having trouble with Mister Fanning . . . yes, I heard that. I couldn't help hearing that . . . what with his voice . . . but I didn't listen behind no doors, Steve Borrow!"

"I know you didn't," he said very gravely. "You're a lot too good for that." He paused, for he discovered that he had come into her kitchen without removing his hat. Now he took it off, and, while he stared at her, he began to turn the hat slowly in his lean, brown hands.

"Staring at folks, that ain't particular polite, is it?" asked Nell suddenly, and she laughed in soft embarrassment.

"I guess maybe it ain't," acknowledged Steve Borrow. "But I was thinking about something. How come that you didn't tell the boys as much as you knowed about me and Fanning fighting?"

She looked down to the floor and dropped her chin upon her little clenched fist in thought. "I dunno," she said at last. "But what right have they got to know what's happened to you? When you were up, they were afraid to yip at you. When they thought that you were down, they come and start snarling. Why, it made me sick. I'd a pile rather be a coyote than a man the likes of them!" Now her eyes shone at him.

"By Harry!" cried Steve, the words pouring out without his conscious volition, "you're square . . . you're fine!" He thrust out at her a hand which she took and pressed with a blush and a slight smile.

"I suppose I ought not to let you tell me such things."

Again he found himself laughing. It was

singularly easy to laugh while she was near. He sat down, the better to enjoy her, but instantly she was up.

"You better be going, I reckon," she said.

"How come?"

"Well . . . you been here about long enough, Steve Borrow."

"I dunno," said Steve. "I ain't tired of you. Are you tired of me?"

She struggled with a laugh and barely managed to suppress it, although it left her eyes shining at him.

"It ain't right for you to stay, though," she said. "They'll be started talking before long."

He understood the inference, and, although it angered him to the heart, yet he turned it off with another smile. "They'll think that I'm afraid to come out, that's all," he said. "Maybe you're thinking that, too?"

"I don't figure that they think that," she said. "I guess since they seen you a minute ago they've been doing a pile of thinking about you and what you are. I watched Gus Loftus's face, while you were talking. He didn't seem none too pleased with himself. I figure that even when his hand gets well he ain't going to pester you with no calling cards of his."

Again she smiled that twisted little wise

smile, and again the sight of that smile saddened him for reasons that he could not quite make out.

"How old are you, Nell?" he asked.

The sudden question took her aback. She sat down and frowned at him. "How come you to ask that?"

"Why, I'm just interested."

"Well, I'm twenty-four . . . was twenty-four in March."

"If you was a man," he said, "I'd call that a considerable lie, Nell."

"What?" she cried, and her eyes defied him. "What are you driving at, Steve Borrow?"

"Twenty-four years?" he echoed. "Why, you ain't more'n twenty!"

"You don't know what you're talking about," said Nell. But she winced, and that wincing meant more than the words she had spoken. He rose from his chair and stood accusingly above her.

"You ain't even twenty," he gasped. "By heaven, you ain't even twenty!"

Now she shrank away and literally cowered in the chair. The more he stared down at her, the more he saw the truth of what he had spoken. For the little lines of age here and there in her face were the lines which weariness will run. But most of all there was something about her meager throat and her bosom that spoke of girlhood. He began to look back fiercely and swiftly into his past. He began to recall a thousand stern and impatient things he had said to her. They returned now and struck like a thunderclap upon his brain.

"My guns," he cried, "you ain't no more'n a kid!"

"Oh, no," pleaded Nell, "I'm full nineteen. But don't you be telling nobody. I can work as well as any growed woman. But . . . but they'd fire me if they knowed I wasn't older . . . and please . . . you ain't going to tell nobody? I swear I'm nineteen, Steve Borrow, on my word and honor!"

IX
"NELL'S GIFT"

Pity was choking him, and he could not speak. In his confusion he began to moisten his lips and to strive to draw a deep breath. With half of his attention only he heard her voice.

"I'll make a bargain with you," she was saying. "You don't tell nobody about me not being twenty, and I'll give you that hoss of mine, that Lady hoss of mine out in the corral. I'll make that bargain, Steve. You need a hoss to ride, if what you said is the truth, and I sure need a place to work, and I'm so used to this place and all the boys, and I don't mind Miss Jessica much, and it'd break my heart to go to another place . . . it'd be worse than the first day at a new school."

The words came tumbling out in a heap, and she was almost sobbing with fear. Still he was thinking back to other things. If she was only nineteen now, how old had she been when she first came? She had seemed a work-worn, taciturn young woman even then, but now he knew that she had been merely a gangling, half-starved child. He remembered how weak she had seemed, and how he had blamed that weakness upon a small spirit and laziness. But all the time she had been simply a child — simply a child.

It moved him as he had never been moved before. There sprang into his mind, why he could not tell, sudden visions of children — bright faces he had seen at doorways as he rode past. He had paid no heed to them then, but now he discovered that they had been printed in his heart of hearts. He looked down, and what he saw, clearing through the haze that obscured his sight, was the work-scarred hands of the girl.

"Nell," he said, "I ain't going to say a word to nobody. I ain't going to say a single word. And I don't want that hoss of yours. Why, that Lady hoss is worth a pile of money to you, Nell. Besides, she's your partner. You keep her. I'll manage my own way. There's lots of places where I'll get a hoss to ride, and darned good wages for riding him. That is, if I feel like working."

She forgot her fear, but not all at once. Only step by step she drew away from the terror of betrayal, and still the shadow of it was lurking behind her eyes.

"You won't say a word, Steve?"

"Not a word. My word of honor goes on that."

"Then shake on it."

He shook hands with her gravely. Then in her great relief, tears rushed into her eyes. "You're all right, Steve," she said. "You're mighty square. Why . . . why . . . I've heard Mister Fanning say that he wouldn't have anyone under twenty on the place . . . not for a minute."

He stood back from her.

"Well," he said, "I'll be going. So long, Nell."

"Steve!"

He turned and found that concern was in her face and her hands were clasped.

"Steve," she said, "I just been thinking what a mighty sad thing it is for me that I didn't know you all these years when I been needing a friend."

"You're all wrong, Nell," he assured her. "I wasn't worth knowing before today. I was just a hound. I was too darned mean to be worth shooting. Them are the facts. It took today to bust the shell off of me and show me the insides of myself. If there's anything decent in me now . . . well, I've got to find out. Leastwise, I'll tell you this . . . I'm a pile happier now without nothing, than I ever was when I had a little ranch of my own and was running this big place."

"D'you mean that, Steve?"

"Every word. When I had all them things, I couldn't think out a sentence that didn't begin with a dollar sign. All them years I never was able to do as much as I've done today, and that's what makes you look at me like you are sorry to see me go. Is that right?"

"It sure is, Steve. And. . . ."

He came back to her and dropped his hands on her firm, strong shoulders. "I'm going to blow around and take a look at things," he said, "and then I'm coming back."

"I'll be expecting you, Steve," she said. "I sure will. When you go outside, are you going to get into trouble with the boys?"

"Me? I hope there won't be no trouble."

"I'm going along," she declared.

"You? To take care of me?"

"I'm going along to . . . to . . . to give you Lady," she said, fumbling for something until she found it.

"Give me Lady! You don't mean it, Nell! Why, Lady is the finest hoss on the range, pretty near. When she gets a saddle on her and gets broke, she'll burn up the ground, Nell. She's a speedster!"

But Nell persisted, shaking her head.

"How would I look on a hoss like Lady?" she asked. "Lady has been fine for a pet. But look how big she is! She's sixteen three, pretty near, or sixteen two, anyways. That's a whole hand higher than the sort of a hoss that I like to ride. But under you she'd be just about right."

Steve Borrow considered her gravely. His heart was leaping at the thought of Lady, but still he hesitated.

"You're only talking," he said. "You're just giving me Lady because you know I'm broke and need a hoss and she's yours to give."

She answered by throwing the door open. "You come along!" she cried, and tugged at his arm.

Far away, sitting in a row, like crows on a fence, he saw the cowpunchers ranged, waiting for his reappearance. He could not stay and argue with Nell under such conditions, and so he went out with her and walked down the steps and straight across toward the corrals, among which he marked the small enclosure where Lady stood, the sleek chestnut glimmering even through the dusk.

In the meantime, as they passed the cowpunchers, the men became furiously busy whistling, or sending up clouds of cigarette smoke, or anything else which would make them seem indifferent. But plainly they could not make out the reason for this sudden interest of pretty Nell in the fallen foreman. When the pair passed on toward the corrals, the cowpunchers detached themselves from the fence rail and began to saunter idly in pursuit, grouping themselves here and there, but managing their movements so that they continually kept Nell and Steve in view.

X

"LADY'S FIRST LESSON"

Lady was busy touching noses with a wise old gelding in a neighboring corral, a broken-down veteran still worth his weight in gold for half a dozen priceless days at the roundups, when his fine spirit and his cunning brain carried him through the labor, but utterly worthless for a long campaign of range riding. With him Lady was conversing as horses do, pricking their ears and touching their sensitive noses and now and then taking a half mischievous, half playful nibble and tossing their heads high thereafter to avoid retribution.

Nell rested her elbows on the fence and watched for a moment. Then she called. Lady tossed her head, reared, wheeled, and came at a gallop so fast that she had to brace her legs at the end of the run. As she slid to a halt before them and shook her head, snorting, because of the presence of the man, Nell stretched out her hands, crooning with delight.

"Ain't she wonderful, Steve?"

"She's the best hoss I ever seen," said Steve with heartfelt gravity. "She's got enough bone and muscle to carry two hundred pounds through the mountains all day . . . unless she's been spoiled and got wrongheaded from too much petting."

"Too much petting?" echoed Nell.

"Sure," he said, "because that spoils a horse. Here she is, a big, strapping three-year-old . . . or ain't she pretty nigh to four?"

"Yes, she's four. But what's wrong with her?"

"She's had her own way too much. She wouldn't stand it, most like, if she got her orders."

"Why, Steve Borrow, look at this!" Nell slipped between the bars and into the corral. Lady danced joyously around her, carrying her sixteen two of solid bone and heavy muscle as lightly as a frisking dog. "Stand!" Nell ordered. Lady was suddenly turned to stone. "Up!" Nell stated next, and waved her hand aloft. Up went Lady on her hind legs and hung trembling and balanced aloft. "You see?" said the trainer, and, as she spoke, she walked under the dangling forelegs of the great mare and so stepped away again, while Steve Borrow gasped.

"Down!" Lady dropped lightly to all fours, and then fumbled at the hand of the mistress for sugar, got none, and tilted one ear back quizzically.

"She's a pretty neat trick horse," said Steve, "but what would she do with somebody on her back?"

"I don't know," said Nell. "I've never had the time to break her. I've always kept putting it off. But she doesn't mind bareback. You see?" While she spoke, she led Lady to the edge of the corral and, climbing up on the fence, slipped onto the rounded back of the chestnut.

"Now, girl!" Off went Lady at a smart trot which ended at the first word of command.

"And I've never seen you working with her," murmured Steve. "How come that?"

"Because I've never had time during the day. There was always too much to do. But I've come out after dark, and we've had our fun then. Nice old girl!"

She slipped down from the back of the big horse and walked again toward Steve, and the mare followed. When Nell stopped on the farther side of the fence, Lady stopped behind her, and above her shoulder raised a lofty head and stared at Steve, with eyes that glimmered through the evening shadow.

"And you still mean it?" asked Steve. "Still want me to take her?"

"With all my heart," said Nell.

"By the Lord, then," cried Steve softly, "I'll tell you this . . . I'd rather have that hoss than a hundred thousand!"

"Truly?"

"Because she means more'n money. It means that, when I'm on her, I've got the foot of everything in the mountains, pretty near. But the first thing is the breaking of her, and the talk comes afterward."

He thought that Nell was about to speak, but she changed her mind and said nothing, while he went off to the barn and took from the peg his own saddle. That, with all else that was his, really belonged now to Fanning, but out of twenty thousand dollars Fanning would certainly spare him one saddle. He returned, carrying it slung over his arm, and found that by this time the cowpunchers had closed up to the fence and were talking with Nell.

"But," said someone, and he thought that he recognized the voice of Mullins, "I dunno what to think about a gent that takes presents like that from a girl that don't know no better."

"That's the way with some hounds," said another. "They sneak around and talk pretty, and they get on in the world that way. They talk big till they. . . ."

Steve had stepped a pace toward the

group, and then paused. "Look here," he said, "I can hear you boys talk. Now, if you aim to talk like that so's to make me understand what you think about me, you don't need to waste all that strength and word power for nothing. I know you hate me, and I know why you hate me. So that settles that. If you're just aiming to rile me by talk like that, I'll tell you this . . . that I don't get riled up easy, but that, when I do . . . now that I ain't the foreman and don't have to think of Fanning's interests . . . I'm going to do no arguing. I'm just going to grab for a gun. Is that straight? D'you understand that?"

He had spoken in the most reasonable manner, and now he waited. So that if any one of the crew wished, he might step out and pick the fight for which they seemed to be waiting. But no one stirred. The murmurs died away to silence. Each man shrugged his shoulders and made himself busy in one way or another, either rolling a cigarette or smoking one, or staring at the mare on the farther side of the fence.

At length, when no voice spoke, he turned again to the corral, climbed the fence of it, and dropped his saddle and bridle upon the topmost rail.

The saddling was easily done. For Nell

kept the head of Lady in play with her talk and her patting, and the big mare only swung about two or three times when the saddle was set first upon her back and the cinches were drawn taut. Then she reared, with her ears plastered back against her head, but that was all. At the command of Nell she dropped back again and with a snort or two submitted to the punishment of those biting girths.

The bridling was a little more difficult to manage. Lady had ideas of her own about the freedom of her head, and, when the hands of Steven Borrow reached up toward her ears, she would swing away and even rear to get out of his touch. Yet it was managed in the end, and there she stood, tossing her head, working her ears whimsically back and forth, more like a mule than a horse, and keeping the bit in play, so that it never stopped chinking. She was fretting to and fro, also, acting as if her feet were sore, and she wished to keep changing the burden of her weight from one support to another.

Steve now unbarred the gate, approached Lady, and placed his foot in the stirrup. At this she swung her head about and sniffed him from hip to shoulder. But, as she was swinging her head back to face the front again, he raised himself with a lurch and dropped lightly into the saddle.

Beneath him Lady sank, as though the muscles of her back could not endure the weight. He felt her crouch and tremble, like an immense cat, beneath him.

"Steady, Lady!" cried Nell.

At once the mare stood up, snorting, and stretched her head eagerly toward her mistress. But Steve Borrow drew her head in again, ruling her with a stern curb.

"Never mind," he said to Nell. "I'll handle her, I guess. Take 'em by and large, horses are like kids. They got to be *made* to mind, not coaxed into it."

"But," cried Nell, "Lady has a terrible temper, and if you anger her. . . ." She paused, breathless.

"Nell," said the ex-foreman, "it's five years since a hoss has throwed me, and I break 'em every roundup! Don't you worry about me and Lady. Move along, girl."

But Lady, when he shook the reins and spoke to her, simply braced all four feet, lowered her head, and stood fast.

XI

"THE END OF THE CONTEST"

There came a slight chuckling from the men, and a few low oaths of expectant excitement.

"Step out, girl!" Steve said, growing a trifle angry.

Yet he was rejoiced to meet resistance. In the days of his high office on the ranch he had never dared to let himself go. The strong, hot temper, which was continually on the point of bursting forth, he had been compelled to control and restrain with an iron hand. Now he felt that he could do as he pleased. There was no need for him to set an example. He was free, wonderfully and beautifully free to use his whole strength and to use it as he pleased.

From the long years of repression it seemed to Steve Borrow that there was stored up in him an incalculable force of electric energy, stored as batteries store a current, and now ready and waiting to be loosed in a wild abandon. He waited another instant. He looked to the side. Nell had buried her face in her hands. How

104

could she guess that a battle royal was about to commence? At any rate he touched the mare with the spurs.

It was like touching a match to a sky-rocket. Lady left the ground and headed toward the nearest star that was just beginning to burn down into view through the late radiance of the evening, now dying in the sky.

As for the unbarred gate, she paid no attention to it. There was another part of the fence nearer, and the fact that the fence was high made no appreciable difference. She cleared that fence with the first tremendous bound, sailed into the unfenced, open beyond, and then straightway started to jump imaginary fence after fence, shaking herself violently at the height of each leap.

Steve Borrow sat motionless in the saddle and chuckled to himself. He could break the heart of any horse that ever lived, if it trusted to straight bucking to get him out of the saddle. Then there was a stronger jar and a lurch to one side. Now the leap into the air was straighter up — solely an effort to gain height, with no attempt to cover ground ahead of her. And when she landed, it was upon stiffened forelegs. In a word gentle Lady had begun to sunfish.

As she did so, there was a groan of recognition and appreciation from the cowpunchers, every one of whom had been racked in the saddle by that most deadly form of bucking. But the groan changed into a shout of excitement, as Lady added another fine flourish to her style of bucking. She began to land upon only one forefoot, and the result was that, after the shock which snapped his head forward and threatened to break his chin against his breastbone, there was a secondary blow that twitched his whole body to the side, like the snapping of a whip, and flung his head convulsively over on his shoulder.

It was the most improved and deadly form of the most terrible sort of bucking, and the cowpunchers cheered and groaned in unison: "A sunfisher! Get her, Steve!"

For most horses, once they have found their proper style of bucking, usually stay by that one form. Since Lady had so suddenly and unexpectedly developed these talents in bucking, there was not a man present whose heart did not go out to the tortured rider.

But Steve Borrow seemed almost to welcome that fierce battle. Disdaining to cling to the girth with his spurs, he used them, instead, to urge the mare to new efforts, and at the same time his heavy quirt slashed her on shoulder and tender flank, or else he swung his legs back and forth and rolled the pricking rowel along her neck and again far back on her haunch. Indeed, he was riding, as befitted one long known as the finest rider who ever drew on gloves for the Fanning outfit.

But every plunge of the great horse was a hammer blow at the base of his skull and a spine-breaking wrench to the side, and under that relentless assault Steve felt himself weakening. It was no sudden defeat he saw in prospect. There was still a hope that he might outlast the mare. But she seemed to possess inexhaustible strength, or else it was as if the earth she touched refreshed her strength. At any rate, up she went, as though driven from tremendous springs, with wild squeals of rage and hate. She was bucking with the strength one would have expected of her size, but she was bucking with the agility, the handiness, the tirelessness of one of her mustang ancestors, before the hot blood of the Thoroughbred had crossed and recrossed upon her stock. But in the pinch she reverted to the older type. The sixteenth of her that was mustang suddenly possessed her whole heart.

How Steve first knew that he was beaten was by the fact that he could not hear the shouting of the men. Or were they actually silent in wonder? Next he could not swing his spurs to rake the mare's sides. And finally he could not wield the quirt except feebly, ineffectually. Still the hoofs of the mare thudded in the soft dust, and still that dust rose, scorching and stinging his throat and nose with its alkali fumes. Still Lady was hurling herself as high, it seemed, as ever, and the blows fell ever thicker and faster on his brain.

But the reality was far other than it appeared to the rider. Now Lady was bucking in one place, and around her in a circle gathered the cowpunchers, whooping and shrieking like demons. For this was an outlaw in the making. Not one of them, except Steve himself, could have sat the saddle in the face of such a struggle. The longer he stayed the more they yelled.

Now they began to see victory for him in sight. For Lady was pitching with less and less violence. To the stunned, sick brain of Steve it seemed that he was being flung as high into the air as ever, but in reality the leaps of the mare were almost ludicrous imitations of her former efforts. Her head was hanging; her squealing had stopped, and now she grunted and groaned with each shock against the earth. She was swaying a little from side to side in her growing exhaustion.

Nell, frantic with excitement, strove to reach the horse, shrilling: "They're killing each other! Don't you see? Stop it! Let me get to Lady!"

But the cowpunchers forgot all courtesy. They knew that even now, if it were heard by the mare, the voice of her mistress would end the battle. So they raised their own voices and shouted her down and barred her away from the inner circle, where the clouds of dust that Lady knocked up were drifting thick and white upon the air.

Lady was reeling drunkenly, yet keeping to her work with a gallant abandon. Still in the saddle, Steve Borrow reeled back and forth and with a feeble hand struck at the air with his quirt, doing no harm to the mare, but at least defying her to do her worst.

There was something sublime, something ridiculous about it, until with a groan Lady dropped down from her last leap and stood motionless, with her four legs braced wide apart and her head dropped to the dust — a figure in stony white, with a white rider sitting limp and drooping in the saddle, for the dust had powdered them both thoroughly. There was a last frantic yell of triumph from the cowpunchers. After that the voice of Nell broke through the comparative silence, calling: "Lady! Poor girl!"

Now the wearied, beaten mare gathered her trembling legs under her and stepped, staggering, toward the familiar voice of the mistress. The cowpunchers gave way. They let Nell run to the horse and throw her arms around the dusty head. But Steve was no longer in the saddle. At the first forward move of the mare he had swayed far to the side, lurched, and then pitched to the ground on his face.

The cowpunchers, who hated him, picked him up, wiped from his face the dust, and carried him to a place beside the watering trough, where they could splash water over him.

Suddenly one of them came running to Nell. "Nell," he exclaimed, "Steve ain't waked up. You know about them things. Won't you . . . ?"

"I hope he's dead!" she cried. "Oh, see what he's done to Lady! See . . . oh, I hope he's dead!"

"I think he is, Nell," said Mullins, for it was he.

Her change was femininely sudden. "You don't mean that? Oh!"

In a flurry of running she reached Steve and dropped to her knees and pressed her ear against his heart. There she crouched for a time, and then she sat up and raised a hand to the silent, awed cowpunchers.

"Boys," she said, "he's all right. He ain't dead. He's just shook up a pile. Will you get a couple of blankets for carrying him into the house . . . and some water fit for him to drink . . . and a little whiskey . . . quick!"

They scattered into thin air. When Steve Borrow opened his eyes, he looked up and saw between him and the stars only the face of the girl. Just behind her and above her shoulder was the head of poor Lady, still trembling. But no one else was near. He closed his eyes again.

"She beat me," he said. "She beat me, fair and square."

He heard her sob: "Oh, no, you beat poor Lady! She stopped bucking before you fell."

He drew in a great breath. "Nell," he said, "you ain't saying that just to make me happy?"

"No, no."

"Then, thank heaven," gasped Steve. "It . . . it's a terrible thing, Nell, to get beat for the first time . . . even by a hoss." He opened his eyes again a little later. "Nell," he said, "I was aiming to hit the trail alone. But I wonder, would you come along?"

"Hush up," breathed Nell. "You ain't strong enough to talk so much. You're talking kind of silly, Steve."

"Honey," said Steve, "I can feel your hand under my head, trembling."

"Oh, Steve," murmured the girl, "I'm nothing but a cook."

"And I ain't a got a penny in the world," said Steve Borrow. "Nell, that's why we'll fit."

Phil, the Fiddler

Published in the December 30, 1922 issue of Street & Smith's *Western Story Magazine*, "Phil, the Fiddler" was Faust's last published story of that year. It appeared under the George Owen Baxter pseudonym. It is a family drama in which is chronicled a fatal division of the Rivals — of Joshua, the stepson of Henry Rival, cousin to Phil, the Fiddler, and a "fearless truthteller" in the twenty-eight years of his life. Once Joshua proposes marriage to Hilda Surrey, the trouble begins.

I
"JOSHUA DECIDES TO WED"

Those who doubt that the name chosen for a child influences its character must have admitted that, if the name did not make him what he grew to be, then Mrs. Rival possessed a touch of prophetic insight when she looked into the Bible and found for her newborn son the name of Joshua.

He grew up tall and straight, wide-shouldered, thick-throated, deep of brow, and dark of eye. He stepped into an early manhood. While he was still a scant fifteen, his fellows ceased calling him Josh. From that time on he was known solely as Joshua, and Joshua alone. No one dreamed of using his last name. Rival was unheard, but through the ranges he was known as Joshua. Not that he achieved his reputation through battle, but one glance of his solemn, black eyes had power to send a shiver up the spine of the merrymakers. So they called him Joshua.

His elders had dreaded him even in his childhood because of a trenchant tongue that spoke the truth and shamed the devil in them on all occasions. He was a fearless truthteller, indeed, was Joshua. And although men loved him for it the less, they respected him the more. He became known, moreover, as an upholder of righteousness. When he denounced wickedness or exalted goodness — which he did upon slight provocation — men and women and little children listened to Joshua's words in wonder and fear. On such occasions he stood straight and set his jaw and half closed his eyes and raised his handsome face — it seemed that an almost divine spark dwelt within him.

Not that his life was entirely an expression of spiritual righteousness. He could look behind the face and form of spiritual things with fully as sharp a glance. For instance, he was great in a horse trade. By his adroit management he had rolled back the burden of the mortgage from the wide lands of his stepfather, Henry Rival. The herd multiplied under his fostering care. The Rival finances rose from debits to credits, and their bank account mounted by swift thousands. Not only was the ranch cleared of debt, but new acres were purchased. Where no man had dreamed of raising anything but cattle for three generations, Joshua, in a fertile,

lowland half-section, sank artesian wells —
and, behold, the water leaped forth, and the
fields became green all the year.

All of this before he had reached his eight-
and-twentieth birthday! Was it any wonder
that men, even old men, became silent
when Joshua entered their midst, and that
women widened their eyes and folded their
hands and listened to his voice? Yet he cherished his words, spoke seldom, listened
much, and, of course, the fame of his
wisdom grew.

His activities included much more than
business. If a crime were committed in the
county and a criminal were to be pursued,
Joshua, on his great black horse, was foremost among the pursuers. He could have
been sheriff, if he had raised his hand to get
the office. But, although he loved the ardor
of the man trail, he would not give himself
to it utterly, for he was, in short, a man four-
square to every wind that blew, as the poet
sings. If one had asked him, Joshua himself
would not have been able to tell in what
field he was most distinguished, for what
pursuit he was best fitted. In the meantime,
the dollars flocked in jingling herds, and his
fame continued to grow.

But, as the sages know so well, woman is
all too blind to even the most eminent vir-

tues. Yet, even though the sayings of the sages were known, who could imagine that the bright-faced Hilda Surrey could say no to Joshua? She did not say it definitely or in a ringing voice, to be sure. As a matter of fact, she was frightened within an inch of her life. She looked down in terror and wonder and saw that the great man had actually taken one of her hands in both of his while his voice softened and lowered.

"Hilda," he said, "there is a time when a man should marry and make a home for himself. That time has come for me. But, to make a home, a man must have a wife. And I have looked around me for three years and seen only one face . . . it is yours, Hilda, my dear. You see, I have waited. I wanted to make sure. But at last I know that there can be no mistake. Hilda, say that you will marry me."

It was a statement of something that must be done, rather than a request. Not that Hilda objected to this. Neither did she object to the patronizing manner in which he patted her hand while he spoke. She was simply filled with an uncontrollable desire to get away. That desire expressed itself in action when he ceased patting her hand and put his arm around her. He had taken her silence for acquiescence. Indeed, how often had even the elders of Hilda been able to answer him?

"As for the marriage," he was saying, "there is no time like the present. Spring is the accepted season for weddings. Customs should be observed. Suppose we select two weeks from Wednesday. . . ."

She slipped out of his loose embrace. He found himself with both arms awkwardly extended toward her, almost in a position of entreaty. If Joshua detested anything in the world, it was to appear awkward, even before an audience of one. But there was one thing which he hated even more, and that was to appear in the light of a beggar for favor. He dropped his hands to his sides and stared at her with a gloomy frown.

But, no matter what her actions, she had grown wonderfully attractive. A bright color had swept into her smooth, brown cheeks, and great, blue eyes flashed at him in wonder and fear. They were like the eyes of an imprisoned deer, seeing freedom even through the bars and yearning for it. The heartbeat of Joshua quickened.

"I . . . I," stammered Hilda, "I . . . can't, Joshua!"

He hardly heard the *can't;* he was too busy drinking in the melody of his name upon her lips.

"You can't?" he echoed mildly. "This is a free country, Hilda. What prevents you? Perhaps you have promised your parents that you will not marry before you're twenty-one? Is that the reason?"

He took a step toward her, his spurs jingling. And Hilda shrank away. It was not unpleasant to see her wince. It made him conscious of the breadth of his shoulders, the strength of his arms.

"No," she was saying faintly, "it isn't that."

Joshua sighed. Of course, a man of his wisdom knew that women are foolish, unreasoning creatures. It was a shame that he should have to argue a point with one of the sex. But he shrugged his shoulders and resigned himself to a debate, just as he would have entered a struggle to beat down the price of a man whose land he wanted to buy to swell the Rival domain.

Somewhere in the old house a violin leaped faintly and suddenly into a dancing rhythm. That was his cousin, Philip Rival — Phil, the Fiddler, as half the range called him. The lip of Joshua curled. Had he not that morning directed Phil to ride fence on the south line? Here he was, as ever, idling — and with a fiddle! He would have something to say to the wastrel, the loafer, later in the day. In the meantime, to business — if he could only get the singing of that infernal violin out of his ears for half a minute.

"I have to go, Joshua," she was saying. "I . . . I really. . . ."

"Sit down," said Joshua.

She slumped suddenly into a chair, very much as though he had caught her by the shoulder and forced her down. There she sat in an attitude which was very familiar to Joshua — her eyes wide as she looked up to him, her hands clasped in her lap. When he spoke, women usually fell into some such position. He spread his legs, folded his arms, and looked down upon her.

"Now let's get to the heart of this thing," said Joshua. "You say that you can't marry me . . . and you say that you have to go now. Let's take one thing at a time. That's the best procedure. Very well. Item number one . . . why do you have to go?"

"I . . . my . . . you see," she murmured, "my mother is canning cherries this morning, and she expects me back before. . . ."

He raised his hand. He smiled. Her simplicity was touching. "I think," he said with a slight emphasis, "that, when she hears you have been detained by my proposal of marriage, she'll excuse you for being late."

"Oh, yes," said Hilda. Moistening her lips, she sank back in the chair a little and continued to watch him with fascinated eyes full of dread.

"So much for that," said Joshua, "so much for . . . confound that violin! What was I about to say? Ah, yes . . . having the matter of your sudden departure disposed of, we come back to the prime question. You said that you can't marry me. What prevents you from marrying me, Hilda? We have to understand the obstacle, before we set about removing it, eh?"

He smiled down at her with a gentle, good nature that surely would make her feel more at ease. "Name it, please," he urged.

"It's hard to name exactly," she said, "only. . . ."

She paused, and Joshua sighed again. If women would only learn to complete their sentences and their thoughts!

"As a matter of fact," he said suddenly, "you're simply afraid. Isn't that it?" He thrust out a long arm and pointed an accusing forefinger before which she shrank again.

"Perhaps I am a little afraid," she murmured.

He watched her fingers, twisting nervously together, and he smiled. He was beginning to feel more and more at home.

"If there is anything else, try to tell me, dear," he said as a teacher draws out a child.

She grew a little braver. Her lips parted. "Yes," she said, "there is something else."

"Good," he said. "Now we'll get somewhere. Tell me what the silly reason is that you can't marry me?"

"Because, really, I'm afraid that I don't love you. I'm so sorry, Joshua, but I really don't."

II

"SOMETHING NEW
TO FIGHT"

Imagine what that other Joshua of old felt when one crossed his path unwilling to follow his will and the will of the Lord. So it was with this Joshua of the Western ranges, for it seemed to him that what the girl had just said smacked of blasphemy. He listened to her, not with grief, but with compassion. Yet he was a little baffled, also, for a new thing had come into his ken. The word love was not often included in his vocabulary. Even in the Bible, where he read it so often, it had little meaning to him. There was something weak and unmanly about that word. When he conceived of God Almighty, it was a misty face, a cloud behind a cloud — but the vague face was always young, stern, frowning — a face not unlike that of Joshua Rival. For frowns were what Joshua was best fitted to understand.

Now, however, a contrary concept was brought into his ken like a strange star foreboding shipwreck. Love! She had just said that she did not love him. But of what importance was that? For his part, he had not allowed his mind to dwell an instant on this phase of marriage. His viewpoint had been that of the man who "amassed a comfortable sum and took unto himself a wife, and she bore male children to him," namely, Joshua Rival, Junior, and. . . .

He shrugged his shoulders to get rid of the formula which, for the past three years, had been running through his brain. He could see now that he had really made up his mind in the very beginning — that evening when he saw the sweet face of Hilda as she danced with Phil, the Fiddler, at the Charity Dance. But he had set himself a goal before he would seriously consider her. When he had added that northeast section of the Parker Ranch to the Rival Ranch — when the Rival place was well rounded out — then, and not till then, would he have had the time to let his mind sink to lesser matters than fortune building.

But had he been wise in staying in the girl's background all this time? Strongly, the old saying came back to him, that women are apt to be light-headed and unable to appreciate important affairs, important men. Now, in the full course of his forward career, he was brought up short and jerked back on the rope of — love! After the blow was struck, it suddenly cut through him with an insistent sting. He knew what it was. He knew this love that had always meant nothing but mealy-mouthed weakness to him.

It was a great flowing of one soul toward another soul. It was a famine which could never be filled. It was a pain which would never end. It was a desire to possess that which could never be possessed — yes, not if she were his wife in the eyes of the law, not if his ring were on her finger, not if she called him husband and obeyed his word — still she was not his until that dread of him should go out of her eyes and in its place come a dim flame of tenderness — of love! For the first time in his life, he bowed his head before a problem greater than himself.

"No!" cried Hilda. "Don't do that!"

He looked up hastily in hope. She had risen from her chair. Her face was flushed. Her eyes were soft. He saw a thousand little things in a glance — something about the blue shadow beneath her eyes, the delicate curves of that half-childish mouth — the way the throat line slipped past the ruffle of her collar, so round and white as though it were perpetually full of song — and the light that stirred in her hair as her head moved. Her beauty struck him to the heart. The violin, far off, was singing, singing of her.

What was she saying?

"Oh, Joshua, I can't bear to hurt you!"

She was pitying him! His face went black. He strode to the door and cast it open.

"Phil!" he thundered.

But the violin went on. With the opening of the door it had become more trenchant. And it was speaking more clearly than ever of Hilda and love, of love and Hilda in an ecstasy.

"Phil!" he roared again and stamped his foot.

"Well?" called Phil, the Fiddler, and a harsh note came as the music ended.

"Stop that noise!"

"All right!"

He slammed the door behind him and faced the girl. "Well," he said, "you don't love me. That's all that stands between us?"

"Yes." She nodded.

He spoke with a savage abruptness. He was too badly hurt to speak otherwise. She was silent, too frightened to answer. For the first time in his life it did not please him to inspire fear in another.

"Why," he cried, smiting one big hand into another, "I wouldn't have you, if I didn't have to fight for you! It's what I'm made for . . . to find obstacles and break them down, smash them. D'you hear? Why, I . . . I live by it. Look at the ranch. My stepfather had to borrow money from the banks every year to run it. Every year came a loan for running expenses and to pay interest, and every year a bigger loan than the year before. He used to have to beg for money from the bankers. But, after my mother died, I took a hand. I was twenty-one, but I ran the ranch. I carried the burden of the ranch and Henry Rival. I don't know which was heavier. But I carried 'em both at twenty-one. In seven years, I've changed things. There's no debt. The ranch is twice as big. There's a better stock of cows and four times as many of 'em. And the banks . . . curse 'em! . . . they beg to get our business!" He paused. The recital of his success had poured new strength and courage into his veins. "Now you say you don't love me. That's a new thing to fight. And I'll fight it. I'll win!"

He stood over her. He lowered his voice, but the strong tremor of it shook his body. "I'm going to make you love me, Hilda. D'you hear?"

"Yes," she whispered.

"Don't say it that way," he gasped, recoiling a little. "Good Lord, Hilda, do you hate me?"

"No, no! Oh, no!"

He turned from her and stalked to the window. He dashed the curtain aside and looked out into the white blaze of the sunshine on the burned fields. He saw the tall form of his cousin, Phil, the Fiddler, lounge past and pause under the fig trees to admire the yellow-green of the new leaves. He turned on his heel.

"Hilda!"

She had dropped back into the chair. His voice jerked her out of it in a panic. What the devil was the matter with the girl? Was he an evil spirit seen at midnight?

"Do you love some other man?"

"No," she said faintly. "No, Joshua."

"That's good." He sighed. "Something popped into my head . . . but never mind. I have to go into town on business. But this evening I'm coming to see you. I . . . let's see . . . we'll go somewhere together. Where shall we go?"

"I don't know," murmured Hilda.

"I'll think of something to do. Only . . . I can't dance, Hilda. Perhaps you'll teach me?"

Her glance lowered. Was it in embarrassment and pleasure, or simply toward the huge, riding boots which encased his legs and feet? He flushed.

"Of course," said Hilda. "Of course, I'll teach you."

"I'll learn quick. You're going to see a lot more of me from now on. And . . . look here, you've got to have things around you that'll make you think of me. I saw the Sawyer girl a couple of weeks ago. She had emerald earrings. I'll get you a pair of earrings today while I'm in town. What kind do you want? I'll get you a pair that'll make people stop and look twice at you. You'll find that I'm not small, Hilda. I do things in a big way. I'll get you the finest pair of earrings in town!"

"Yes, Joshua, but. . . ."

Why was she so red and white?

"Good bye," he said. He turned toward her again at the door. "You won't be out of my head all day," he said. "You'll haunt me, Hilda, like a mirage that keeps slipping over the desert . . . a blue lake when the canteens are empty. Good bye, Hilda. Remember that I don't ask for a thing until I've fought for it."

He was gone.

In the harness room he got his saddle and bridle and stepped outside. The sunshine burned on his neck and the back of his hands. He found that he was covered with great beads of perspiration. His nerves were

130

gone. It was as though he had just witnessed a horse race in which his horse had lost. A month from now there would be a different story to tell.

He saw Phil, the Fiddler, under the fig tree in the same position, hands on hips, head bent back, eyes wandering up through the new leaves and on to the pale blue of the sky overhead.

"Hey, Phil!" he called.

The Fiddler turned slowly toward him. The leisure of his movements always angered Joshua. Today it maddened him.

"Why aren't you out riding fence?"

"That old Nell horse kicked me in the leg. Lamed me a bit."

He took a step to show. There was a pronounced limp. Joshua remembered that when he looked out the window there had been no trace of infirmity in the walk of the Fiddler.

"That's a lie!" roared Joshua.

"What did you say?" said the Fiddler mildly.

Joshua stared into the pale blue eyes that met his glance so calmly. There had always been something about the Fiddler which disconcerted him, and never more than today. On the hottest day this man seemed cool — as he was now. It was doubtless because he lived without friction. For the Fiddler was incapable of effort. Joshua fought for what he got. But all the Fiddler needed came to him without the lifting of a hand. When Joshua's mother married Rival and joined her small, cash fortune on a luckless day to the big, bankrupt rancher's assets, Joshua had found a cousin of his own age living on the place — Philip Rival, whose father was the black sheep of the Rival family and had died the year before in prison, leaving a wife who survived him only a month, and this penniless child. But a home had been given the waif by Rival, the rancher.

From the first, Joshua had fought to supersede Philip in the esteem of Rival, but he had never succeeded. He won more respect, but less affection. If he worked all day while Phil went swimming, at the end of the day Phil avoided a whipping with a well-timed jest which brought a roar of laughter from Rival. When Joshua, with superior bulk and brawn made hard by labor, tried to beat Phil in fair fight, he had been astonished to find that in the lazy muscles of his cousin there was the elusive speed of a cat and a cat's strength.

In every way, that for which Joshua struggled with main might was given to Phil as a birthright. If Joshua practiced night and day with rope and gun to win the applause of hardy, old Rival, Phil, without training, could step out at the critical moment and do strange things with the rope or with his weapons. Beast and man obeyed him; he cajoled them into subjection. The ranch hands, who one and all hated Joshua, worshipped the very ground under Phil's feet. The unbreakable mustangs, which even Joshua's fine horsemanship and matchless strength could not master, were wheedled and coaxed into usefulness by Phil, the Fiddler.

So it had gone on from the first. When Joshua went out and earned his way through school, Phil, the Fiddler, stayed at home and took up the violin. There was not a shadow of doubt that the violin of the Fiddler was dearer to Rival than the education for which he respected Joshua. Manifestly, it was unfair. And now the fortune which he had built for Rival would be left, probably, half to him and half to the idler, although that was a point on which he would make himself sure when he saw the lawyer today.

But he found himself saying as he faced those quiet, blue eyes: "I didn't mean to call you a liar, Phil. But I saw you walking without a limp a while back."

"You didn't look close enough." Phil yawned. "That horse broke me all up."

He yawned again and stretched his long arms, then smiled in the face of his cousin as though he knew that Joshua knew he lied, and challenged the other to tax him with it. Although Joshua loved nothing so much as a fight, he had never forgotten that terrible day long ago in their childhood when they had matched fists, and he had come out second best with a split lip that had left an ineradicable scar. So he made caution the better part of valor.

"I know that you've taken it easy," he said slowly. "You've never done a lick of work. But I want to ask you one thing . . . did Father make me the foreman on the ranch or did he not?"

"He did," said the other.

"And are you supposed to be working under me?"

"Sure."

"Then I order you to saddle a horse and ride that fence!"

Phil, the Fiddler, sighed. "All right," he said. "You're the boss. Soon as I get into my boots, I'll take the horse." He sauntered toward the house.

As for Joshua, he hurried on to the corral, roped a powerful horse, and flung his saddle on the back of the gelding. A moment later, he thundered past the house. From the road he looked back, and he saw in the front window, neatly framed, the picture of the Fiddler sitting and laughing beside Hilda Surrey.

III

"FRAMED —
FOR A FORTUNE"

There was no need to spur Joshua on this day, but that sight galled even his very soul. Had she told the Fiddler? Were they laughing at him? He went cold at the thought. Then he drove the spurs home and darted down the road.

Yet, he told himself, there could be nothing in his fear. In the first place, the girl had told him that she loved no other man. In the second place, when she did fall in love, it could not be with the lean, ugly face of the Fiddler, with that hawk-like nose, that outthrust of chin. Still, there was a horrible doubt in the very soul of Joshua, and he went on with contracted brows. He had looked upon Phil as a burden and a nuisance before. Now he began to regard him in the light of a menace. And a devil came up in the eyes of Joshua.

When he reached town, he went straight to the office of Camper. He found the plump-faced lawyer wreathed in smiles at the sight of him. He had always detested

Camper. He had always doubted his ability. But Rival had known him years ago, when Rival himself was newly making his way in the West, and he had clung to Camper as legal adviser for the sake of Auld Lang Syne — an emotion that never could have budged Joshua from the path of efficiency. But, only a short time before, when Joshua wanted to learn things about Henry Rival which his stepfather was unwilling to tell him, Joshua had gone straight to William Camper and discovered that the lawyer was perfectly willing to talk about his client's business for the sake of a handsome retainer. So the money had changed hands.

For that matter, Joshua was always ready to buy information. Dollars to him meant simply power. He could get all the money he wanted from the estate. All its financial affairs were in the hands of Joshua. But, since the prosperity of the ranch was his own prosperity, he had hitherto used the funds for no private purposes. Now it was time to make a change. In the first place, he had to learn what dispositions Rival had made in the will which he had recently drawn up. In the second place, he had to have money with which to besiege the girl.

He was hardly in his chair, when he blurted out his question. "And the will, Camper?"

Camper neatly avoided the direct answer. His palm had not yet been crossed with silver, so to speak. "Wills are queer things," said Camper. "Never would guess how people will act when it comes to making out their wills. Knew a man that cut off a brother living in Alaska without a cent. Millionaire, too. But he didn't remember his brother for a cent. 'Why?' I asked him. 'A man that hasn't the sense to live in a warmer climate than Alaska hasn't the sense to spend my money,' he said. There he was. I couldn't budge him. There was another old chap. . . ."

Joshua shrugged his shoulders. He saw that he could not shock the information he wanted out of the lawyer by surprise and blunt questions, so he changed his tactics. "All right, Camper," he said. "I know that business comes in slowly these days. I have a hundred dollars that isn't working today. And I want to find out what I get in that will my stepfather made out last week." It was sufficiently to the point. He wondered how Camper could avoid making an answer.

"When I was a young fellow," said Camper, "I saved up a hundred dollars. Looked to me like enough money to buy half the world. Well, sir, I took that money and started to buy the finest horse in the

West. Went to a big auction and saw a beauty. Big, bay mare with an action like a running river. But when I started bidding, they shoved the price right up to two hundred, and I went home broken-hearted."

Joshua grinned as he caught the inference. He drew forth his wallet, counted out two hundred dollars, and laid them on the desk. The other picked them up carelessly and shoved them in a crumpled wad into his coat pocket.

"That stepfather of yours," he said, "is certainly an ungrateful man."

Joshua turned pale. "Has he put a joker in the will?" he asked huskily.

"You can call it a joke, if you want to, but if I had a stepson who made me half a million or more, I'd be inclined to favor him over a worthless loafer who spends his time playing a fiddle and flirting with half the girls in the country who. . . ."

Joshua stiffened in his chair. "Wait a minute," he said, the matter of the will growing dim in his mind. "You say Phil is a good deal of a hand with the women?"

"Didn't you ever watch him at a dance?" asked the lawyer.

"No," said Joshua thoughtfully. "Not to speak of."

"There's a lot to speak of, if you watch

Phil," said Camper. "He has a great line with 'em. They follow him in flocks."

"Women are queer," said Joshua bitterly. "But Phil . . . how does he manage it with that face of his?"

The lawyer glanced into the dark, handsome countenance of Joshua and smiled faintly. "Looks don't count with the girls," he said. "Lord pity me if they did! But the finest woman on earth married me. Poor Alice. When she died, my lad, she took the sun out of my life. I never saw another like her."

"Humph," grunted Joshua.

"Besides," said Camper, "Phil has a face no one can forget, it's so ugly. And he has a way of looking at people as if he meant what he said to them. If he tells a girl she's pretty, and that he can't sleep for thinking of her, she believes it's gospel."

Joshua loosened his collar and drew in a deep breath. That picture of Phil and Hilda at the window began to mean more and more to him. "The will," he said suddenly. "What about that?"

"Fifty-fifty," said Camper.

Joshua rose from his chair. "Half the estate goes to Phil?" he gasped out. "I knew it! By heaven, I knew it! I've slaved like a dog. I've made every cent Rival has. And this is what I get for it! Besides, where would he have been, if he hadn't had my mother's money in the nick of time?"

"Ruined," agreed Camper. "He would have been ruined."

"That's his gratitude!" said Joshua through his teeth.

"Pretty bad, I admit. But you're to have the running of the ranch. Phil can't touch the management."

"But he gets half the income?"

"Right."

"I do the work, and he gets as much out of the place as I do. I sweat my life away, and he sits still and twiddles his thumbs. Makes no difference. For every dollar I get, he gets a dollar!"

In his rage, he walked up and down the office, looking for something he could seize and break. Then it seemed to him that the steady, pale blue eyes of Phil looked in on him. He grew suddenly sober. "Camper," he said, "what would make Rival change that will?"

"He's set his heart on Phil," said Camper. "Mighty fond of that boy."

"And all I am is his drudge!"

"You might put it that way. It's rather strong."

"Camper?"

"Well?"

"What does Rival hate worst in the world?"

"A snake." Camper chuckled. "He was bit once when we were out on a hunting trip. Never saw a man drink so much whiskey in my life. It killed the snake bite, but it nearly killed Rival, too."

"I asked you what he hates most in the world," said Joshua fiercely.

"Why, he hates a card cheat . . . and so do I," said Camper virtuously.

"Then Phil is a card sharper?"

"Eh? Why, I've played with Phil. He's straight as a string."

"I tell you, we're going to prove that Phil is a cheat."

"Nonsense! I'd trust Phil as I'd trust my brother. Going to sit in with him at a little game of poker tonight, as a matter of fact."

"Then," cried Joshua, "tonight is the time we prove that he's a cheat!"

"What the devil are you driving at?"

"Isn't there such a thing as a marked deck?"

"Well?"

"If a marked deck were found in Phil's pocket. . . ."

Campbell sat, stiff and pale, at his desk. A great loathing rose in his eyes. Quickly he turned his head from Joshua and stared through the window, across the street. By ill fortune, he saw the looming figure of the new bank building going up there. It represented to Camper the thing he wanted most in the world — money. And here in his office was a rich man, or one who would be rich, waiting to be bled. He drew out a handkerchief and turned back to his guest, mopping his forehead.

"A thousand dollars," said Joshua.

"Son," said Camper, "I've seen Phil, the Fiddler, work with guns. He's a man-killer if there ever was one."

"Two thousand!" said Joshua.

"Two thousand for what?"

"Five thousand dollars!" said Joshua.

"I got to be excused," said Camper. "See you again tomorrow. This is my busy day."

"Ten thousand dollars cash . . . the minute I get the estate!"

A vision rose before Camper's eyes, a vision of gold. Suppose he had this note for ten thousand, would it not be a club through which he could extract far larger sums from Joshua?

"You'll put that in writing?" he said.

"Yes!"

Camper reached for a pen and paper. **If I become sole heir to my stepfather, Henry Rival, I promise to pay. . . .** The pen flew swiftly across the sheet.

IV
"THE CARD GAME"

It was the one talent which swelled his income, the skill which Philip Rival possessed with the cards. Not that he could manipulate them illegally. Indeed, he dreaded to learn a gambler's tricks for fear the temptation would be too great for him, for he loved the card table, the silences, the whisper and slip of the cards as the deal sent them flashing around the table, the stony faces of the players as they took up their hands. In the eyes of the men he mined for information. No matter how like stone they made their faces, before he had played half a dozen hands he began to find traces of expression. There was a hidden gleam when a hand was strong, and there was a differing sense of what the strength was.

At the table where he sat this night, for instance, William Camper was a conservative, but, when he held so much as a full house, there was a subtle change in his manner which Phil, the Fiddler, knew of old. The lawyer grew a little rigid of body, although his well-schooled face did not alter in a single line. On the other hand, there was Jack Fanshaw, who played a good game, except that now and then he gave way to temptation and would bluff on nothing at all. It was a good bluff that he ran, except that a faint smile, hardly discernible, played about the corners of his lips. Other men thought that it meant a strong hand, but Phil Rival had come to know that it meant bluff, pure and simple. And Lefty Michaels, when he had even three of a kind and believed that his luck was "in," was unable to keep the gleam out of his eye. As for Hal Goshen, the last of the five at the table, he was a newcomer, but, before five hands had been played, Phil had worked out some of his weaknesses. By the time they had been playing for an hour, Phil had won some singular hands.

For one thing, Lefty Michaels had run up a large bet and lost on three jacks against three aces in the hands of Phil. With a wretched pair of nines Phil had had the courage to see a hand of Jack Fanshaw's in which there was nothing at all. Three of the other men at the table took these winnings as a matter of course. They had played with Phil, the Fiddler, before, and they knew that he was hard game, but it was not unnatural that Hal Goshen should have looked upon the winner somewhat askance. He took advantage of a moment during which Phil had left the table to start opening his heart.

"Look here, boys," he said, "I take it that we're all amateurs . . . all of us in this game?"

"Of course," came the ready assent.

"Well," said Goshen tentatively, "it looks to me like one of us is sure looking through the backs of these cards."

It was the cue for which Camper had been waiting since the game began. He was glad that it had come as early as this, for the strain on his nerves had become terrible.

"You mean that Rival is winning pretty regularly?" he said. "I don't wonder that you're surprised, Goshen. But Rival is straight as a string. We've all played with him before, and we all know that he's honest. But it's a fact that he's a hard one to beat. I don't think I've ever won from him over an evening's play."

"Nor me," declared Michaels, and Jack Fanshaw assented.

"He's a stone wall," said Fanshaw, "but I keep hoping that I can break through the wall and get to him."

"Well," said Goshen, "I guess you boys know him. But still, it looks sort of queer to me . . . unless he uses doctored cards. Not that I'm accusing him, mind you . . . but. . . ." He let his sentence end in suspense.

"Why, make sure for yourself," said Camper hastily. "I got a little magnifying glass in my vest pocket right now. Take it and give the backs of these cards a good look. That glass is a jim-dandy. It'll show up anything that's wrong."

"Thanks," said Goshen, and he took the proffered glass. "Mind you," he added, flushing a little as he saw the constrained expression on the faces of the others, "I'm not sure. But I just want to cut out the tenth chance that there's anything wrong."

It was like a dispensation from Providence to Camper, for he had dreaded having to open up the talk of suspicion. He watched the other take a card and study it carefully, then another, another — and his heart failed him. Had the work been done so cunningly that even the glass did not show it? All that afternoon Camper had had an expert at work on the pack that he had managed to introduce into this game, and he dreaded lest that wandering artist should have done his task with too delicate a touch.

But now Goshen stopped, seized a card, and looked up wildly at the others.

147

"By heaven," he whispered. There was as much horror on the faces of the rest as though they had seen a ghost.

"You don't mean that you've seen something?" they breathed.

"I . . . I hope not," stammered Goshen. He reached for another card, exclaimed faintly, then examined another. Suddenly, he seized Jack Fanshaw by the shoulder and gave him the glass and the last card he had been looking at.

"Right up in this corner," he said. "You see that little blur? It's hard to see, even with the glass at first, but once you've found it, you can find it again on any sort of card . . . just that little smear of red."

"That's an accident," said Fanshaw, muttering half to himself. "The dye on the back of the cards might of run a little bit if a moist fingertip touched 'em."

"I'll prove it to you," declared Goshen. "This is an ace of diamonds. Find another ace."

An ace of spades was quickly secured and turned on its face.

"Look there," pointed out Goshen, disdaining the use of the magnifying glass now that his eyes were accustomed to the secret.

Now they could all see it — a tiny blur of red in the exact center of the intricate enmeshing of red lines which patterned the back of the card.

"And here's a king," went on Goshen, full of his discovery and talking swiftly to anticipate the return of Phil, the Fiddler. "Look here. There's a spot up here in the corner of the card. Here's a queen . . . the spot is near the corner, but not right on the border. Here's a jack. The spot is still further away from the corner. Look through the rest of the deck, boys. I tell you that every card in the pack is marked. Phil, the Fiddler, has been daubing 'em . . . that's why he's had the good luck!"

"Hold on!" exclaimed Lefty Michaels. "Phil ain't the only man sitting in on this game. There's five of us. I say that any one of the rest is a pile more apt to have done this dirty work than Phil. Why, I know Phil. I've ridden herd with him. I know him like a brother and am attached to him the same way. I tell you, he can't do a crooked thing!"

"Facts is facts," said Goshen. "I ain't accusing any man, except that Phil has been winning . . . and these cards are marked." He stood up from the table, a slender little man, his face twitching with rage and excitement. "I say that every man here is going to be searched," he declared, "and the gent that we find the crayons on is going to get

149

pumped full of lead! That's the way they handle skunks like that in my part of the country, and it's a pretty good way!" He dropped a hand instinctively upon the butt of his gun as he spoke.

The door opened. Phil, the Fiddler, came back smiling. His smile went out as he faced the gloomy party, every man upon his feet.

"Start on me," said Goshen.

Without a word the search began, pocket after pocket being emptied.

"There's a dauber been working on these cards," said Goshen. "We're going to locate which one of us is the low hound."

"Good Lord," breathed Phil, and looked wildly around at the others until his glance rested upon Camper. That was the only man beside Goshen he could suspect. The honesty of the others he was sure of as he was sure of his own.

The search of Goshen was completed. That of Camper followed. Although they brought out a queer jumble of papers and trinkets, nothing faintly resembling a crayon was found. Phil shook his head in sad wonder. If it were not Goshen, the stranger, or Camper, the tricky lawyer, it must be one of his old and tried friends, Lefty Michaels or Jack Fanshaw, and his heart grew cold at the thought.

Little Goshen faced him. His voice was sharp and shrill. "Now your turn, Rival."

"Blaze away," said Phil, smiling faintly. "Go as far as you like with me, boys."

Goshen reached into the breast pocket of Phil's coat. In his hand, as he withdrew it, was a slender strip of red-tipped crayon. He tossed it down upon the table and leaped back, his gun conjured into his hand. Every other man in the room drew — except Phil.

He stared at the crayon like one entranced. Then his wild eyes turned to Camper, for that was the man who had been sitting on his left side — that was the only man who would have had an opportunity to slip that damning crayon into his pocket.

"Camper," he said, "if what I think about you is right, the Lord forgive you."

"You talk about the Lord and forgiving!" exclaimed little Goshen, his whole body, except the hand which held the gun, shaking. "Why, you yaller dog, when we get through with you. . . ."

"Wait a minute!" gasped out Camper. "Boys, I want you to listen to me for one minute. What made Phil do this, I don't say, but I can lay to it that it's the first time. So'll the rest of us. I say that Phil has had enough of a lesson. He'll never try this one trick again. I say let him go. And let's keep our mouths shut about this."

"That sounds right to me," said Michaels and Fanshaw in a breath.

They had pocketed their weapons and were staring at the floor, quite unable to look poor Phil in the face as their shame for him became a burning thing.

Goshen, who saw that the body of opinion was turned against any violent measures, stepped to the table and scooped up the cards and the crayon. "The rest of you can do what you want," he said. "How it comes that you can let a skunk like that wander around loose to trim others the way he's been trimming me is sure something I can't understand. But, no matter what the rest of you do, I'll tell you what I'm going to do . . . I'm going to start in and spread this all over town. I'll make a rattlesnake a popular thing around here compared with Phil, the Fiddler."

He turned on his heel and stamped out of the room. The other three prepared to follow, but, first, Lefty Michaels came suddenly and impulsively to Phil. He caught his hand and wrung it violently.

"Phil, old man," he said, "this looks black as the devil. But if the whole truth was out, I know we'd find that you had a good reason for doing it. I'm not going to do any more thinking. I'm just going to trust in you, and in the end I know that you'll come out on top. Good bye, old man. Keep your head up. This ain't the end by a good sight."

He followed the rest. The door closed behind them, and Phil, the Fiddler, went to the window and looked out into the night.

All was quiet. The stars shone more brightly than ever before, it seemed to him. Far away through the town he heard the pleasant voices coming in faint groups, and one by one. They were his friends an hour before; they would despise him in an hour more. His last hope to clear the mystery was gone, for, if Camper had put the crayon there, if Camper had put the deck into play, would he have made the plea for merciful silence?

Phil ground his knuckles across his forehead and sighed.

V
"HENRY RIVAL'S OPINION"

He could not endure going back to the ranch while this cloud hung over him, so that night he rode straight out into the hills. He spent the next day wandering, but in the afternoon he knew he would have to come back. It was the thought of Hilda Surrey that drew him with an irresistible power. So, in the dark of the evening, he rode his sweating horse back to the ranch and put it up in the barn.

Coming toward the house, he passed Shorty, out with a lantern — Shorty, his worshipper and most constant henchman — Shorty, whom he had taught to shoot and ride — and Shorty stopped as though shot, stared at him with great eyes, and said not a word.

That was the way persons were taking it, then. If Shorty were silent with horror, how would those who felt less kindly toward him act? How would Joshua, for instance, receive the news? The lips of Philip Rival curled as he thought of his cousin. It seemed to him that all which he most detested in the

154

world was gathered and summed up and perfectly expressed in the form of his big cousin. In the hall he paused and unbuckled his cartridge belt and the revolver deliberately. He dared not be wearing deadly weapons when he faced the sneer of Joshua. The temptation would be too mortal. Yet, was it not better, a thousand times better, to be hanged for murder than to be detested for cheating at cards?

He lounged against the wall, head down, sick and weak. A card cheat! When he looked up again, he heard the rumble of Henry Rival's voice in the room at the end of the hall. The door was edged with lamplight. How familiar it was — and how familiar was the room beyond it, and the rough, kind face of Henry Rival! How would Rival greet a cardsharper?

When men face the gun, it is less terrible than the expectation of facing it. It seemed to Phil, the Fiddler, that there was an eternity of shame and pain between him and that door. Why was it that he could not raise his head in the consciousness of innocence? No, the very presumption of his sin which existed in the minds of others was a weight crushing him. By this time even Hilda Surrey knew. What would she say? What could she say?

Suddenly, even the dread of Henry Rival faded to nothingness. What was his opinion compared with the opinion of the girl? He opened the door and found that they were waiting for him. They had heard his footsteps in the hall. In vain Henry Rival looked down at his paper. The hand that held the sheet trembled. In vain Joshua stared at his book. The sneer of righteous contempt curled his lip. Anger suddenly welled up in Philip Rival. What right had they to damn him at the first report without waiting for his explanation?

His uncle lowered the newspaper. A draft caught it and tumbled it noisily across the floor. "You got up your courage, eh?" Rival said. "You came back, after all?"

"Had you rather that I stayed away?" asked Phil sadly.

His uncle made a vague gesture, and even in the gesture his hand was shaking. A thousand emotions seemed to be working in him — rage, shame, grief, and all their variants. And Phil, who loved him like a father, looked wistfully upon him. The face of Rival was like a forested mountain, so densely covered with an unkempt mass of wiry whiskers that the features were hardly distinguishable, but there was the fire of the eyes and the outward thrust of the chin — a Rival family feature — which even the whiskers could not quite obscure.

"Rather you stayed away?" echoed Henry Rival. "Well, there's some who might have. There's some that would have gone off to do something that would make people forget, unless they could come back and prove they were innocent. Is that right, Joshua?"

Phil set his teeth. It was an old habit, this habit which Rival had formed of referring everything to Joshua. As usual, Joshua merely looked up and nodded. It was enough. A red mist swam before the eyes of Phil, the Fiddler.

"That," said Phil, "is what I've come to do."

Henry Rival smote his hand upon his knee. "Phil!" he cried. "It was a lie, then?"

Joshua faced suddenly toward the new-comer.

"It was," said Phil.

"Thank heaven!" cried his uncle. "Then let's have the proofs. We'll start out tonight and lay them before everybody. We'll have somebody's head for this! Why, every man in the mountains has heard about it already. I've been living in a fire! Good boy . . . good, old Phil . . . I knew you'd be out working to get your proofs. What are they? Who played the trick?"

"I have no proofs," said Phil slowly. "But I'm going to get them."

"You have no proofs?" The hope died out of Henry Rival's face. A gloomy anger settled upon him.

"Uncle Henry," cried Phil, desperate, "don't you know that I couldn't have done a thing like that . . . cheat my own friends in a card game? Why, that's lower than a snake could get."

"Lower than a snake?" thundered Rival. "It's lower than anything in the world. I'd rather that you'd been brought home dead than have that story go the rounds! What'll they say? It was bad enough when your father. . . ."

The hand of Phil went up. "No more of that," he said slowly.

"Have you come here to tell me what I can talk about?"

"What you talk about is your own business until you touch on my family."

"I say the Rival name is black as the pit after today. Self-respecting men will turn their backs on me! And it's through you and. . . ."

"Uncle Henry," said Phil, "you can say what you want to me and about me. You have the right to talk as much as you want. But leave my father out of it. You've sworn to me a thousand times that he was innocent . . . that the rest of 'em put the blame on him . . . that he was perfectly innocent. . . ."

"What he did was white as snow compared with card cheating," declared Rival.

"It was," said Phil. "But I do not cheat at cards. I'll swear to you by anything you can name."

Joshua cleared his throat, and Henry Rival turned sharply upon him and then nodded, as though his stepson had spoken.

"That's right. Taking oaths don't prove anything. We've got to have facts from you, Phil! I'd walk on fire to get 'em. I'd fight ten men to prove that you're innocent. But would I be a fool to fight in a lost cause? Phil, who do you suspect?"

"Camper."

"You infernal, impudent puppy! You dare to accuse my old friend Camper of cheating?"

"He sat beside me . . . he was the only man who had the chance to put the crayon in my pocket."

"By the Lord," groaned Rival. "It's too much. Why, I trust William Camper as I'd trust myself. A man who could accuse him is just the sort of man that would cheat at poker with marked cards. Am I right, Joshua?"

As usual, Joshua looked up and nodded.

"You," said Phil, gasping out the words as he turned on Joshua, "get out of the room!"

"Do you wish me to leave, Father?" said Joshua mildly.

"Certainly not," thundered Rival. "Since when have you been giving orders in my house, young man?"

"I can't talk to a man when there's a rat around to listen," said Phil. "You double-faced hypocrite, Joshua!"

"No more of that!" exclaimed Rival, springing between them.

Joshua, indeed, had risen and slipped his hand significantly into a hip pocket.

"There's no fear of a fight," sneered Phil, the Fiddler. "I have no gun, but even without one the yellow dog is afraid of me. I say that, if we're going to talk any more about this, he leaves the room!"

"You'd better go, Joshua," said Henry Rival kindly, turning on his stepson. "I know all you could say. Phil lies. You're afraid of no one. But I won't risk you in this sort of brawl. You're too valuable to me, Joshua. Leave the room."

"Not until I've wrung his neck for him," vowed Joshua, growing more violent as Rival interfered.

"Not a step toward him," said Henry. He

dragged Joshua to the door and thrust him out. Then he faced Phil again. "Card cheating, then gun fighting, then highway robbery, then murder, then hanging! Phil, I can see your life spread out before me as clear as though you were on a road and I were on a hill looking after you."

"Thanks," said Phil. "I didn't know you had that much faith in me."

The sneer turned the forehead of the father red with fury. He stamped to his desk in the corner of the room. He jerked open a drawer. He threw down a document on the top of the desk.

"Read that," he commanded.

"It's your will," said Phil, with a flash of insight. "It's your will, and it disinherits me. Why should I read it? I take it for granted."

"It was drawn up by Camper for me today. The man you accuse fought for you, Phil. He begged me not to cut you off. He pointed out that you're young, that the lesson will change you . . . he talked to me with tears in his eyes. Now, like an ungrateful hound, you bite the hand that cherishes you! I tell you, I've learned more about you today than I dreamed of during these twenty years. I was going to make that just a tentative will to change, if you showed yourself a better man a year from today, but now it goes into the vault and will never be altered. From this day, you leave my house and my life."

VI

"A GREAT IDEA"

When a man has reached the limit of rage, there is a recoil, just as a rope that has been overstretched snaps back. So it was with Phil Rival. His fury had risen past the boiling point as he listened to his uncle talking. But, when he parted his lips to speak, he found that his anger was gone. Instead of an unjust man making a snap judgment, he saw one who had acted in the place of a father to him since his boyhood — as kindly as he was hot-tempered.

"Uncle Henry," he said, "I see the way you look at it, and I don't blame you. As far as the money is concerned, I'm glad that you've made up your mind to cut me off. I've done nothing to make the ranch prosperous. That's Joshua's work. Let him take the cash and the credit. But what cuts me is to leave you like this . . . in a passion. I hope that you're saying more than you mean. To-morrow you may put on a softer pedal. I'll tell you where I'm going. I'm going up to Jackville in the mountains. If you want to write to me and wish me luck, you can address me there."

"I'll see you hanged before I wish you luck!" roared Henry Rival.

Phil sighed. "Very well," he said. "That's your idea tonight. In the morning, you'll change. You're too just not to change. Remember that I don't hold any grudge. A thing like this has to come to light. It's like murder. It can't be buried. When I'm cleared, I'll come back and ask you if you've changed your mind about wanting to see me. But as for the will, let that stay the way it is. It's Joshua's money. He can keep it."

If one should beard a lion and see the monster merely arch his back and grunt with content, one could not have been more surprised than was Henry Rival at this quiet speech from his nephew. He saw the tall fellow walk from the room, heard the outer door open and close. Still he stared in apathy. Then he roused himself as he heard a beat of hoofs, tore open the door — and ran into Joshua.

"I came to see if I couldn't talk you into being a little easier on Phil," began Joshua.

But Henry Rival rushed to the outer door, flung it open in turn, and saw the figure of Phil melting far off into the night. It was too late to undo what had been done. He came wearily back into the library and found Joshua already there.

"Joshua," he said suddenly, "what makes Phil hate you?"

Joshua raised his brows. This was a new tone for Henry Rival. Certainly it was the most unexpected on this night of all nights. "He may be a trifle jealous," said Joshua carelessly. "He wishes that he had a head for business, you know."

"The devil he does," snapped the older man. "You don't know him, if you say that. And jealous? There isn't a jealous bone in his body. He's just been telling me that he doesn't want a cent of my money . . . that it ought to go to you, every bit of it."

"That would be too bad," said Joshua, his eyes brightening in spite of himself. "I never wanted to see Phil cut off."

Rival grunted. "I'm not so sure about what you wish. But what I know to be a fact is that I'm not going to cut him off. I was crazy mad today. Tomorrow I'll call Camper back and have him make a new will for me. I'll leave a majority with you, Joshua. You've been a good boy . . . you've worked hard. But . . . say a third . . . yes, the last Rival blood is in Phil. He has to have something."

"Quite right," Joshua said, but there were

165

ashes in his heart as he listened.

"I knew you'd agree, Joshua," said Rival kindly. "Now that Phil is gone, I'm going to see more of you, my boy . . . a good deal more. I'm going to bed. I'm tired out. I feel as though Phil had taken away half of my heart with him when he left me, because . . . blood is thicker than water, you know."

He started for the door, paused as though about to say something more, changed his mind, and went on.

Left to himself, Joshua dropped into a chair with clenched teeth and hands buried in his hair. He had failed. All that effort, all that planning. Now he had changed his portion from a half to two thirds — a beggarly increase! Besides, how could he tell that he would not get even less? As Rival had said, blood is thicker than water — much thicker. And, in the course of years, Phil's supposed crime would be forgiven and forgotten. He would be reinstated, perhaps become dearer than ever because of his present absence.

The long strain was beginning to tell on Joshua. He felt his strength giving out. He could not continue forever playing his part of respect and even affection toward Henry Rival. In his heart of hearts he had always hated the wastrel for his inefficiency, and for his loose methods.

He raised his head. If right received its just dues, the ranch and all that was on it belonged to him, decided Joshua. He had the industry to develop it. He had the brains to make the most of its possibilities. For instance, there was the half-section of irrigated land. It had brought in a net profit of fifteen thousand dollars last year, more than the entire ranch had ever produced before the genius of Joshua appeared to reclaim the place from its foolish ways.

Yet, here was this ignorant old dotard ready to deed away the labor of Joshua and give it to another wastrel! Joshua raised his fist and brandished it at the ceiling. Blood spoke to blood — blood is thicker than water. For his part, he thanked heaven that there was no drop of Rival blood in his veins. For his part, he only cursed the unlucky day that had made his mother marry Henry Rival.

He went outside. He could not endure the closed room. Under the stars there was more breathing space. He came up behind the bunkhouse. There was a stir of voices within. Joshua, forgetting his own troubles for the moment, stole closer to listen. Nothing was a dearer delight to him than an opportunity to overhear others when they were least aware of it. It was a chance to glimpse their secret minds. He loved it above all else. It gave him a feeling of mysterious power.

It was the voice of Shorty that he heard first. "I stayed close to the window. I heard the old man giving Phil the devil. Told him that he was cut off and wouldn't get a cent out of the ranch. Everything went to Joshua. So I say that, when that hound has full charge, I'm going to move on!"

Joshua gritted his teeth. He would make Shorty pay for that little speech, if he lived.

"Sure," said another. "All that's stood between us and a bad time has been Phil. Poor old Phil! I wonder what come into his head?"

"I dunno," said a third voice. "If all was known, most like it would be found out that some friend of his got into trouble and needed money terrible bad. And Phil had to make a quick turn to make the raise, so he done that."

"That's going pretty strong, though."

"Phil was the kind that would do anything for a friend."

"Right!" came the ringing chorus.

It was like a blow in the face to Joshua. Even in this moment their faith clung to the fallen man. A righteous anger burned in

Joshua. What blind fools they were!

"That sour-faced Joshua," said Shorty's drawling voice, "will raise merry blazes with us in ten ways every day now that Phil's gone."

"He sure will. Phil kept him down a little. He's afraid of Phil."

"Ain't he got reason to be? Old man Parker was telling me the other day about a fight they got into when they was both little shavers. Joshua was twice as big and broad. But he couldn't get his big hands on Phil. Phil danced around and cut him to pieces till Joshua busted out bawling and begged Phil to stop and said that he wouldn't bother Phil no more."

There was a groan of disgust and derision from the cowpunchers. Joshua, in the darkness, beat a hand against his face in rage and mortification. That battle out of his boyhood would never be forgotten, so it seemed. With all his soul he yearned for a chance to blast those men in the bunkhouse — sweep them from the earth! Fire was too good for them!

"But I hope that Phil don't go and make a fool of himself," said Shorty. "He must be fighting mad. First thing you know, there'll be a gun fight, and, when Phil gets into a gun fight, there'll be a killing, and he won't be the man to die. He's too fast with a gun. That's what's the matter with him."

So it was that the great idea came to Joshua. In a trice he had almost forgotten and forgiven what Shorty had said about him in the first place. He wandered back to the house lost in a brown study, and so into the library. There, in five minutes, he made up his mind grimly.

He took the telephone which connected with the bunkhouse — that was one of his first installations to modernize the ranch — and called for Shorty to come to his office. In another moment Shorty was before him.

"Shorty," he said, "I've called you in to give you a confidential message. I don't want a word of this to get to the other boys."

Shorty blinked.

"There's been trouble in the house," said Joshua. "In a word, Phil has been disinherited for that rotten business in town. He has just left the ranch, swearing that he'll come back and get Mister Rival."

Shorty swore softly.

"What I want you to do, Shorty, is to slip out of the bunkhouse in a few minutes and stand guard tonight. You'll get a month's wages for the work. And . . . don't let a syllable get to the other boys. You understand?"

Shorty nodded, his eyes as round as saucers.

"That's all," said Joshua. "Mind you, I don't want you to try to stop Phil, if he comes back tonight. Just give an alarm. Personally, I think that poor Phil will change his mind, when he has a few hours to think things over, but I can't take chances. Mind you, not a syllable to the others, for Phil's sake."

But when Shorty left, overawed, there was a pleasant consciousness in Joshua that within five minutes every man in the bunkhouse would know as much as Shorty himself knew.

VII

"IN PHIL'S DARKEST HOUR"

To Phil, as he started from the house that night, the black heads of the upper mountains loomed like a promise of harbor and oblivion. Rumor toiled slowly up those long slopes. Perhaps he could outdistance it, and the story of his shame would never arrive at his destination with him.

At least, it was some such blind hope as this that drove him on, with his head high, his eyes straining forward. Presently, the horse swung sharply to the right at a division of the road, in the fork of which stood a schoolhouse. Phil, with an oath, drew his mount to a halt. But he did not immediately turn back to the original path. There was a reason for that turn the mustang had made. It was the trail that led to the Surrey place, and many a time the old horse had cantered along it with Phil on its back. If it had seemed very hard to leave the range without seeing Hilda again, it was now doubly painful.

Lost in his thoughts, he was hardly conscious that the horse had begun to walk forward again. When he recovered himself, he was a mile closer to Hilda, a mile farther from the trail he had chosen on starting. With a sigh, he brought his horse into a canter and sent it on resolutely toward the Surrey house. He dreaded Hilda and her scorn like fire. But he dreaded still more leaving the country without seeing her.

The trees which enshrouded the Surrey house grew up dark before him. He tethered his horse under an outlying cottonwood and went in on foot to the house itself. The porch, where he had expected to find the entire family on this warm evening, was dark. The two windows that marked the dining room still glimmered with lamplight. He stole up and looked inside.

There they sat — Hilda's mother and father at opposite ends of the table, Jack Surrey on one side, Hilda on the other. A hot discussion had kept them long past their usual time of rising from the table, and still they were fighting over the disputed ground.

"But it all comes back to what I said in the first place," said Mrs. Surrey. "Bad blood makes bad blood. His father was bad before him, and now Phil has gone the same way."

"I don't see how you can say such a

thing!" cried Hilda. "How many times has he sat right here at this table . . . and we've all been glad to have him."

It was such a purely feminine argument that Phil, in the outer darkness, could not avoid smiling.

"What sort of sense does that make, Hilda?" said her father. "You sure are talking foolish, honey."

"I'm not," said Hilda, her head high, her face flaming. Ah, how the heart of Phil leaped as he watched her. "I'd like to know what could be more sensible? Haven't we all known Phil, and known him to be the height of honesty and generosity?"

"Until the pinch came," said Mrs. Surrey. "Then he wasn't equal to the strain. He cheated his own friends at cards! That's the lowest of the low."

"There's no proof," said Hilda.

"No proof? The cards daubed and the red crayon found in his pocket after he'd done the winning? What sort of proof do you want?"

"Someone put the crayon in his pocket," insisted Hilda.

"'Well," said her father, "I give up. When a woman gets hold of some fool idea, there ain't no use trying to talk her out of it. You can go right on thinking that he's as innocent as the angels. The rest of the country will go on thinking that he's guilty."

"Not all!" cried Hilda.

"Anybody been found that agrees with you?"

"Jack," said Hilda, "are you dumb?"

"What can I say?" said Jack.

"When he rode up in the face of that stampede two years ago, and you on the ground in front of them . . . when he split that stampede and saved your life . . . you had something to say about him then, Jack Surrey!"

"I'd do the same for him," said Jack gloomily. "But that doesn't cover up the fact that he cheated at cards. I'd rather hear that he'd done a murder . . . a lot rather."

"You're an ingrate," quavered Hilda.

"Look here, Hilda," said her father with a sudden change in his voice as he leaned toward her, "what makes you so strong for Phil, the Fiddler? A body might think that you're plumb in love with that cardsharper."

Hilda sprang up from the table. "He's not a cardsharper . . . and I do love him!" she cried.

"Hilda!" chorused the three, in horror.

"I mean it. I love him . . . I love him . . . I love him! And the more you hate him, the more I love him . . . and you should be ashamed . . . and I won't stay here to hear him insulted!"

After which tumbled outburst, she flashed from the room. Her heels rattled over the porch, then thudded on the ground. Phil, the Fiddler, hastened to find her, and he found her a dim figure, hurrying on under the trees.

"Don't follow me!" she called, when she heard him coming.

"It's I, Hilda," he called softly.

She stopped short, and, when he came up to her in the steep shadow of a tree, he could see that her face was pale, her hands clenched at her sides. How his heart flowed out to her after that revelation which he had heard the moment before.

"Hilda . . . ," he began.

But she cut in on him: "How do you dare to show yourself here?"

He was astounded.

"Who wants to see a card cheat, Philip Rival?"

"I've come to swear to you, Hilda, that I'm innocent. It was a plant. . . ."

"Who'll believe you? Where are your proofs?"

What devil had possessed the girl that she would stand up to fight for him against others and attack him so fiercely when they were alone?

"I have no proofs," he said.

"Go get them, then," she said. "Why, until you find them, I'm ashamed to be seen with you."

"I'll leave you, then," said Phil bitterly.

"By all means . . . go!"

"Hilda," he said suddenly, "is this all you have to say to me?"

"What better thing could I say? You tell me that someone has made a plant against you, that you are innocent . . . and I tell you that you should go and force the man who made the plant to confess what he did. You should have your proofs in writing. When you have that . . . oh, Phil, I'll be the happiest girl in the mountains! Or if I could help you to get what you want to have, I'd crawl a hundred miles on my hands and knees through the desert to do it."

She had come suddenly toward him, and the tremor of her eagerness was an electric thing. It filled the air. It made the heart of Phil, the Fiddler, proud.

"If I could get it," said Phil. "But how can a man be made to talk?"

"How is a child made to mind?" cried Hilda fiercely.

"Do you want me to horsewhip him?"

"If a man lied about me and damned my character," said Hilda, "what would you do to him?"

"I'd kill him, of course."

"I'd expect you to. I know you would. But, oh, Phil, when they've ruined your good name, you're going to slink away out of the country, I suppose, and hide your head. If . . . if you do, never speak to me again."

"Hilda," he said miserably, "I'm not sure. I don't know who did it."

"How many men were in the room besides you?"

"Four."

"Who were they?"

"Lefty and Fanshaw, a stranger named Goshen, and Camper."

"Lefty and Fanshaw never would harm you, Phil," she said instantly and with a perfect surety. "They'd die for you, both of them. It's either Goshen or Camper."

"Suppose I try the wrong one?"

"When you find out he's wrong, then go try the other. It must be one of the two."

"Hilda, how can I take a man and tie him and torture him? Good Lord, I get a cold chill at the thought!"

"Then think of another thing. If you're not proved innocent, every day of my life will be a torture."

"Hilda," murmured Rival.

"Don't touch me!" she cried sharply. "I won't be touched by a man the world calls a card cheat. But if my good name were touched, and I suspected who might have started the lie, do you know what I'd do? I'd chloroform them . . . I'd tie them hand and foot . . . and . . . and . . . I would feed them into a slow fire until they confessed the truth and wrote their confession out . . . and then I'd call in the town and show them a dog worth hanging. . . ." The tirade trembled away to nothing on her lips. "Oh, Phil," she sobbed out, "my heart is breaking!" But she cried an instant later: "Don't touch me . . . don't come near me!" So she fled away beneath the trees and was gone into the night.

But for Phil it was as though the starry sky had parted and he had seen the gold of heaven shining through. In all the years he had known her, he had never once spoken to her of his love, and yet she had known and loved him in return. Was it not like a gift from heaven that the knowledge of her love should be opened to him in his darkest hour?

Hastily he went back to his horse, mounted, and turned into the road. But the way he took was not toward the mountains — it lay straight to the town.

VIII
" 'HELP! MURDER!' "

When Shorty left the house, it was to do exactly as Joshua had expected. He went straight to the bunkhouse, and there he told the cowpunchers what he had learned. A solemn discussion followed.

One and all, they agreed that strange and terrible things were apt to happen in that house of Henry Rival before the morning.

"Because," as Scotty said, "suppose all of us was to go out and stand guard, how could we keep Phil away, if he wanted to come back? Look how the trees and the bushes come right up to the house. We've all gone hunting with Phil and seen how he can stalk a deer. He can just drift along through brush where another gent makes enough noise for an army . . . but Phil never makes a sound. He's got a talent that way. A wildcat couldn't go smoother or softer. I say that, if Phil swore he'd come back and finish Rival before morning, he'll do that same thing."

"Kill his own uncle?" gasped out Shorty.

"Not in a thousand years. He ain't built that way."

"I dunno," said Scotty. "There ain't no telling what a gent will do when he gets mad enough."

Such was the feeling in the bunkhouse, when Shorty went out to stand guard. But, in the ranch house proper, Joshua had gone back to the desk and picked up the will. Slowly and carefully he read it through. It was perfectly clear. In case of death, the entire estate went to — **my beloved stepson, Joshua Rival.**

For the first time in his life, Joshua was glad his mother, when she had married Henry Rival, had had her son's name legally altered from that of his father, Jenkins, to that of his stepfather, Rival. The very name, Rival, gave him a better claim to the fortune of the rancher. So, for the moment, he was the sole heir to the whole Rival estate. But before tomorrow night, all would be changed. Phil would be reinstated — before tomorrow night, if Henry Rival lived. For that reason he must not live. He must die in the night, and by violence.

It had become entirely clear to Joshua. He could see that he would be a fool to hesitate for an instant. Yonder were the men in the bunkhouse, convinced that Phil had sworn to return before morning to commit the crime. Phil himself was wandering toward the mountains. His very destination was known to Joshua, so that the apprehension of Phil would be the easier. As for Joshua, was not his position perfectly clear in the eyes of the law? To protect his uncle's threatened life he had hired a cowpuncher to stand guard all night. He had offered a month's pay out of his own pocket to Shorty. Certainly that would clear him of any shadow of blame.

It only remained to explain how Henry Rival, after a murderous threat against him, could have gone calmly to bed. But that could be made clear easily. All men knew the blunt and hearty nature of the old rancher. He would simply testify in the court of inquiry that Henry Rival had laughed the threat of Phil to scorn and had vowed that he would not lose a wink of sleep on account of it.

So all the lines were cleared for action. There was only conscience to hold Joshua back. But not for nothing had Joshua learned to use his brain. He worked out his theory without a flaw. The world needed efficient workers. The world needed men who made the best use of great opportunities. He was such a man. In the hands of Phil Rival, the big ranch would disintegrate; in the hands of Joshua, it would develop and develop. Its boundaries would spread, its stock increase, its farm lands would be doubled and trebled. It would become a show place. Thousands of new settlers, attracted by the romantic story of how he had created a fortune out of a desert, would throng into the country. In the place of the rambling old ranch house, there would arise a veritable palace from that white stone which abounded in the hills of the ranch. As mistress of the ranch, beautiful Hilda Surrey would hold sway in the lofty rooms of the mansion. She would be a queen worthy of such a king.

But all this led to other prospects. The town itself must not develop without his guiding hand. Already he had worked into the interests of the new bank. He would gradually acquire more of its capital stock. He would put his huge shoulder to the wheel and roll it faster ahead. The old bank would begin to stagger, and finally it must go down. Then Joshua would sit enthroned in the only bank in the county, the financial dictator. When he said — "Come." — the dollars would advance; when he said — "No." — they would remain in the vaults of the bank. Once the bank was his, the rest of the town would be quickly swung into line. His word would be law.

Why not? He had the brains, he had the power, and, above all, he had the abiding patience to wait while each scheme developed and became ripe. The vision of his approaching greatness swept in rosy tints before the mind of Joshua. Lifting up his head, he wondered, with a sort of glad humility, if the community would ever sufficiently appreciate his greatness.

Between him and all this splendid future there arose only one wall — the life of Henry Rival. Was it a wonder that he shrugged his shoulders at the thought of the miserable obstacle? No, not for an instant could he hesitate. The future waited for him, beckoned to him. Woe to the sluggard. What was Henry Rival in the scheme of the world? Merely a wastrel, a spendthrift, a useless squanderer of what the labor of another heaped up. Plainly, heaven did not care for such a man or what became of him.

In a sort of blissful content at the ease with which he had seen the clear way to action, Joshua went up the stairs, not to his own room, but to the room of Philip Rival. Still, heaven was with him. On the wall, from a peg, hung the holster containing one of Phil's weapons.

He drew out the revolver, and behold! It was Phil's favorite gun. There was not a cowpuncher on the place who could not testify that Phil many and many a time had declared that old Colt to be the king of revolvers. He had praised its close shooting, its matchless ease of action, its mysteriously perfect balance. He had said that he would rather walk on one leg than enter a fight without that well-known old gun. Yet, here it was, left behind him, with all his belongings, on account of the haste in which he had ridden into the night.

When Joshua gripped the weapon and lifted his head, he saw two pictures — Henry Rival lying murdered in his bed, and Philip Rival standing on the hangman's trap door, protesting his innocence in vain to the last. They were pleasing pictures to Joshua. They meant that the world had no place in it for idle sluggards. They meant that brains will be served. They meant that there is a system of economy and a regard for profits in the eternal mind of heaven. So, smiling to himself, with a light heart, a steady hand, and a clear conscience, Joshua went down to do the deed.

It was perfectly simple. He opened the door. The instant he set hand upon the knob there welled up in him a mysterious assurance that all was safe, that he would come upon Rival sound asleep, that his footfall, crossing the floor, would make no sound, and that the revolver found on the floor would hang Philip. With all those sweet assurances, he swung the door open and stepped inside.

But at once the voice of Rival spoke from the bed at the farther side of the big room. "Phil, lad, is that you?"

"Yes," whispered Joshua.

"Ah, boy," said the old rancher, "I've been lying here, cursing my hot temper and my quick tongue. But I never loved you more, Phil, than when I was cursing you for a knave. I knew all the time that you couldn't have done the dirty trick. Come over to me, Phil, and take my hand and tell me that you forgive me. Why, Phil, when I saw your violin and thought that I might never hear it played again, it turned me to a woman. The tears ran down my face."

The infernal old doting idiot, thought Joshua to his dark heart. It was well, indeed, that he had decided to strike the blow tonight. In the morning the will would be changed.

"Light the lamp on your bedside table, will you?" whispered Joshua, only dreading lest his voice should be known.

"Certainly," said the rancher, scratching a match and raising the chimney of the lamp. "But why all this whispering, Phil? Have you lost your nerve?" He touched the match to the wick, the flame ran nimbly around the circle, and, when the chimney was replaced, Henry Rival shaded his eyes with his hand.

"Haven't lost my nerve yet," said Joshua aloud.

"You!" growled Henry Rival. "Joshua! What are you up to here, at night?"

"You're not glad to see me, eh?" said Joshua. "You'd a lot rather talk to the card cheat?"

"None of your impertinence!" barked Rival. "And . . . get out and let me sleep. What do you mean by coming here and making a mock of me?"

"I came to tell you one true thing."

"I'm tired of having you around for a sort of walking conscience to tell me true things. Keep it until morning." He turned his back on Joshua.

"Turn back," said Joshua. "I came to tell you that you're a useless fool, and, because of that there's no place for you in the world. Turn back and look at me."

When Rival turned, he was looking in the face of a leveled Colt.

"It's Phil's gun," said Joshua. "He'll hang for it!"

"Ah," breathed the old man. "You devil!"

Joshua pressed the trigger. It seemed to him that the head of Rival was jerked back as the bullet struck before the roar of the explosion thundered into the ears of the slayer. Joshua walked calmly nearer and leaned to make sure of his work. There was no doubt of it. Death had been instantaneous. The old rancher lay on his back with his arms thrown out, a smile on his pale lips, and his dull eyes fixed on the ceiling.

Joshua threw the gun on the floor, then ran to the door. "Help!" he shouted. "Shorty! Help! Murder!"

IX

"PHIL USES POKER TACTICS"

What filled the mind of Phil, the Fiddler, as he galloped his mustang toward town, was the inescapable truth of what Hilda had told him. It was one of the four men who had been with him the night before that must have dropped the crayon into his breast pocket, and Fanshaw and Lefty Michaels were naturally out of the reckoning, which narrowed the field to Goshen and Camper.

From which should he try to force the confession? All his natural suspicion centered around Camper, but the fact that Camper had actually pleaded for him with his uncle that day had shaken Phil's confidence in his judgment. It seemed impossible that Camper could have filled such a double rôle. Accordingly, he picked out Goshen for his target.

It was eleven when he reached the town and entered the hotel. A sleepy night clerk gave him the number of Goshen's room, and he climbed straight to it.

In answer to his knock, the voice of

189

Goshen called out instantly. It was like such a little terrier of a man to be awake in an instant.

"It's Camper," said Phil, deepening his voice as artfully as he could. "Have to see you, Goshen. Very important."

"With you as soon as I get a light," said Goshen cheerfully.

Phil heard him scratch a match, and then a glow of pale light slipped through the crack beneath the door. Presently, the key was turned, and the door swung open.

"Come in, Bill," began Goshen. "What . . . ?"

But the fist of Phil Rival entered before his body, an iron-hard fist driven with the speed of a snapping whip. The blow landed flush on the point of Goshen's chin, and he crumpled soundlessly to the floor. Phil entered, locked the door again behind him, tied the hands of the senseless man behind his back, and lifted him to the bed. His lip was curling in distaste for his work. It was not his practice to take men unaware and strike them down by treachery, but the fierce voice of Hilda Surrey was never out of his ears. *I would feed them into a slow fire until they confessed the truth!*

So he hardened his expression and his voice as Goshen at length opened his eyes and blinked up at the ceiling.

"What the devil . . . ?" he began.

Phil shoved the cold nose of his Colt beneath Goshen's chin. "I'm here on business, Goshen," he said slowly. "If you peep, I'll blow the top of your head off. Talk soft and answer my questions!"

"Rival," breathed Goshen, and then was silent, watchful, with his teeth grinding softly.

"Goshen," said Phil, "I've heard the whole of the dirty business. You framed the deal, and you put that crayon in my pocket. Now, mind you, I ought to send you to kingdom come for that. But I'm going to give you a chance to get out of town. All I want is your signed confession of the plant, and then I'll swear to give you a running start for your hound's life."

But Goshen merely sneered at him. "You dirty dog," he said. "Why, I'd rather die ten times than double-cross myself like that. Pull the trigger, Rival. You'll get nothing out of me. But when they lynch you, I'll be pulling on the rope."

Without a word, Phil balled his handkerchief and thrust it into Goshen's mouth as a gag. He jerked the chimney from the lamp and held it close to the bare feet of Goshen, so close that the flame licked against the skin for an instant. Then the heart of Rival failed him. He replaced the lamp on the table, leaned above his victim, and took out the gag.

"You swine," gasped Goshen, the sweat pouring down his face.

"I'll burn them to the bone," said Rival. "I'll burn them till you write what I want."

"Burn and be hanged," said Goshen. "You'll get nothing from me."

Phil turned toward the lamp, then shook his head. He could not do it. Every nerve in his body was crying out at the horror of the thing. No, Hilda's idea belonged in the realm of bad dreams. It was too terrible for the hands of Philip Rival.

"Goshen," he said, "I can't do it. You or Camper . . . one of the two . . . put over the deal on me. I suppose it has to be you, but I'd rather be an exile the rest of my life than go through with this deal. I'll ask you one thing. Will you give me your word not to raise the house on my heels, if I leave you here ungagged?"

"I'll give you my word," retorted the other, "to furnish an extra strong rope when they hang you. That's all you get out of me!"

"Very well," said Phil. "Then I'll keep you quiet by force."

In five minutes he had trussed Goshen

hand and foot so that he could not stir, and the gag was fixed between his teeth once more, only loose enough to permit him to breathe. He gave a last glance at his prisoner to make sure that all was safe, blew out the light, and left the hotel, and once in the street he mounted and went for Camper's home.

It lay at the farther end of the main street, a neat little bungalow of modern construction, and the very apple of Camper's eye. There was no difficulty in entering, although the house was unlighted. The door yielded instantly to Phil's hand, and he stepped into an atmosphere rank with strong pipe smoke.

Through the living room, he entered a kitchen, and then went on, trying door after door, until he found the master's bedroom. The pudgy form of the lawyer lay in the bed with the bedclothes in a high mound above him. He snored gently, like a well-fed pig.

Phil himself lighted the bedroom lamp and had replaced the chimney on it before Camper roused himself and sat up in bed, rubbing his eyes. It was a flushed, bewildered face that Phil saw as he turned toward the bed. But all bewilderment instantly was banished from Camper's face as he looked up at Phil.

193

Instead, a wild terror seized him. He shrank back against the pillows and drew up the covers around him, like a frightened child taking refuge from the fear of ghosts. "Phil," he gasped, "why . . . what . . . what're you doing here, Phil?"

"Why," said Phil, smiling, "I got lonely, Camper. I come in to have a little chat with you."

The relief which swept over the face of Camper was ridiculous to see. He uttered a sort of groan as his fear left him, and he sat up in bed. "I was sort of having a bad dream," he said. "And when I woke up and saw that light . . . and you . . . it sort of took my nerve, Phil, d'you see?"

"That's bad," said Phil coldly. "It's pretty bad when a man loses his nerve."

The animation faded from the face of Camper. The surety departed. Terror once more widened his eyes. Phil Rival, at a glance, saw the shadowy guilt in the wretched soul of the man.

"Camper," he said, "are you broke?"

"Broke?" said Camper, his eyes gleaming with a faint hope. "Never broke when an old friend calls on me. Name what you want, Phil. I'll show you that I'm your friend."

"What?" said Phil. "I've still got a friend in spite of what happened last night?"

Camper turned gray. "It was an unlucky business," he said, wiping his trembling lips with the back of his hand. "I'm not one to judge my fellows. Besides, I have an idea that must have been a fixed job, Phil. I can't imagine you doing such a thing . . . I've told everybody in town that I couldn't imagine it . . . I told your uncle today!"

"That's mighty kind of you."

"Why, lad, you don't know the interest that I take in you. I fought out your father's case, you know. Isn't it natural that I should take an interest in his son?"

"Like father, like son," said Phil bitterly. "I wonder, if you worked for poor Dad the way you work for me?"

"Eh?" breathed Camper, his eyes going wild with fear again.

"I forget all the details of Dad's case," said Phil. "There was something in it about an alibi. He always swore that he could get a perfect alibi, if he could only locate a man, but that man could never be found."

"No, that was Jack Turner, and he ran out of the country. He was down in Mexico. Never could be brought to make a statement even years afterward." He cocked his head to one side and stared eagerly at Phil. "What do you know about Jack Turner?" he asked. "Have you seen him? Is that what's brought you in here?"

A strange suspicion seized upon Phil Rival. But the horror of it was too great. He pushed the thought away. But, in the meantime, he could play this situation out as he would have played out a poker hand — on a bluff. There was something about a meeting between Philip Rival and Jack Turner that filled the lawyer with dread. What was it? Was it something that Phil might have learned from Turner? He stared curiously at the lawyer, but he made his face blank as possible. "Yes," he said after the long pause that had terribly increased the nervousness of Camper. "I've seen Turner."

"Ah?" murmured Camper. "And what did he have to say? What yarn did he tell you? Jack always had a great imagination . . . could always spin you a wild yarn."

Camper was growing maudlin with fear. Phil decided to play his strongest card.

"I was with Turner on his deathbed, " he said calmly, "and before Turner died he told me everything." And so saying, he deliberately drew out his revolver.

X

"THE SOUL OF A COWARD"

There was a choked cry of fear from Camper. Then he flung himself on the floor and caught his hands together. "For the Lord's sake, Phil!" he begged.

The sick chill of suspicion that had run through Phil before was now strengthened. This man had had something to do with the downfall of his father. Indeed, his part in the tragedy, which had placed Rival behind bars and thereby brought about a quick ending to his life, was so terrible that he feared murder at the hands of the son of the man he had injured.

"What would you want your son to do to . . . a man like you?" he asked Camper.

"I'd want him to be merciful," said Camper. "I've always been a merciful man myself. . . ."

"What?" exclaimed Phil.

Camper was literally crushed back against the wall by the tone in which Phil spoke. His terror was so unmanly that it made the flesh of the younger man crawl with shame.

"Get up," said Phil.

"Not till you promise . . . not till you put away that gun, Phil."

Without a word, Phil dropped the weapon into the holster again. And William Camper staggered to his feet.

"Now we can talk," said Phil. "Mind you, Camper, I promise you that I don't want your life. All I want is the means of putting my father's reputation right, and my reputation after him. You can do it, Camper. You can write a statement that will clear us both."

Camper looked around him, blinking. He was grinding his hands together. "It means that I've worked all my life for nothing," he said. "If I make this statement, I have to leave . . . my house'll go for nothing. . . ."

"I'll see that the house is sold, and that you get a good price for everything in it. I'll send the money wherever you wish it sent."

"It isn't the money, Phil. But all my friends are here. All of my old friends. My friends are more to me than. . . ."

"Wasn't my father an old friend of yours?" asked Phil suddenly.

Camper bowed his head.

"You sent him to prison and broke his heart. I'm supposed to be an old friend of yours. But you blasted my name and. . . ."

He stopped speaking by a violent effort.

"Phil," gasped out Camper, "lemme tell you how it came about. I was just married. My wife was sick. We were terribly poor. When they came to me and made the offer, I cursed them and told them I'd see them hanged first. They . . . they came again that same night and doubled their offer. I took a gun and told them that, if they came once more, I'd simply start shooting. But they came back a third time and . . . I didn't shoot, Phil. I was weak. I sort of crumpled up under their offers. It was big money . . . and I was young . . . and my wife was sick . . . and. . . ."

"And so you sent my father away to die. . . ."

"No, no, Phil! I swear that I didn't dream that would happen. I had it all planned. Within six months I was going to start the wheels in motion. The governor knew your father and respected him. He'd've gotten Rival out. Besides, I had another way of working things. Turner was always sick of the game. He always wanted to confess that your father was innocent . . . wasn't even on the ground when the thing happened. I was going to get the confession mailed in from Turner before he started for Australia to keep clear of a lynching. But. . . ."

"But my father died before you could do it?"

"Yes, Phil. That was the crushing pity of it. I'll never get over that blow, if I live to be a hundred!"

Phil watched the lawyer turn up his bright little eyes to the ceiling in a sort of holy repentance, and he was seized with almost uncontrollable desire to set his foot on the fat body and crush it under his heel.

"It was very sad," said Phil. "However, that isn't all according to the story which Turner told me."

"Turner didn't know anything of the inside dope!" exclaimed Camper. "I swear he didn't, Phil. I'm telling you everything as straight as a string. All Turner knew is that I went to him and offered him some money, if he'd go down into Mexico and stay there so that he couldn't be called on to fix up the alibi. That's all he knew . . . that and the fact that I had a devil of a time finding him."

It grew upon Phil, the quiet horror of this narrative. By degrees he began to see the full blackness of the tale. His father was attacked with a false charge, his alibi was perfect, and then the enemy corrupted the very lawyer of Rival to carry the bribe to Turner, send him out of the country, and so plant poor Rival in jail, where despair and heartbreak killed him.

Then he saw a desk with pen and paper on it in a corner of the bedroom. "This goes in writing, Camper," he said.

Camper groaned, but the thought of the future was less terrible than the fear of Rival in the present. He stepped to the desk, sat down at it, and began to write swiftly. As he wrote, from time to time, Phil paused nearby and read down the page.

As the story grew, he became sick and sicker, and, when the confession ended and the name of Camper was scribbled beneath it, Phil stood back and fought against the desire to draw his gun in spite of the promise and drive a bullet through the heart of the older man. Instead, he stepped nearer and sat down on the edge of the desk.

"Camper," he said.

"Well?" asked Camper. "Isn't that enough, Phil? Isn't that everything I promised to do?"

"But I've still got some questions you can answer."

"Go on, Phil."

"How did the crayon get into my pocket last night?"

Camper shrank back in his chair, mute.

"I know the whole thing," said Phil, a blind rage sweeping across his eyes. "But I want the rest of the world to know it. I want you to write down that story as you wrote down the first."

Camper had lowered his face and buried it in his hands. "How can you keep from killing me, Phil?" he groaned.

"By watching myself," said Phil sternly, "and by knowing that I've got to get your story down in black and white."

"It was the money," said Camper. "Every man has his price. Joshua reached mine."

"Joshua!" cried Phil, and leaped up from the desk. "Joshua? Did you say my cousin bought you for this last little trick?"

"If I'm bad," said Camper malignantly, "and I've told you enough to show you what sort of things I've done . . . if I'm bad, Joshua is the master devil himself. He's got more twisting ways than a snake in. . . ."

"Joshua," breathed Phil. "Ah, I knew there was something wrong behind him."

"The hypocrite!" snapped Camper. "But he couldn't cover his trail all his life."

"Tell me what happened?"

"He offered ten thousand, if he became his stepfather's sole heir. . . ."

"And you were to do the rest for him? Why, Camper, you seem to have been a sort of omniscient villain. No matter what the task, if the fee is large enough, Camper will undertake to perform the work."

"Phil, all flesh is weak. . . ."

"Don't whine, man. Hang it, don't whine! I'd rather see you brazen it out than whine and try to find sympathy. I'll tell you this . . . you ought to be burned over a slow fire till the flesh rotted away from the bones. But I'm not the sort that can perform such little offices. I'm not a Camper, you see . . . I can't rise to all occasions for the sake of a fee. Camper, sit down and write out the story of what dear Joshua did and said. . . ."

Camper shuddered — then turned again, obediently, to his work.

Phil interrupted him only once. "You're getting clear on this, Camper. Joshua won't!"

"I hope you send him up for life!" snarled Camper over his shoulder, showing his yellow teeth.

In spite of himself, Phil could not help smiling at such cowardly malevolence. "Then give me another concrete proof against Joshua."

"Here . . . in this wallet." He jerked out a slip of paper, and Phil read on it:

I, Joshua Rival, promise to pay to William Camper, if I become sole heir to Henry Rival. . . .

"Perfect," breathed Phil.

There was a clattering of running feet of men and horses in the street. The noisy cavalcade poured up to the house of Camper. They came from the direction of the Rival ranch — evidently they feared that the murderer of Henry Rival would go for Camper next.

"Hello . . . Camper!" thundered a chorus. "Are you safe in there?"

"They've come to save you from me," said Philip Rival. "Answer them, Camper."

"Here!" Camper called, his voice choking, thin and small. "Here and safe, boys . . . all well in here!"

There was a rumble of disappointment, and the crowd surged back. But poor William Camper lowered his head into his hands and wept silently.

Rival took the paper from the desk and read it. All was well. He had enough in his possession now to jail Joshua and clear himself, and, above all, to make the name of his father forever clear.

So Phil stepped outside and stood under the freckled shadow of the tree at Camper's gate. Far in the distance the noise of the mob was dying away as it dispersed to its homes. Philip, turning down the street, went straight for the house of the sheriff.

XI
"JOSHUA IS BEWILDERED"

The shouts of Joshua were not needed to bring the cowpunchers in a rush for the house of Henry Rival. They had heard the bark of the revolver, and every man was out from his blankets and sprinting for the big house in an instant, gun in hand. They stormed in through the front door — they tumbled in through an open kitchen window.

Joshua found himself in the center of a maëlstrom.

"Shorty!" he thundered. "Didn't I order you to stand guard?"

"I stood guard," said Shorty. "I sure done my best. I'd swear that I didn't hear a thing come to the house."

"Go inside," said Joshua, stepping away from the bedroom door. "Go inside and see if anyone came to the house. This is your last day of work on this ranch!"

Through the door they went slowly, reverently. There was no need to tell them what they would find, and no need to explain how it had been done.

"We've got to get on the trail, boys," called Joshua from the hall. "Maybe we can run onto his trail and nail him before morning. At any rate, we have to try. Mind you, I'll pay a thousand dollars in hard cash to the man who gets Phil Rival dead or alive!"

"Very neat . . . very neat," muttered Shorty to himself.

The rest of the cowpunchers moved with a deep-throated grumble that meant business. No matter how fond they might be of Phil Rival, that dead body of the old man had rubbed away the last trace of their affection for him. Not a man in the party, with the exception of Shorty, but would have shot, and shot to kill, on sighting the fugitive.

"He'll go for the Surrey place," suggested someone. "He'll sure want to see Hilda before he gets out of the country."

"Is he as thick with her as that?" asked Joshua.

"Ain't they been sweethearts all these years?" was the response.

Joshua felt as though a chill had blown in the wind in a midnight gallop through his very heart. There was no doubt about it now. Phil Rival must certainly die. No mercy could be shown. If it came to the last crisis, he would even venture on battle himself against his formidable cousin. What a blind fool he had been to keep such a close eye upon business, that he had not heard even a rumor of the fondness of Phil for the Surrey girl!

Now the band was mounted, and they swept along the roads at a smart gallop, with Joshua riding his great, black horse in the lead and the others following in a scattered group. Now and again Joshua turned his head and looked over his men. It was a pleasant experience, this one of riding with his stanch retainers behind him. After a time, he would begin to make them more and more his special men. He would find ways of winding ties about their hearts. He would make himself necessary to them. Perhaps it would be possible to apportion small bits of land to them. Perhaps, when they married, he could give them little cottages. Why not establish a regular tribe of workmen on the Rival estate? From father to sons, they would know nothing but the will of the Rivals. There was something solemn and feudal about the idea that appealed to Joshua. It moved in rhythm with the beat of his galloping horse.

As he rode through the darkness, with the others spurring hard to keep up with the long strides of his Thoroughbred, other ideas came to Joshua. Now that he had absolute power over the estate, he would be kinder. Not that he felt any kindlier toward his followers, but kindness was a good policy. Men were such blind fools that they could not look behind a smile. Joshua would learn to smile. Men could be bought body and soul by a little gentleness, whereas force only made them the stronger to resist. That was the secret of Phil's power, for instance. All these men, until they saw the dead body of Henry Rival, had worshipped Phil. Joshua knew that, and he decided that he would steal Phil's fire and use it in his own cause.

On the whole, it was the most uplifted time of his life, that ride to the house of the woman he loved, the woman who loved Phil Rival. What more perfect than the ability to tell her, at the end of the ride, that the man she loved had been guilty of brutal murder on the body of an old and helpless man? He would kill that love of hers just as he had killed Henry Rival. That bullet had done two great bits of work for him. The future was bathed in a rosy light, a morning light. Nothing from this time on would be too great for him to undertake. Now the house of Surrey grew up before him out of the night, and he put his mind to the work immediately before him.

They came up to the house with a rush of hoofs which wakened the sleepers within. Almost before they dismounted, Surrey himself was at the front door, his son behind him.

"What's up?" they called to the newcomers.

"Is Phil Rival around here? Has he been here?" they asked.

"No sign of him," said Surrey. "After this you don't need to come here to find him. But what's new?"

"Nothing much," said one of the cowpunchers, "except that the dog sneaked back to the house tonight and murdered old Rival in bed."

There was a shrill cry from within the house. Hilda Surrey slipped through the door and confronted Joshua.

"It isn't true, Joshua!" she cried. "Tell me it isn't true?"

"I'm very sorry," said Joshua, stepping at once into his new rôle of gentleness, "but the men have seen Father dead in his bed, and they're wild to get to Phil. I've brought them along. It was my duty."

"If Henry Rival is dead," she answered with a conviction that amazed him, "Phil didn't do it."

It sent a chill through Joshua. It was as though she had pointed an accusing finger at him.

"Who could have done it, then?"

"Someone who wanted to take advantage of poor Phil. Besides, I can prove that he wasn't there."

The flash and roar of a thunderbolt falling before his eyes could not have been more amazing to Joshua. "How can you prove it?" he asked.

"Because he was here hardly half an hour ago."

"There was time for a fast rider with a horse ready to have killed Father and gotten here that much ahead of us, very nearly."

"Not half an hour," said one of the cowpunchers. "Could you swear to that time?"

"I can," said Hilda. "I looked at the clock when I went inside after I talked to him."

"Hilda!" shouted her father. "You've talked to him tonight?"

"Yes. And he's gone from here straight into town. If you want him, go hunt for him there. He told me where he was going."

"It's a plant between them," said Surrey suddenly. "They've worked together to draw the wool over our eyes. Wait a minute, boys. My son and I will join you."

In two minutes they were in the saddle,

and the ride began again. But it was in the direction of town that they moved. There was a faint possibility that Hilda had told them the truth. At least, they had no other clue to guide them. So they poured down the road toward the town until they encountered the figure of a hurrying horseman who approached from the opposite direction. They stopped him with a shout, and he answered with a haloo as he drew rein.

"Who's there?" they called as they jogged on toward him.

"Lefty Michaels," he answered.

"Where you bound?"

"For the Rival place."

"You're going the wrong way."

"How come?"

"There's no one there but a dead man."

"Eh?"

"Phil Rival killed his uncle. We're on his trail."

There was an explosion of incredulity from Lefty. "What sort of talk is this?" he exclaimed. "I got a telephone message from Phil fifteen minutes ago telling me to ride straight for the Rival house, and that he'd meet me there. If you want to see Phil, ride on with me."

Joshua drew up beside Lefty. "Michaels," he said, "what's in the air?"

"I don't know. All I know is that Phil is on fire with something. His voice shook over the telephone. He's excited as the devil about something."

"He's gone back to face the music," decided Surrey. "That's the way with some men. After they've committed a crime, they have to go back to the place, and, when they're arrested, they can't help trying to brazen things out. They have to talk. Phil is probably that way. He wants to get his friends around him. They'll give him a feeling of more confidence. But let's turn back, boys, and head for the ranch house again."

So back they turned, but Joshua no longer rode in the lead. It was very bewildering to him. By all the rules of expectation, and by all that he had heard, Phil Rival should be traveling hard to get into the upper mountains and forget his shame of the night before. But, instead, he was back in their midst. However, he could not escape. The net had been drawn too closely around him. It would have been preferable, of course, to have hunted Phil down with guns. It would be hard to face him and hear his protestations of innocence. But that was a small inconvenience compared with the great gain, so Joshua shrugged his shoulders and sent his black into the lead on the way home.

XII
"DEAD GAME"

They had ridden their horses in a complete circle by the time they got back to the Rival house. They found that others were there before them. Lights burned in various rooms. They heard voices stirring, and, when they threw themselves out of the saddles and swarmed into the house, the first man that Joshua encountered was the tall and solemn form of Sheriff Joe Waters. He was that old and white-haired man whose terrible name was so interwoven with the early history of the mountains that he was hardly more than half fact while one part of him remained pure legend.

There he stood in the hall of the Rival house with his white hair flowing down almost to his shoulders, his hands resting on the butts of his heavy, old guns, and his eyes fixed upon the face of Joshua.

As for Joshua, he would rather have met the devil with horns and fire. What fiend had inspired Phil Rival to bring the avenging spirit to the house?

"How are you, Rival?" the sheriff was saying. "I've come out here to see to some little things, and I've found a sad sight . . . my old friend Henry Rival, lying dead in bed. You've been out hunting the murderer, Joshua?"

"Riding hard," said Joshua, "until we heard that we'd better come here, if we expected to find him. So here we came. Is my cousin Phil in the house as we heard he'd be?"

"Phil brought me out," said the sheriff. "Yes, he's still here. He's in his uncle's room . . . all broke up, poor boy."

"The lying hypocrite!" shouted Joshua, burning with an honest indignation. "Sheriff, if a man is hung for the murder of Henry Rival, it will be his own nephew Philip. We heard a terrible argument between Father and Phil earlier this evening. Father had cut him out of his inheritance because of that shameful card episode. He finally told Phil what he had done. And Phil began to rave at once. He swore that he'd come back before morning and kill Father. Of course, Father paid no attention. Even I couldn't believe there was that much devil in Phil. But I got Shorty to stand guard outside the house. I lay down myself, with all my clothes on, ready for trouble. . . ."

"In your stepfather's room?" asked the sheriff with interest.

"No, in my own room. I thought that, if Shorty gave an alarm, I could get out in plenty of time. But Phil must have come in as silently as a cat. I heard the report of the gun. I ran down and found Father dead and Phil's favorite gun, lying on the floor. If he's in this house now, he should be arrested. You'll be responsible, Sheriff."

"The snake!" snarled the sheriff. "Boys, get Rival and bring him out here! If this turns out to be what it seems to be, you can finish Rival here . . . I'm going on into town. But speaking of guns, let me see that Colt of yours, Joshua, my boy."

"Certainly," said Joshua, and handed over his weapon. To his amazement it revolved in the agile fingers of the old sheriff. Its muzzle was presented within an inch of Joshua's breast.

"Good Lord," he breathed. "Is it a joke, Sheriff?"

"Not at all, lad," said the sheriff. "Just a time for talk. You'll be glad to know that I'm watching you every minute, and, if I see anything that looks suspicious, I'm going to touch off this trigger. Is that clear?"

"Friends," Joshua spoke out, "there's dirty work here. The sheriff is plotting against me.

I want you to bear witness. . . ."

"Bear witness to the way he answers some questions," interrupted Sheriff Waters, "I'm going to put to him and . . . come back, the rest of you . . . we'll let Phil Rival alone with his grief."

They came back in wonder. They stood packed around the sheriff and his prisoner in a close circle, and these were strong men who quivered in that moment of suspense.

"You lay down on your own bed to wait?" asked the sheriff.

"Yes," breathed Joshua, feeling a hand of ice close on his heart.

"That bed wasn't laid on tonight," said the sheriff.

"The wrinkles might have smoothed off," said Joshua.

"We found the will . . . it leaves everything to you," went on the sheriff. "Why would Phil kill his uncle to give the estate to you?"

"He wanted revenge."

"Phil ain't a revengeful man."

"Sheriff, you're taking his side."

"I am," said Waters.

"You're against me?"

"I am," said the sheriff.

"Will you tell me why?"

"Here's one reason," said Waters, and with his left hand he took a small paper from his pocket. "Here's your promise to pay Camper ten thousand dollars when you get the whole estate. Why did you make that promise?"

The brain of Joshua reeled. "He's done a great deal of work for the estate. . . ."

"He worked for Henry Rival, not for you."

"I wanted his influence to show Father that Phil was not a proper man to handle money. I intended to provide for Phil out of my own pocket."

The sheriff smiled. "I have Camper's signed confession," he said. "You can listen to it. Michaels, read this paper out loud . . . and start at the beginning."

It was a strange document to which that circle listened. They heard the fair name of the father of Phil cleared, and in another breath they heard the plot against Phil himself unfolded to the last detail. When the reading ended, there was a faint groan of wonder and detestation.

Joshua heard that groan and read his death in it. "May I see the signature on that paper?" he asked calmly.

"Show it to him, Michaels."

The paper was spread before Joshua's eyes. "It's a forged signature," he said. "It's a game. . . ." He had raised his left hand, as

217

he spoke, to touch the paper. Now he dashed his hand down, and the force of the blow knocked the weapon from the fingers of the sheriff.

Straight ahead leaped Joshua. He snatched a revolver from the holster at Michaels's hip. He plunged on. A blow with his club-like fist sent Jack Fanshaw sprawling. He leaped around the corner of the hallway and fled up the stairs beyond. Once at the head of them, he could turn down the hall and leave the house at the rear — then there was the open air and a chance for flight and safety. If only he could reach the head of those stairs!

The hall roared with a wild tumult of voices. It swept nearer. It bellowed just behind him as they ran around the corner of the hall and came in full view of the stairs. The distance was short, and there were good marksmen in that party, but the light was the treacherous flickering of a single oil lamp.

Half a dozen guns roared. The noise crashed at the ear of Joshua. But still he was unharmed. Here was the head of the stairs. He turned with a shout of triumph to flee down the upper hall, but, as he did so, it seemed that a hand struck him violently on the left shoulder. The force of the blow made him stumble, and he lurched heavily against the wall. There was another blow against his left thigh, and he crumpled to the floor.

He was done. Burning pains were thrusting through and through his shoulder and his upper leg. They had shot him twice, and, sprawling on the floor, he looked back and saw the old sheriff standing at the rear of the rest, with the gun poised in his hand.

At least there would be one life to pay for this. Joshua jerked up his own gun, but, before he fired, a third blow fell against him. The roof seemed to crush about him, then darkness swept across his eyes. It was only an instant of blackness. Then, out of the dark, he heard a voice saying: "A skunk . . . but a dead game one!"

He looked up. A dozen faces leaned above him. "I'll beat you yet," said Joshua. "The law will fight on the side of an innocent man."

A wave of dizziness struck his brain. Their voices became a disunited, meaningless jumble coming from far away, but striking with a strange force on his eardrums.

"And when I'm free, I'll get . . . Joe Waters . . . first . . . then Phil. . . ."

So he died.

The Gold Trail

A Reata Story

When this story appeared in Street & Smith's *Western Story Magazine* on January 6, 1934, under the George Owen Baxter byline, it was titled "Stolen Gold.". It was the fifth short novel to feature Reata who had proven to be one of Faust's most popular characters among readers. In all there were seven short novels in the Reata saga. The first of these, "Reata," appears in THE FUGITIVE'S MISSION (Five Star Westerns, 1997). The second, "The Whisperer," is to be found in THE LOST VALLEY (Five Star Westerns, 1998). The third, "King of the Rats," is to be found in THE GAUNTLET (Five Star Westerns, 1998). The fourth, "Stolen Gold," is to be found in STOLEN GOLD (Five Star Westerns, 1999). With this tale the saga continues with Reata's efforts to retrieve the gold stolen from the Decker & Dillon Bank.

I

"STOLEN GOLD"

Inside his roll of bedding, Pie Phelps had forty pounds of gold in a chamois bag. He had loosened the tie strings of the bag, worked the bag into a sausage shape, more or less, retied the mouth of the sack securely, and then lashed it inside the blanket roll. He felt that he had lashed it very firmly, but in that he happened to be wrong, and that was why the shadow of the law fell across his path.

The nature of Pie Phelps was as large and liberal as his mouth, which divided his face almost from ear to ear, and, although he knew perfectly well that the forty pounds of gold were part of the stolen money of the Decker & Dillon Bank in Jumping Creek, Pie almost honestly felt that it was now his own. So, as he rode across country, his mind was at rest. For one thing, it was Sunday, and if Sunday does not always produce good deeds, at least it is likely to cause a state of rather sleepy confidence. When Pie Phelps came across the hills and saw the long, low bunkhouse of the Lester Ranch, and when he heard the musical *ding-dong* of the cook's bell and the cook's voice, faintly and far away, telling the boys to — "Come and get it!" — Pie saw no reason why he should not ride up to the house and sit down at the table.

It was true that Colonel Lester had taken a leading part in the search for the stolen money when that treasure was lodged in the Jumping Creek marsh. It was true that the colonel's formidable foreman, Steve Balen, had been the straw boss in handling the workers. But Pie Phelps did not feel that any considerable suspicion rested on him. All that people could know with any surety was that he, as he had related, had been held up by a fugitive in the middle of the night, forced by the stranger to help in the saddling of four horses, and then driven into accompanying the man in the first part of the other's flight. All of these things were true, except that the fugitive had used not a .45-caliber Colt to compel him, but a forty-pound sack of gold. In fact, that was a far more persuasive weapon, for, although Pie Phelps looked like a caricature of a man, he had plenty of courage.

The people at the ranch house would be more than a little excited, when he dropped in for lunch. They would be sure to ask him a lot of questions about his strange adventure, and they might offer him some sympathy because he had been robbed of four horses. He grinned a little as he thought of a ten-thousand-dollar payment for four ordinary range bronchos. He was on his way north, where he would settle down in a part of the country where people had never seen his face before. There he might change his name, turn his gold into greenbacks, and then buy for himself just the sort of a small ranch that had always been his dream.

He was full of these comforting plans — unlucky Pie Phelps! — when he rode up to the side of the old ranch house, dismounted, and turned his mustang into a corral. He then carried his saddle and the heavy bedding roll and the bridle to the open shed which communicated between the kitchen-dining room and the bunk-house. After that, listening greedily to the sound of knives and forks against tin plates inside the kitchen, he retreated to the pump, filled a basin with water, and covered his face and hands with suds. His washing did not include neck and ears. Pie Phelps was only interested in presenting a good front.

As he dried his face and hands on an unsoiled section of the coarse, yellow, roller towel that hung beside the kitchen door, he looked at the trees that loomed on the other side of the hill. He could see, also, the red tip of the pyramidal-roof of the house of Colonel Lester, for the moment the colonel had bought the property, he had left the old ranch house for the hired men and built for himself and his daughter a huge mansion with a Georgian porch of slender white pillars. To Pie Phelps, who had once stood in awe in front of that porch, it had seemed as impressive as any church façade or the front of any bank.

Pie had not neglected to wet his hair. He now took a big-toothed comb that hung by the towel, looked in a cracked mirror that was nailed against the wall — too low for the comfort of such a tall man as Pie — and whipped the wet hair into place. The part ran back two or three inches from his low brow and then was lost in a confused jungle of disorder. But Pie had made his toilet, and he was proud of it. Being alone, he enjoyed himself for two seconds by lowering his eyelids and then turning his head to either side. He had heard a man say that a big mouth is a sign of character. Without stretching his lips, Pie could see that he had lots of character.

Now he climbed the steps, rapped at the open door of the kitchen, and walked in. It was a big room — this end devoted to the uses of the cook and his big stove, the other end filled by the long table. That table was now surrounded by the men of the ranch, and at the farther end of it appeared the tall form and the narrow shoulders and the ugly face of famous Steve Balen. He was one of the few men in the world who deserved the title of "two-gun man," because he could shoot straight with left or right; he was almost the only one of the two-gun men who was able to lay claim to a life of sterling honesty at which no one had ever dared to point a finger of accusation.

When Steve saw the stranger come in, it could not be said that his face lighted in the least. But having a load of string beans on his knife at that moment, he emptied the cargo into his mouth so that he could point more freely with the knife to the end of the table, opposite him. Around the beans, Steve Balen managed to say: "Lay another place, Doc."

The rest of the crowd gave Pie Phelps at least more attention, if not a more rousing welcome. Some of the men half pushed back their chairs and turned sharply to the newcomer. A little murmur ran around the table. Two or three waved their hands. One man said: "Hello, Pie."

When Pie sat down, a grim-faced man on his right muttered: "How's things? Caught the gent that robbed you of them four hosses?"

"Ain't caught him yet," said Pie Phelps. "Goin' to get the runt, one of these here days."

"Yeah? He was a runt, was he?" asked Steve Balen from far away.

"Well, I dunno," retracted Pie. "He wasn't so dog-goned big. Just about average, maybe."

"Yeah. That's what I heard you tell the judge," said Steve Balen, and there was no ring of conviction in his voice. "I guess the gun that he pulled on you must have been man-sized, though."

"Yes, it looked like a cannon to me, all right," agreed Pie. He was glad to have a loaded plate brought to him. Over this he leaned, steadied the edge of it in the firm grip of his left hand, and began to work with his fork, giving it a good, free scooping motion that cleared long furrows through the heaps of food. With his face inclined away from the gaze of the company, he was free to remember certain details of the other night, and how the voice of Steve Balen had rung nasal-hard and clear from the face of the cliff down which Balen and his men were climbing in pursuit of the criminal.

Pie Phelps had started his meal when the others were half through. He was catching up nobly, toward the end, but he lingered to roll a cigarette and enjoy a fourth cup of acrid coffee before he went out to catch up and saddle his mustang, which by this time would have filled its belly with water and would have grazed on some of the sun-cured grasses that still grew around the edges of that capacious corral.

It was this final delay of Pie's that caused the trouble, because, when the other men trooped out from the kitchen, shuffling as cowpunchers will, walking with their knees well apart, Steve Balen, who was a tidy man, as a straw boss or a foreman ought to be, picked up the narrow bedding roll that had fallen down from the horn of Pie's saddle, where it hung from a peg on the wall.

When he picked it up, his eyes opened a little. The extra forty pounds made him exclaim: "What's Phelps got in here? Half a dozen guns?" With that, he gave the bedding roll a hard shake. This was where chance and a bit of carelessness in the tying of a single knot proved hard on Pie. For the weighty, little bag of chamois leather broke loose from its fastenings and slid out onto the floor of the shed.

Two or three of the other men saw the thing and looked casually at it. But the teeth of the foreman were set hard as he picked it up. He deliberately untied the mouth of the bag, dipped his hand into the contents, and then allowed a sparkling yellow shower of metal dust to pour back into the chamois sack.

"This here," said the grating voice of Steve Balen, "is sure the gun that robbed Pie Phelps of his four hosses, and a piece of his time."

Everyone had seen it, by this time — that is, everyone except Pie, who now came out with the fumes of strong coffee in his throat and the fumes of tobacco sweetening his nostrils. Then he saw tall Steve Balen standing there with a gun in one hand and the bag of gold in the other.

"Well," said Balen, "it was sure a whale of a heavy weapon that gent pulled on you, the other night. Dog-gone me, if I hardly blame you for givin' right up and doin' what he wanted you to do."

Pie Phelps, as has been stated before, was no coward. He regarded the chamois sack with a calm eye, lifted his glance to Balen, and then inhaled heartily on his cigarette.

"Well, Steve," he said, "what about it?"

"Dog-gone me, if I know," answered Balen. "What you think yourself?"

"Dog-gone me, if I know what to think," said Pie Phelps. "I been wonderin'. Would you call it thievin'?"

This fine point caught the attention of all the cowpunchers far more heartily than the more spectacular feat of the man's capture.

A 'puncher said: "How would it be stealin'? The money was give to him, wasn't it?"

"Maybe you'd call it receivin' stolen goods?" said another.

"He might do a lot of suspectin', but, when he took the sack, how would he *know* that they was stolen goods?" demanded Balen.

"That's right," said another 'puncher. "Dog-gone me, if lawyers don't have a pretty hard time figgerin' things out. I wouldn't be no judge for love or money, says I. *Keepin'* the goods after he heard tell about the stealin' of them . . . that would be the worst thing ag'in' Pie, I reckon."

"We'll have to go up and see Colonel Lester," said Steve Balen. "There ain't no doubt in my mind that you're as crooked as anything, Pie, and dog-gone me, if I would want to take the blame for doin' nothin' about it!"

II
"JILTED"

There was plenty of trouble up there behind the white columns of Colonel Lester's house. It had started half an hour before, when Agnes Lester, under the big trees south of the house, steeled herself to say to Tom Wayland: "We can't be married next month, Tom."

Tom Wayland was such a big fellow and such a handsome fellow, and the mirror had told him so often all about himself, that it required time before the full weight of this speech struck him. He fairly reeled under the impact, however, when the blow came home. Then he stared at the smallness of the girl, and the big blueness of her eyes, and it was all he could do to keep himself from sneering. Someone had said that all small men have small natures. Tom weighed two hundred pounds, and, therefore, he agreed with the remark. He said to himself that the girl was a fool. But that, of course, was apparent. Otherwise, she would never have been capable of saying such a thing to him. But even if she were a fool, she was the daughter and the only heir of Colonel Lester's square miles of ranch. Therefore, Tom did not sneer. He merely said: "This is a terrible thing, Agnes."

"I don't think it's terrible," she answered. "You don't care about me, Tom."

"You haven't any right to say that," he declared.

At this, she put her head a bit to one side thoughtfully. "I don't suppose I have," she answered, "but none of us is such a very mysterious creature. I dare say that you've seen through me like glass. And I think I've been able to look a little way into you, Tom. I know that a lot of marriages are not romantic. I know that it would be a very good thing, in a way, if the Wayland and the Lester properties were joined. I'm sure that Father and your father and you have a lot of interest in that. But I'm selfish *and* I'm romantic. I want to be in the center of the stage, when my marriage comes along."

He was so angry — because everything she said was true — that he turned quite white. He put a hand behind him and gripped it hard. Truthfully, it must be admitted that he wanted to punch her pretty little face for her. He knew, above all, that this was unfair in nature, because pretty girls should not have enough brains to see through the big, powerful brains of their masters — men. He wanted with all his might to hurt her. Afterward, he would arrange matters with the colonel. That would be easy.

"Agnes," he said, "I've known for a good many days that you've been feeling differently about me. Ever since that day down on the island in the marsh . . . ever since the day that pickpocket, Reata, was run off your father's place . . . ever since that day, you've felt differently about me."

"Yes," she said. "That was when I began to make up my mind."

This cool admission staggered him. "One glance at a pickpocket, one look at a sneak thief, and you change your mind about what men should be? Agnes, is it because you wanted to see me pick up the little whippersnapper by the nape of the neck and throw him off the place? Great heavens, my dear, a fellow of my size could not touch a little rat like Reata."

She shook her head. Truth was in her like a cold poison and it had to out.

"That isn't the reason you wouldn't touch him, Tom," she said.

"You mean that I was afraid of him?" said Wayland.

"All the men were afraid of him, when they knew that he was the one who had killed that horrible monster, Bill Champion," she said.

He was fairly checkmated. There was no move open to him. He could feel that his face was working with his rage and with his open and discovered shame. That was why she looked a little away from him as she went on: "Tom, I'm going to ask you to tell my father that our marriage can't go through. If I tell him, there will be a frightful scene. He's so sure of his strength and his control over me that he may do some dreadful thing. After he's delivered a judgment, he's much too proud to change his mind. I want to beg you to go to him and tell him that we simply don't care for one another enough to marry."

"Well," said Tom Wayland, "I'll do it. I have to do it, if you ask me to."

She did not even say that she was sorry. She merely thanked him. He went off with his head whirling. If he had been sure of anything in the world, he had been sure of her. If he had been sure of anything, he had been certain that she was just a sweet, little, clinging sort of a thing that a husband could pat on the head now and then, while he went about his more important affairs. She was good enough to look at, and her husband would be envied. That had about summed her up.

Now she had turned into this soft-voiced, soft-eyed seer and bold speaker of the truth. Suppose that a lamb should stand up and hit a lion between the eyes and knock the lion stiff — yes, it was like that. However, he was quite determined to play the part of a man.

He went straight to Colonel Lester, who had just come in from his daily ride — or parade — across his range. As the colonel pulled off his gloves in the hall, Tom Wayland said: "Colonel Lester, I've got to tell you something. The thing isn't going through. Between Agnes and me, I mean. It can't go through."

The colonel turned from him, placed his hat on the rack, laid his gloves on the table, and brushed some dust off his coat. "You mean the marriage?" said the colonel gently.

Tom Wayland knew that a terrible river of anger was being dammed up behind the teeth of the colonel, but he blundered on: "It can't be worked. I'm sorry. I thought. . . ."

"You're sorry, are you?" said the colonel. "When the plans that *I* have laid are to be shattered, when the fortune that . . . when the forethought of years is to be . . . when a young puppy dares to jilt my child!"

This speech was not exactly coherent, and yet the meaning of it was clear enough. The last phrase came out with a good, hard ring to it. The colonel wanted some good grounds for his rage, and he found a good basis for it in his last words. Every man has a right to be wroth, when his daughter is cheaply esteemed and treated.

The colonel took a breath to let out another terrible blast, but Tom Wayland bowed to the blast. He forgot his good, manly intentions.

"*She* isn't the one who's being jilted," he said.

"The insufferable arrogance of the young fellows who can have the . . . ," began the colonel. Then he saw that the last response of Wayland had altered the matter a good deal and required a refitting of words and measures. "Agnes?" said the colonel, panting a little because of the pressure of excess steam. "*Agnes* is the one who is not pleased?"

"Colonel Lester," said Tom Wayland, "I don't want you to let her know that I've told you. I came here to take the full blame on my own shoulders. But then I saw . . . I felt . . . I knew, all at once, that it wouldn't be right for me to let you dream that I could ever treat you or yours without the greatest respect, and affection, and esteem. I have to tell you the truth!"

Tom Wayland began to be noble, as he worked into this speech. He began to make a few of those fine, wide gestures that start with the hand on the heart. He was shocked when the colonel merely said: "You and your truth! Where's that ungrateful brat?"

"Agnes is outside under the trees," said Tom Wayland. "But please, Colonel Lester, please don't let her know that I've spoken to you in such a way as to. . . ."

"I'll be the height of tact. She'll know nothing," said the colonel. "But I'm going to get to the root of this nonsense."

If there was one thing, above all else, upon which the colonel plumed himself, it was on his possession of the most exquisite tact. He walked slowly out of the house now, and gathered himself, and arranged his features. He presently produced a smile, but the smile furrowed a face that was half red and half white.

When he got beneath the trees, he found Agnes reading in a hammock. Yes, just lying there, stretched out, one hand under her head, reading — in a hammock! Oh, these infernal young lazy females who waste their time on silly romances, and who, at their sweet pleasure, do not hesitate to smash to pieces the profoundest schemes of their parents — and then lie down again in the hammock to the next sickly sweet chapter! The red cover of the book was to the colonel like a red flag to a bull. Yet he constrained his voice to say gently: "What are you reading, my dear?"

"The cookbook, Father," said Agnes, and she sat up dutifully in the hammock.

"The which?" said the colonel, going a trifle blank.

"The cook has never been able to bake real Boston beans," said the girl. "I love 'em . . . on Saturday nights, don't you?"

"Humph," said the colonel.

"I mean," said Agnes, "that, when you're hungry in the middle of the night, it's always nice to find some cold baked beans with bread and butter. Don't you think so?"

Baked beans? Bread and butter? The colonel threw good nature and tact to the winds.

"You can bread and butter your beans when Tom Wayland is walking out of my house forever?" he shouted suddenly. He raised his hand and shook his forefinger, also his entire fist, at the girl. She stood up. "The plan which would affect the entire future of this county . . . the cultural future of the West . . . the whole effort toward which I have been pouring out . . . in short, the work of my life is what you're throwing over your shoulder for a pot of baked beans!" shouted the colonel.

She did not appear to notice the lack of sequence in these remarks. She merely said: "I thought Tom would have to put the blame on me."

"Confound it," roared the colonel, "on whose shoulders *does* the blame belong?"

"On mine, I suppose," said the girl.

"Then march into that house this minute and beg Tom Wayland to forgive you for being a fool!" commanded the colonel. He wished for his riding whip to give his gesture more dignity; there was plenty of force in it, at that.

"Do you want me to ask Tom to consider that I haven't talked frankly to him?"

"Do what I tell you," said the colonel.

"A man who would let me do that . . . would you want me to marry such a man?" she asked him. She was neither pale nor red. She was simply steady. Something — just a trace — of this calm iron had been in her mother. The colonel felt as though a dreadful ghost had looked in upon his soul.

"Go . . . instantly!" he shouted.

"I can't go, Father," she said.

Colonel Lester actually swallowed the first ten words that rushed into his mind. The effect was to choke him and make the eyes pop out of his head. At last he gasped: "Go . . . to your room . . . and stay there!"

She went, her head a little bowed, the red-backed cookbook tucked under her arm.

III
"REATA'S VISIT"

The colonel stalked back toward the front door of his house in such a fury that his heels banged down on the ground in a sort of goose-step that shook his entire body. Just as he was swinging in toward the steps of the porch, Steve Balen and half a dozen others came up with the big, loose form of Pie Phelps striding among them.

"Colonel," said Steve Balen, "here's the gent that passed the four hosses to the thief that stole the gold out of the marsh. Just now I shook down a forty-pound sack of gold dust out of his bedding roll. I guess the crook bought him, all right. But what we wonder is . . . what we oughta do with him?"

There are such things as sudden transferences of the passions. The colonel made a perfect one at this instant. The fury that was ripened and on tap under high pressure in him was instantly turned loose on Pie Phelps.

"The scoundrel!" shouted the colonel.

"Put him down . . . down" — he was about to say into the dungeon, but remembered himself in time — "into the sub-basement. Lock him up there. Tie his hands and feet. Leave him in the dark with a guard at his door. Let him have some solitary darkness for reflection . . . and . . . and . . . send for the sheriff. If there were *men* in this part of the world, they wouldn't ask me what to do with . . . with horse thieves and . . . and rascals . . . they'd hang them up to the first tree!" He indicated the trees beside his own house, and then strode through his front door.

Steve Balen said: "Well, dog-gone me, the chief is kind of upset. I guess we'd better take you down into a nice cool cellar and leave you there for a while, Pie. Stud, you and Bill take him down there and lock him up, and the pair of you take turns watchin' him, till the sheriff sends out. Dog-gone me, if I ain't sorry, Pie, but you heard what the boss said."

"Sure," said Pie, looking toward the tree. "I heard, all right. The cellar is good enough for me."

"Tuck," said the foreman, "you sashay into Jumpin' Creek and get hold of the sheriff or somebody. I'm a deputy, all right, but I don't want to have that ride all the way in and back."

★ ★ ★

That was why Pie Phelps sat in the darkness, close to the door of that dingy cellar room, and communed through the panels with his watcher.

"Supposin' that everything was to go wrong," he said. "What would happen in the court? I mean, suppose that they was to find me guilty of something?"

"Receivin' stolen goods?" said Bill, on the outside of the door.

"How would I know they was stolen?" queried Pie sadly.

"You wouldn't guess it?" Bill said. "Not with Steve Balen hollerin' off the top of the cliff to stop that thief, and the rest of us yappin' pretty loud?"

"I had a cold in the head, and I wasn't hearin' very good," said Pie.

"I dunno that I'd tell a judge and a jury about havin' a cold in the head," said Bill thoughtfully.

"No, I dunno that I will," Pie answered, on second thought. "But supposin' that they socked me into jail, what you think it would be?"

"I dunno. Receivin' stolen goods is bein' a fence. A fence gets socked pretty hard. I dunno. Maybe ten or a dozen years."

"Ten or a dozen chunks of hellfire!"

howled Pie Phelps. "Lemme out of here!"

"Dog-gone me, I'd like to, but I can't," answered Bill.

"Lemme out!" Pie Phelps shouted. Then, realizing to the full his unhappy condition, his voice sank into the longest and the deepest of groans.

A good many events were being prepared by chance at this moment. For one thing, when Tuck cantered into Jumping Creek, he intended to go straight to the office of the sheriff. And there was the sheriff, waiting as a good sheriff should, with a goose-quill toothpick laboring earnestly to remove a bit of corn husk from between two molars. So before the middle of the afternoon the sheriff in person should have arrived at Colonel Lester's ranch to receive Pie Phelps into his custody, and, if he had done so, perhaps everything else would have been changed.

But when Tuck was cantering his mustang blithely down the main street of Jumping Creek, it just happened that he saw Sim Matthews come around a corner — good old Sim Matthews who had been away south of the Río Grande for two years and who was loaded, everyone said, with tales about the romantic Mexicans. And Sim ran out into the street and hailed his friend, and dragged him off his horse with big, happy hands, and pulled him into the Trotting Fool Saloon.

Those powerful hands restrained Tuck, who was quite weak with happiness at seeing his friend and the pungent smell of whiskey which favored the air of the Trotting Fool.

Even by one hand, Sim Matthews was able to hold his friend, while he ordered and paid for drinks with the other. Together they hoisted the glasses and laughed in one another's eyes.

"You dog-gone old worthless piece of rawhide, Sim," said Tuck.

"You blasted son of a wall-eyed Paiute clam eater," Sim said affectionately.

"I gotta go down the street and leave word with the sheriff, and I'll be right back," said Tuck.

"Sure. I'll walk along with you," said Sim, "soon as we've had one more drink. I wanna tell you about what happened to me in Chihuahua, though, when I met up one day with a lean slice of bacon by name of Honorario Oñate, or some sort of moniker like that. . . ."

Time, which had taken a good look at the pair who leaned at the bar of the Trotting

Fool, promptly disappeared from the place and did not return to lay a startling finger upon the conscience of Tuck until the dark of the night was spread over the town.

Just after twilight a rider came over the hills on the very trail which Pie Phelps had ridden. It was Reata, riding without song or whistle, down-headed, young no more in spirit. The little dog, Rags, who ran ahead of the trotting mare, did not need to hurry to keep ahead of the smoothly shuffling forehoofs of Sue. Her head was down, like the head of her master, but for all her shuffling she would not stumble more than a mountain sheep. For all the gauntness of her outline, and the crookedness of her neck, and the miles she had put behind her, there was a storm of tireless speed locked up in her tough body.

Reata, when he saw, at last, the glimmering lights of the ranch house, instead of continuing toward it, swung to the side and rounded the hill until he was close to the mansion of the colonel. He rode up among the trees, dismounted, and approached the house gloomily. For he was coming, as he had promised, to see Agnes Lester once more. He was going to say good bye before he left this part of the world forever; if need were, he was going to tell her why — that he had lived too long with thieves to escape from their influence now with ease. He would even tell her, if the occasion demanded, that he was the thief who had stolen the gold from the Jumping Creek marsh. Could he go further? Could he tell how Pop Dickerman and Harry Quinn and the others had bamboozled him, until he was convinced that hidden treasure was the rightful property of the first man to find it? He doubted it. She was a gentle thing, trusting, dear, and true, this blue and golden girl; but, even to her faith, there would be a limit.

Looking up toward the house, he saw that all the windows were dark on that side of the place, except one in the second story. And at this open window sat a girl with the lamplight glowing on her golden hair.

To Reata, the thing was clear. Chance had placed her in his full view solely so that he would be able to see her with no trouble. For, if he presented himself at the door, he would very likely be ordered from the Lester place, as he had been ordered once before.

The thing was extremely simple — for Reata. He stood under the window and whistled. The little dog, Rags, sat down at his master's feet and looked attentively up as though he knew what it was all about.

At the whistle, the girl leaned out over the window sill, holding a book in her hand.

"It's Reata," he called to her.

As though the name were a blow, she swayed back out of his view. Was that all? Would the shade be drawn down indignantly? No, she appeared again.

"I can't come down," she said.

"Then I'll come up," said Reata.

"You can't," was the guarded whisper. "Father won't let me see a soul."

"I'm not a soul. I'm only a Reata," he said. "May I come?"

"They won't let you into the house!"

"I'll walk up the wall then," he said.

At that, he pulled from his coat pocket the forty feet of his rope, sliding the leather round of it, pencil-thin and strong as steel cable, through his expert fingers until it was a double strand. Then he threw, and, with the end of the long noose thus made, he caught the projection of the wooden hooding above the window. He swayed back, putting his weight against the line, to make sure that it was strongly fixed. Then, as he had promised, he simply walked up the wall, handing himself along the rope with his powerful arms, and walking up the boards at the same time. He made the thing seem simple, but a circus would have paid him to do the trick in public.

She was protesting all the way, although, with the grip of both hands, she steadied the lines, until suddenly he was seated on the sill of the window.

"Quick! Come in, or they'll see you against the light," she commanded.

"Put out the light then," said Reata. "I can't come into the colonel's house till he invites me."

IV
"A FRANK TALK"

When she went to the lamp and leaned over it, all her face and hair were lost in flame color. Then at a breath she was a part of the darkness. He could hear her coming toward him, but she was almost at the window again before he could make her out. But seeing was not important. He had his memory in place of that.

"This isn't all right," he said. "If somebody came in and found you talking to a tramp on your window sill, there would be trouble. But I promised to come back, and here I am."

"I'm glad you came. I would have come down," she answered, "but you see I have to stay in my room."

"Ill?"

"No, I'm being punished."

"You?" said Reata. "Punished? Kept in your room? No, I don't believe that."

"It's the truth."

"Not for something you've done, but something you didn't do," said Reata.

There was a bit of silence in answer to this remark. It extended long enough to show that she did not want to continue the subject.

"I've come to say good bye," said Reata then. "I'm drifting out of this part of the country."

"How far?" she asked.

"A thousand miles or so."

"There's something wrong, then," she said.

"Not with the country," answered Reata. "It's my country. I know all this part of it. I've got all the mountains put down in my mind so that I can walk around 'em, and tell you what the back looks like when I see the front. I know where the rivers go and the way they run. I know the water holes in the desert. It's all my country and it's the best in the world. The trouble's with me." He paused there, to gather his courage. She said nothing, but he felt that she was with him. "Listen," said Reata, "I want to come clean to you."

"I want you to," said the girl.

"Because I'm saying good bye, I can talk out, can't I?"

"Say anything you want," she told him.

"When I saw you the other day," he began, "it was like hearing a song that fits right into your memory. Afterward, you can whistle it. D'you mind talking to me like this?"

"No, I like it."

"I went off star-gazing and daydreaming. But, now, I want to tell you why I was down here in the marsh. I was looking for the gold. That night, I went back and got it."

"You were the one? Well, it had to be someone like you."

"I'm going to tell you another thing that'll be hard for you to believe. I didn't know that stuff was stolen from the Decker and Dillon Bank. The people who told me where to find the stuff in the tree let me think that it was cached there by an old miner. Can you believe that?"

There was a bit of waiting. "I want to believe you," she said. "Pretty soon I shall."

"Anyway, when I found out that I'd been tricked, I didn't take any of the stuff. I got to thinking things over, and I saw that, much as I liked this part of the world, it wasn't the place for me. The fact is, I've been what Tom Wayland called me. I've been a crook. I've been jailed for crookedness."

"That was all wiped out by the governor of the state," she answered, "after you got rid of Bill Champion."

"Not even the governor can wipe out such

things," said Reata. "You know how it is. I can feel the crookedness in me. I'm a lazy fellow. I like to take the easiest way. And the easiest way is the crooked way, especially when you're around a lot of people who know how to give you wrong starts. Going straight ought to be a habit. I'm going to go away somewhere and try to get into the habit."

"I understand," she said.

"That's the whole story," said Reata. "I'll say good bye and get out of here before somebody walks in on you. Sometime I'm going to see you again, when I'm on my feet and standing straight."

"When you're older, and turning gray, and when you're hard from handling money and watching the dollars? Is that when you'll see me again?" she asked. "I won't want to see you then, Reata."

His mind reached out after these words, but he could not understand them very clearly, they were such a shock to all his pre-conceptions of her.

"You've been frank with me, and I'm going to be frank with you," she went on suddenly. "When I saw you out there in the marsh, making that big mastiff helpless, and then freezing Tom Wayland cold with fear, it wasn't like a song, to me. It was like hearing good steel ring. I've kept on hearing it, ever since. That's why I hate to have you go away."

"I'm getting a bit dizzy," he told her.

"Don't," said the girl. "I've been trying to find the same ring in other men, and I haven't found it. That's why I'm confined to my room tonight. I told my father that I couldn't marry the man he wanted for me."

"Wayland!" exclaimed Reata. "It's Wayland that you mean!"

"Yes, it's Tom Wayland."

Reata said nothing. His heart was beating so hard that speech would have been very difficult for him, even if there had been words in his mind. "What should I do?" he asked her at last.

"Follow your way," she answered. "It may bring you back across my life, one of these days."

"If you'll say the word. . . ."

"I don't want to say it," she replied. "There's no good in saying it. You're a free man, Reata, and I want you to stay free. We like each other a lot. That's true, isn't it?"

"When I think what you mean," began Reata, "when I think what you would be if. . . ." She began to laugh. He stopped, amazed and angry.

"It's no good, Reata," she told him. "You

see how it is. If we really can mean anything to one another, words will never say it. Talking wouldn't help. Talking is only good for the sort of life that I'm leading. I talk to men and women, and men and women talk to me. We have our jokes and pleasant times, and every day is sweet and pretty . . . and small. Suppose that I tried to pull you into this sort of a life, and suppose that you were willing to come. After a while, you'd be like the others. Just small and trifling."

"It sort of staggers me," said Reata. "It makes me want to fight."

"What does?"

"Your talking like this. You ought to be sort of sweet and gentle and a little silly and childish. Instead of that, you talk like a man. It makes me sort of mad."

"Not like a man," she answered. "I know what you mean. I have a pretty face and nice big blue eyes. I know how to use 'em, too. I've worked and worked to look sweet and simple and all that. But even when I'm talking out and out to you, Reata . . . well, there's a mile of difference between this talk and man talk."

"Aye," said Reata, "there is. But a fellow would have to be on the jump to keep even with you, I suppose."

"Do you think so?" she asked. "Maybe. I

don't know. A pat on the hand and a smile wouldn't be enough for me. I'm sure of that."

"You know," Reata said, "a minute ago I thought this was turning into a regular love scene. I was about to reach out and get hold of your hand. But, by Jiminy, look how things have turned out."

"Well," she said, chuckling, "you told me the truth about yourself, and I had to give you an even break, didn't I?"

"Thanks," said Reata. "I wish I had some light on this subject. I've thought that I could see you in my memory. But not the sort of a girl you've turned out to be."

"It isn't safe for you, if I light the lamp," she said. "Here's my hand, Reata."

"It's not a whale of a big hand," he said.

"It'll hold onto a friend very hard, though," she said.

"I'll bet it will," said Reata. "I'm saying good bye, and wishing Tom Wayland a lot of bad luck."

"Bad luck? It would be worse luck for him, if he married me. Before long, he'd want to give away all the Lester acres and beef to charity, if he could give me away with the rest. There's another thing I ought to tell you. There was that fellow you hired the four horses from that night."

"Hired 'em?" said Reata. "Well, that's right. What about him?"

"Pie Phelps is here in the house."

"Thunder, no! Is that his name?"

"Yes, that's his name. He came here for lunch today. Steve Balen found the sack of gold in Phelps's blanket roll. My father was in a fine fury, at about that time, and he had Phelps put down into the sub-basement, and a guard placed over him."

"Thanks," said Reata. "I suppose . . . confound it, I suppose I ought to do something about it."

"I imagined that you'd think that," she answered.

"But why?" he argued. "I paid Pie a hundred times over for what he did for me. He's lost the pay and the horses. But that isn't my fault."

"No, it isn't your fault," said the girl.

"Why should I burn my fingers on account of Pie Phelps just now?"

"There's no reason," she answered.

"Still, to lie there in the dark till the sheriff comes . . . I can't let him stay there. Am I a fool, if I try to get him loose?"

"I suppose you are," said Agnes Lester. "Reata, there's a wide-awake armed man down there, every moment. And isn't it true, as people say, that you never carry a gun? Would you really go down there and risk your life for a fellow like Pie Phelps?"

"I'm a fool," said Reata. "You don't want me to go, then?"

"Oh, I want you to be your whole self."

He caught her suddenly, and drew her closely into his arms.

She made no resistance, but she said: "Please don't, Reata."

"Why not, when I love you, and you half love me?" he demanded.

"Because I'm a silly thing," she answered. "If you kiss me, I'll begin to belong to you from that moment. That's no good, is it? If you follow your own life and your own way, as you ought to, maybe you'll never see me again . . . and I don't want to sit here the rest of my life with nothing but an aching in my heart."

He kissed her hand, instead, and kept his head bowed over it for a long moment, although he could not tell whether there was more love or awe or astonishment in his mind.

V
"FLIGHT"

Since the house was built on the side of a hill, there were plenty of cellar windows along the lower wall of the building. When Reata had slipped down to the ground and shaken his rope loose from the window gable above him, he went straightway to that row of low, squat windows and began to try them. The second one moved under his hand, and he slid into the damp darkness of an underground room.

He closed his eyes and made his outstretched hands serve him as guides until he was able to locate a door that opened onto a narrow hallway that presently carried him to steps down which he descended to the subbasement. A faint glimmer of light warned him to go slowly. While he was approaching the corner of the lower hall, he heard voices from nearby, one that of a stranger, and one that of Pie Phelps, muffled by a partition. Reata could recognize the accents of the fellow from whom he had secured the four horses on the night of his flight.

The nearer speaker was saying: "Maybe he ain't in town at all."

"I wish he'd come," said the stifled tones of Pie Phelps. "I'd rather be in jail than layin' here where things are crawlin' all around me."

"When you get to jail, you're goin' to have a long rest, son."

"Yeah, I'll have to take what's comin' to me. I wonder if they'd really give me as much as ten years?"

"Sure they would, and laugh as they done it. You take a judge . . . he don't care what he gives you. He don't figger it's a good day if he don't hang somebody or send him up for life, and if he don't give ten years, he kind of loses his appetite and mopes around a lot. Givin' sentences is a sort of exercise for a judge. It makes him feel good."

There was a deep groan from Pie Phelps.

"Look at here," said the guard. "Suppose that you was to open up and do a little talkin'. They'd let you off, if you turned state's evidence."

"What's that?" asked Pie Phelps.

"Why, it's where you take and spill everything you know about the gents in the game that are higher up than you are. Like the gent that come along that night, and hired you and your hosses with the stolen gold."

"Would they let me off, if I talked about him?"

"Sure they would. Nobody knows who done the trick that night. If you could spot him for the law, you'd be let right off, likely. You know who he was?"

Reata listened intently, and his heart sank as he heard Pie Phelps answer.

"Sure, I know who he was, all right."

"Well, then, you don't have to be afraid of no jails or no judges, neither. All you gotta do is open up and talk."

"Yeah, but how could I do that?"

"How couldn't you?"

"This *hombre* comes along, and I know that he's getting away with something, all right. I take his money, and plenty of it. I sell him the hosses. So what call have I got to stab him in the back, afterward?"

"Hold on. You'd spend your ten years in the pen, instead of takin' a whack at a gent that don't mean nothin' to you?"

"I dunno," said Pie Phelps. "Somehow I can't hear myself standin' up and swearin' the law onto the trail of a gent that didn't do nothin' wrong to me. Maybe I'll weaken, when the time comes, but I sure hope that I won't."

"You got me beat," said the guard. "Listen to me. . . ."

Reata heard the next words only faintly. He was venturing a glance around the corner of the wall, and he saw, not twenty feet away, a tall cowpuncher who sat on a box, facing a door that closed up the end of the hallway.

The thin, weighted coils of the lariat that instant flew from Reata's hand. He had to make a difficult cast, for the ceiling was not much higher than the top of the peaked hat of the guard. But the noose slithered through the narrow space and dropped over the guard's arms. The jerk on the rope slammed the man flat on his back, and, before he could shoot, Reata — his bandanna pulled up the bridge of his nose to serve as a mask — was leaning over him with the guard's own gun in his hand.

"Just take it easy," said Reata. "I won't hurt you. I won't even gag you, if you'll take it easy."

He saw the face of the fallen man contort as he rolled the body on its side, then rapidly lashed hands and feet with lengths of twine.

"Me . . . done in like a washerwoman," muttered the guard.

Suddenly Reata heard a quickly drawn breath. He realized what was coming, but, before he could clap a hand over the parted lips of the cowpuncher, the wild yell of —

"Help!" — went pealing down the hall and vibrating up through the ceiling above them. He was tempted to repay the guard with a tap over the head from the long-barreled Colt. But the mischief was done. He turned the key in the lock of the door and jerked it open, then leaned over the startled face of Pie Phelps, who sat agape on the floor of the dark room, his hands and feet lashed together.

Reata, as he slashed the bonds with the edge of his knife, said rapidly: "Want to take your chances with the law, or come with me?"

"Law? Damn the law," Pie Phelps responded, lurching to his feet. "I'll go with you."

He went, on a dead run, behind Reata down the length of the hall, while that bawling voice of the guard betrayed them from behind, yelling: "Help! Help! Pie Phelps is loose, and a gent with him! They're boltin' for upstairs! Help!"

Reata, still coiling the forty feet of his trailing lariat as he ran, reached the head of the steps. It was big Pie Phelps who carried the lantern that gave them light, for Pie had had wit enough to snatch the lantern from the peg on which it hung. With that light they found the upper hall, then turned down to the door which stood open and through which Reata had made his entrance.

As they disappeared through it, more light flung toward them with the opening of still another door. Voices poured at them. A revolver boomed like shaking thunder in the narrow confines of the hallway.

Reata slammed the door behind him, and locked it, hearing the voice of Steve Balen shout out: "Foller on here. Sam and Lefty, come on outside with me! We're goin' to get 'em!"

Pie Phelps was already through the window, and Reata slithered out after him, where little Rags began to leap up and down like the head of a shadowy fountain at his feet.

"Now, if they want me, they surely gotta pay for me," gasped Pie Phelps. He had taken not only the lantern, when he had dashed out in the last cellar room, but he had also snatched up one of the guard's Colts. Reata struck the edge of his palm across the fellow's wrist and made the gun drop to the ground.

"No shooting, you fool," he whispered. "This way."

He led him on the run through the trees to the place where Sue waited. Behind them,

Steve Balen and the others were rushing among the trees, and from the house came the heavy battering against the locked door in the cellar.

But Reata already had Pie Phelps in the saddle on Sue. He himself clung to one stirrup leather, and, as the mare broke into a lope, Reata followed with gigantic strides at her side.

They cleared the trees. Behind them voices were shouting: "They're on hosses. Saddle up! Saddle up!"

Beyond the trees, the ground dipped into a hollow, little valley, where some sleeping horses sprang up and scattered before them. The noise of Reata's lariat was instantly over the head of one of them. A noose in the slender rope he then worked between the teeth of the mustang, and so could rule the animal by that grip on the lower jaw. Reata leaped onto the back of the half wild horse. There were ten seconds of frantic bucking, and then, grunting at every stride, the broncho set sail after Sue, who was disappearing with Pie Phelps in the saddle and Rags in front of it, over the rim of the nearest hill. Over that hill, in turn, the mustang carried Reata, and, glancing back, he saw a stream of half a dozen riders come pouring out from the cloud-like shadows of the trees around the house of the colonel.

Before him, Pie Phelps, like the good fellow he was at heart, was reining in the speed of the roan mare until Reata ranged up beside him. Then the pair of them headed north for the broken ravines of the foothills. It would be very strange if even Steve Balen could catch them in that chopped and confused wilderness.

VI
"TROUBLE STRIKES"

Reata and Pie Phelps, by the time their horses had corkscrewed two or three miles and a hundred devious turns into the foothills, were safe enough, unless chance played against them. They simply pulled up and spent the night in a good camping place under the big trees, with a trickle of water running down the side of the clearing. Pie Phelps was in high spirits. Concerning his misadventures of the day, he said: "It's all in a life. I been on the run before. I'm on the run ag'in now. And what's the odds? If I had had that forty pounds of gold on the horse, it would've beat me, because I wouldn't've had the nerve to chuck the stuff away. I'm forty pounds lighter, without losin' no strength whatsoever, when you come to that."

He added, after Reata had wrapped himself in a blanket with little Rags lying close to his head as a guard: "How about shovin' along through Chester Falls tomorrow? I got a coupla pals up there that would give us a hand-out and a change of horses . . . because it's goin' to be my turn to ride bare-back tomorrow."

"Chester Falls?" Reata repeated. "I've heard that there was a gang of Gypsies there recently."

"Sure there was," said Pie Phelps, yawning. "Had a letter from my friend up there, about seein' their show. They got a strong man with a face like a cat, whiskers and everything. And the boss of the gang is a woman, dog-gone me, if she ain't, and she smokes cigars all day long. But the prime number is the bareback rider. My friend writes that she's a gal worth seeing. Slim as a magpie and just as dog-gone pert and smart and dances on the back of a gallopin' hoss like it was a dance floor."

That thought held Reata as he closed his eyes for sleep. He had been thinking, since he first saw Agnes Lester, that all the other women of his life had been made dim and uncertain shadows, but the mere mention of the bareback rider made his blood bound. If they stood side by side — Gypsy Miriam and golden-headed Agnes Lester — what man in the world would know how to choose?

He began to think of that hollow valley in the mountains where he had worked in a dream that lasted happy weeks, building the cabin where he and Miriam were to settle down after their marriage. That dream had ended when she told him, one day, yawningly indifferent, that she was tired of the thought of marriage, tired of him, also. Something more than his vanity had been hurt, and there had followed those empty, endless days when the very sun in the heaven had been no more than a pale, storm-ridden moon to him. Then he had found Agnes Lester and set his life to a new tune. But here, at the mere mention of the bareback rider, the old emotion came storming up and putting an ache in his heart.

He muttered aloud: "Wherever we go, we don't go to Chester Falls."

"Hey, why not?" asked Pie Phelps.

But, receiving no reply, Pie was silent. He knew that he had fallen in with a leader, rather than a companion.

They were up with the dawn, and soon on the trail. Trouble hit them an hour later. It was as Reata asked Pie Phelps how he had been able to identify him on that other night in the darkness, and Pie answered without hesitation: "Well, as long as you keep that little snipe of a dog along with you, folks are sure going to recognize you every time, old son."

Right at the end of the words, Pie clapped his hand to his shoulder and yelled. Into his yell chimed the ringing report of a rifle. As Reata twisted in the saddle, he saw riders come pouring out from a cloudy woodland up the slope, just as he had seen them issue, the night before, from the trees around the house of Colonel Lester.

Pie Phelps, groaning with pain on the bare back of the mustang, raced it behind the lead of Reata over rough and smooth for five heartbreaking miles, with the blood spreading constantly over his left side. Then they doubled back into a cool, shadowed ravine and heard the hunt go roaring past them.

In that ravine, Reata bandaged the shoulder of his companion. It was not a bad wound. The high-speed rifle bullet had clipped through the flesh without touching bone or tendon, but there had been a good deal of blood lost.

When they went on again, Pie Phelps was riding the roan mare, and Reata was bareback on the mustang. Reata had a silent groan deep in his own throat, for the only thing to be done, so far as he could see, was to get Pie Phelps at once into the upper country where they would have to spend ten days of isolation until the wound was well closed. It was another stroke of fate, he felt, to pin him down in this country from which he was trying so hard to escape.

Pie Phelps wanted to go straight on to Chester Falls, but Reata pointed out that, if Pie had friends in that town, other people were apt to know it, and the manhunters would be fairly certain to look first of all inside those friendly houses. So they kept on straight for the higher mountains, and, before they were an hour on the way, luck struck them again with a heavy fist.

In a great, broken country like this, where whole armies could have been lost without the slightest trouble, there was not one chance in ten thousand that Steve Balen and his men would be able to sight the fugitives a second time, but that was exactly what happened. A little dust cloud rolled up a valley, topped a ridge, and turned into half a dozen hard riders. Balen was after them again. Well, let Balen push his men forward as hard as he pleased, they were not apt to catch Reata as he jockeyed the tough little mustang along. Certainly they would never get within hailing distance of Sue.

But two miles farther on, coming down a hillside, the mustang stepped on a loose stone — and went on with a dead lame right shoulder.

Pie Phelps, when he saw this, shouted:

"There ain't any use. Everything's ag'in' us! Take your mare, Reata. She's goin' to run you out of sight over the edge of the sky in no time. I never sat on anything like her. Let Balen and the rest of 'em get me. I might've knowed that Steve Balen would get me. He *always* gets what he wants. There ain't ever a man he's started for that he ain't brought home!"

"Stay in that saddle!" commanded Reata. "Stay there till I tell you to leave it. If they haul you in, they're going to haul me in, too. Keep going, and we'll make luck come to us."

They broke over the rim of a hill, and, coming through a dense growth of trees, Reata saw a main road below them, a white streak winding through a broad-bottomed valley. Down that road moved a long train of covered wagons drawn by old horses and mules so thin with age or bad rations that their heads were down, every one, and their ribs stood out, skeleton-like. Here and there appeared men on prancing, sleek little mustangs, the very pick of an entire range, and the sun flashed on brilliant housings, and on gay scarves that waved from the hips of the riders.

"Greasers?" asked the pale-faced Pie Phelps.

"Gypsies," answered Reata. "It's Queen Maggie's gang. Those are her black mules in the lead. There she is on the driver's seat. Ride fast, and maybe I'll be able to get 'em to put you up and hide you from Balen. Come on!"

He got the last strength and the last speed out of the crippled mustang, as they charged down the slope and up to the lead wagon of that procession.

There was a little rush of the Gypsy men on their sleek, bright horses. They came swooping about the two fugitives and then split away, recoiling to each side and shouting: "Reata! Reata!" The women, putting their heads out of the wagons, and the little children, leaping down and running up the road, echoed in shrill choruses of fear and anger: "Reata! Reata!"

It was an ominous welcome for him, but he could not wonder at it. They had paid heavily for the two visits that he had made to the tribe, and perhaps they were expecting to pay heavily again. It was not strange that the sun began to wink on drawn knives and guns; it was only odd that they did not follow the natural impulse and start using the weapons. Perhaps the blood that showed down all one side of Pie Phelps was the sight that restrained them.

Right up to the leading wagon rode Reata, and there he saw Queen Maggie close up, her face set in sullen lines, her big cigar tilting at a resolute angle between her teeth. She looked more like an Indian squaw, or an Indian chief, than ever. She wore the same battered old man's hat, and a man's coat, and the look of her hands and her heavy jaw was mannish, also.

She stared straight before her, as though she could not see Reata as he wheeled his staggering mustang beside her. As though, above all, she could not hear him calling out: "Maggie, I'm down and out. This poor devil is drilled through the shoulder. Take him in. There's a posse after him. It'll come popping out of those trees yonder, any minute . . . and then it'll be too late to do anything. Take him in and hide him in the wagons, and I'll make it the best day in your life. Look here, I've got no money now, but you can trust me, when I promise. You know that!"

She parted one side of her mouth, while she kept a firm lip and tooth hold on the cigar in the far corner. "You never brought us nothin' but trouble, Reata," she said. "You've beat my men, and you've grabbed Miriam, and, when she come back, she was never the same. I'll never lift a hand for you!"

"Hi!" shouted the Gypsies, in a deep and angry chorus.

Up from the rear, on foot and running with a savage haste, came the cat-faced strong man, his hands reaching out before him in a significant way. For how many days now had his prayer been that one moment only, this man would be given into his terrible grasp?

Someone also came past him at a swinging gallop, riding that sleek, black stallion that Reata remembered so well. It was Miriam, with a twist of yellow silk around her head, and another of blue silk about her hips.

He called, with his hands out to her, for he knew that she could overrule even Queen Maggie, if she chose.

"You see me beaten, Miriam! Make them take in this friend of mine!" He pointed back over his shoulder toward the trees that crowned the opposite slope.

Strangely enough, she did not look at Reata, but hard and earnestly into the face of Pie Phelps. Then, openly, she sneered and shrugged her shoulders. "Are you making friends of stuff like this, Reata?" she asked. "Have you dropped that far into the muck? Well, we'll take him in. Help him, there. . . ." She broke into a flood of the Gypsy jargon.

Queen Maggie, slamming on the brakes so that the wagon after one groan and shudder stood still, sprang up from her place and began to shout back. Two or three rattling repartees from the girl left her silenced. She threw up her hands and made a gesture of surrender. After that, things happened.

No matter how those Gypsies might hate Reata, and for reason, they loved and followed their bareback rider with sufficient enthusiasm to forget that hatred now. She actually rode up to the strong man and grabbed him by the yellow-striped neckcloth that he wore about his huge throat, and kept her grip, pouring out words at him, until he threw up both hands and groaned out an assent.

It was he who literally lifted Pie Phelps off the ground, as the wounded man dismounted, and carried him inside the third wagon of the caravan.

The girl went on shouting her orders. The Gypsy men began to laugh.

"Now!" she called to Reata. "One minute and I'm with you!" She darted into the wagon where Pie Phelps had disappeared, and came out a moment later, with Phelps's hat on her head and struggling her arms into a man's coat.

"Maggie," she called to the queen, "when they come, tell 'em that Reata and his friend held us up. Don't blame Reata! The men they're chasing held us up and made us give up our best horse to take the place of the lame mustang. That's why all our men have lined out chasing the crooks!"

"Reata!" called Queen Maggie.

"Aye?" he answered.

"Miriam comes back to us?"

"If I have to tie her hand and foot and bring her like a parcel," he answered.

"Then go on . . . and luck with you, you wild fool!" shouted Maggie, and she began to laugh in her stentorian voice.

VII
"THE GOLD TRAIL"

It made the strangest picture of a rescue that Reata had ever seen. He and Miriam raced their horses across the road and over the wide field of grass beyond with the whole crowd of Gypsy men streaming after them, firing, yelling in a tremendous chorus, and laughing between shots, between yells.

Looking back over his shoulder, Reata saw Steve Balen at the head of his men come storming down the slope. Would Maggie be able to send them on, or would wise Steve Balen pause for a time to search the caravan?

Reata had the answer for that in another moment. He saw Balen, in a swirl of dust, halt his horse for an instant at Queen Maggie's side. Then Balen rushed his horse on in pursuit.

Reata began to laugh in turn. Catch him now — catch him when he was mounted on Sue with no wounded bulk of a man to encumber him? That mare, at least, would never take a false step, never stumble. Cast steel might go lame, but never she. Neither would they overtake the black stallion with Miriam feathering him along like a jockey. Fresh as the stallion was, it was fairly matching, stride for stride, the tremendous rush of the mare. Afterward her long stroke might wear the stallion out, but by that time they would be well beyond the reach of Steve Balen.

Already the Gypsies were lagging behind, although they had ridden as hard as though they were in earnest. How could the horses of Balen and his men hold the pace? They could not. From the top of a high slope, before dipping into the forest beyond, Reata saw the Gypsies drawing rein. Behind them, Balen and the rest all pulled up, also, giving up the manifest absurdity of that chase.

Reata laughed as he looked down at them, and then swept the mare into the coolness beneath the trees. They came down into a long valley full of the voices of water, for innumerable little streams broke out from the rocks, here and there, and ran themselves white on their way down to the central creek that ran in a powerful undulation over its rough bed, like waves of the sea which blow into white foam, now and then, and seem to race with the wind. There was good, soft turf underfoot to ease the steps of the horses, and stretches of burning bright sun, and places of quiet shadow.

This was his country at its best, with the big mountains on each side looking down and giving peace to the scene, but the exaltation ran suddenly out of the heart of Reata. When he glanced aside, he saw that the head of the girl was high, and she was smiling to herself. In the old days, he would have said that it was happiness in being beside him that made her smile, but he felt that he knew now, that she was happy because of any one of those thousand mysterious reasons which are sufficient to keep a girl smiling, to the maddening of all men.

He fell into gloomy thought. "You might as well go back now," he finally said.

"Not yet," she answered calmly.

A moment later she unsheathed with a whipping motion the rifle that was fitted into the long holster under her right leg. The butt of the weapon pitched into the hollow of her shoulder. Only then he saw a movement, a stir, a racing form through the dapplings of shadow in a grove. The rifle swung with it for an instant, then spoke. The deer that he had barely marked leaped into the air and fell lifeless.

"We'd better eat before we say good bye," she told him. "You look a little pinched and drawn, Reata. What's the matter with you, old boy? Struck a lean patch?"

He said nothing. There was growing up in him a sort of savage distaste with life and, above all, with himself. He who had bent over the hand of Agnes Lester, only the night before, now to be finding the whole image of her turning dim, while music rang in his ears and quivered through his nerves as he looked at the Gypsy girl — what was he to say of himself?

He went methodically about the hanging up of the deer, but, when that was done, the girl would let him do no more.

"You're going to be the big chief for once," she told him. "You're going to sit still while the squaw works for you. Roll a cigarette, chief, and pull up your belt a notch. I'm going to do some venison steaks for you."

She worked without haste, but with wonderful speed for every touch of her hands accomplished something. She kindled a small fire, breaking up a bit of dead brush with her gloved hands. Then she carved the meat she wanted in thick, red slabs. A stack of them. After that, she let three pieces fairly burn over the coals.

"The outside pieces go to charcoal, Reata," she told him. "The juicy inside piece is what the chief eats."

Out of his own small pack she had found the coffee and the coffee pot. With snow water from the creek she made the mixture and soon had it steaming on a fire of its own. She cut off a strip of clean bark and laid it before Reata. Then, for she had managed to have everything finished at once, she laid before him coffee, hardtack, and that central thick slab of venison that had been protected from the fire by the burning of the two outer layers, and into which had run the juices of the wasted pieces.

"But what about you?" he asked.

"Ever hear of a squaw that ate when her man was eating?" she asked him cheerfully. "No. You never did. Besides, squaws don't have to eat. They look at the big chief, feeding his face, and that's food enough for them."

He knew her well enough not to argue the point. He simply said: "Not even smoking, Miriam?"

She shrugged her shoulders. "The big chief doesn't like to see his squaws smoke," she said.

"Why d'you talk like this?" he asked. "Does it do you such a lot of good?"

"It doesn't hurt you," she answered.

"No? But it does." He stared at her.

"Go and tackle that venison . . . it's getting cold," she advised him.

He fell to on the venison.

Well, here was another comment on his human nature, his too-human nature. No matter how much he was hurt by the flippancies of this strange girl, his appetite became raging the instant he tasted the meat. He was able to sit there and feast and almost forget his mental troubles. The very shame he had felt *because* those troubles could be so forgotten melted away from him. He finished the best meal he had had in many days. Then he sat back and rolled a cigarette and lighted it, and sipped the thick, black coffee she had made. It was exactly the kind he liked and that only Miriam knew how to compound. Vaguely he stared at her.

"You're a queer devil, Miriam," he said.

"Feeling full up, or want another whack at that venison?" she asked him.

"Full up," he said. "Go on and answer me."

"About being a queer devil?" she said. "So are you. We're all queer devils."

"Men are no good," he replied. "Everybody knows that. But girls ought to be good."

"I'm a mighty good cook," said Miriam.

"There you go." He nodded at her.

"Tell me what you've been doing," she asked. "Where've you been? What devil have you been raising?"

He pondered this question for a time. It was very strange that, no matter how wild-headed she might be, no matter how well he knew that careless and flighty nature, he also knew that whatever he told her would be locked up as in a secret safe, a secret which all the forces in the world could never tear from her. He could talk to her freely, he felt.

He said: "You know there was a fellow who swiped the Decker and Dillon gold out of the Jumping Creek marsh?"

"I know," she said. "Everybody knows, by this time. Fellow who ran the gold up the track on a handcar, and dumped it over a cliff, and flew down the cliff like a bird, and then got away safe and sound. Sounds like a fairy story. He a friend of yours?"

"That was my job," said Reata.

"Hi!" cried the girl. "Your job? I should have known it! Tying up one of the guards and not having the nerve to tap him on the head when he yelled. Why, Reata, whenever people run into a crook who's afraid to draw blood, they'll soon know that it's you."

He stared at her again. "You despise me

for that, I suppose?" he asked.

"Don't bother about what I think. Gypsies have queer ways of thinking."

"You're not a Gypsy," he told her. "Maggie told me you weren't. Your blue eyes tell me you're not."

"Blood doesn't matter," she answered. "It's the living that matters. I've lived Gypsy, and I'm Gypsy to the bone."

"All right," muttered Reata, frowning.

"So you're on the run because of that business?" she asked him.

"No, not because of that. This fellow Phelps . . . the one I left back there with the caravan. He was the one who gave me the horses that night I was getting clear with the gold. I gave him a bag of it. Well, they spotted the gold on him the other day. He was locked up. And I had to get him free. They chased us. You saw the end of the chase."

"That sounds like Reata. But you're fixed up now, boy," she told him. "You got enough hard cash to last you the rest of your life."

"That stuff? It was stolen money, Miriam. Swiped out of the Decker and Dillon Bank in Jumping Creek."

"That makes it all the sweeter for old light-fingered Reata."

"I've changed that," he told her. "I'm not using stolen money, Miriam."

"Hi!" She laughed. "The boy's washed himself as white as snow!"

"The one thing I wish that I could do before I get out of the country is to get that stuff back. Twenty-one more sacks of it. Get it back to Decker and Dillon. Then I'll be free to leave the country."

"You're wanting to leave the country?"

"Aye, and I'm leaving it."

"Look," she said. She pointed toward the shimmering green of the meadow, to the leap and shine of the creek, to the high, still rising of the mountains. "Leave this? This is what you love, Reata!"

"I'm getting out," he told her.

"The trail getting too hot even for Reata?" she asked.

His gray eyes had a glint of yellow in them, a quickening of light that she had seen before and that she knew very well. Men knew it better than she and had learned to dread it. She surveyed, leisurely, the breadth of his shoulders and the sinewy cords at his wrists. He had made trouble in this world, and he could make more trouble — very much more.

"Too many people know I've been a crook," he said. "Too many around this part of the world. I want to go straight, but I'm a fool. The first pull takes me down a dark alley . . . and hell starts popping."

"I know," she said.

He brooded on her more gloomily than ever. "There's a better reason," he said. "I've found another girl who's too good for me."

He did not see, blank as his eyes were, the sudden gripping of her hands, but she kept on smiling. Smiling is the special talent of a woman.

"There're the little troublemakers, eh?" said the girl. "She's a blonde beauty this time, I suppose?"

"Golden. Blue. That sort of thing," said Reata.

"Ah?" said the girl.

"Money, breeding, name, all that sort of thing, too."

"And a little dizzy about old Reata?"

"She could be," said Reata honestly. "But I'm getting out."

"Kind of tough on her?"

"She told me to go. She knows things. You know the quiet sort of a girl, Miriam? Quiet, very still, with a mind that keeps thinking? Too deep for me. I felt like a fool when she was talking. I could see how much she was over my head. She's another reason I'm getting out."

"Poor Reata . . . not worthy of her, eh?" asked the Gypsy, her smile suddenly turning into a grimace.

"You know how far I'm unworthy of her?" he asked. "Let me tell you something. The last time I saw you, you were laughing at me. Not laughing. Worse than that. You were yawning. You were tired of me. You sent me off . . . you remember how?"

"I remember how," she said rather faintly, looking down to the ground.

"It was sort of the end of everything. There wasn't any heart left in me. I was empty. You know . . . with you poured out, I was empty. Well, to show you the sort of a weak-headed fool I am . . . I run into this other girl, and pretty soon I almost forgot you. You're glad of that, of course."

"I suppose so," she said.

"Then I leave her the other evening, and come up here, feeling that the world's at another end. I'm never going to look at her again, because I'm not worthy of her. Then I see you. And then . . . well, I don't care how worthy she is. I don't care such a lot about her at all. And I wish. . . . You'll laugh at me. I wish I was back there in the valley, whacking away at the cabin where you and I were going to live. See what I am? Fickle as a fool. Any way the wind blows is the way I travel. Now go ahead and laugh."

"Suppose you did settle down, how long would you last?" she asked him. "You've got plenty of enemies who want your blood. How long would you last?"

"I don't know," he said gloomily.

"And every girl you know . . . that's another address where people can look you up. Quinn and Salvio and Dave Bates . . . they ought to be friends of yours, but are they?"

"They pulled me in on the Decker and Dillon game. How am I to call them friends?" he asked her.

"They came up to the caravan today, all three of them. Remembering what the Gypsies did to Harry Quinn, and almost finished, I thought it meant a fight, but that wasn't in the air. They simply wanted to ask questions. About you. They thought that you might have looked me up."

"Quinn, Salvio, Bates . . . all three of 'em? That's strange," he said.

"Is it? Well, they were all on the road together, with a lot of horses carrying loads. Not a lot. Half a dozen."

"With horses carrying loads?" He jumped to his feet.

"Which way did they travel, Miriam?"

"Right down the road, but faster than the caravan was going. What about them? If they're not friends, what about them?"

"If I've got 'em in the open . . . ," he said through his teeth. "The double-crossing. . . ." He whistled, and Sue came swiftly toward him, watching him with her wise eyes.

"You're off, are you?" asked the girl, her voice hard, her eyes still harder.

"I've got to start," he said. "I'll be going back toward the road. That's your way, in part."

"Never mind my way."

"You're not coming?"

"I'm riding alone."

"What's the matter?" he asked. "All at once it looks as though you've started hating me. What's the matter? What have I done?"

"Nothing," she said. "Get going . . . and have luck, Reata."

"But it's true," he insisted. "You're practically hating me now."

"I'm only hoping that I never see you again," she told him, with a sudden outbreak of bitterness.

That pulled him up. He stared at her with blank, hurt eyes for a moment, and then mounted the mare. "I'm sorry," he said. "I don't understand anything. I'm a dummy for fair. Tell Maggie that she won't lose by taking care of Pie Phelps. I'll pay up to the hilt. So long."

She merely waved a hand as she turned away. She would have called out carelessly, cheerfully, but she was unable to speak. She went blindly toward the black horse. Men, she kept telling herself, are not the only things that matter. There are other things that go to the making of a world and a life. But the mere naked telling did her very little good. There was a pulse hammering at her temples.

Well, he had been there, and with a gesture she might have brought him back to her — with a smile, even. She had chosen to let him go. It was true, as she had told him, that he had too many enemies in this world, and the happiness that he might try to find with a wife would not last long. They would find him — the manhunters. But, in the meantime, as he drifted through the world, how many others would he find capable of making him forget her? Yonder there was the creature who had, he said, a mind so deep. A blue and golden woman, he had called her.

Well, the sky was blue and the sunshine was golden as she rode on the black, but she hated the world through which she moved.

She would have dashed to pieces the whole wide wall of the horizon and replaced it — she knew not with what. She did not care.

VIII
"DICKERMAN'S MEN"

That camp which Harry Quinn and Gene Salvio and Dave Bates had made was securely hidden beyond a steep ridge, beyond the rushing of a creek, and in a tangle of profound darkness among the trees and the underbrush. They had the best of good reasons for secrecy as to their place, because they were carrying with them some seven hundred and fifty pounds of gold. They had the burden on three good, strong horses. They had three other horses to carry them. They had three Winchester rifles, and at least one pair of Colts apiece, together with plenty of ammunition. But, in spite of all of these safeguards, they were ill at ease. For men with stolen treasure are bound to feel that danger may drop on them from the empty sky or rise among them out of the solid ground.

Danger, in fact, was coming toward them, slowly and surely. There was only one man, with a roan mare beneath him, and in front of him the little, wagging tail of Rags as the dog scented out the trail with the hair-trigger accuracy of his small nose. Up to the later part of the afternoon, Reata had been able to trail the cavalcade of six horses down the road. Then he overshot the mark and had to turn back with Rags who, by this time, had the proper scent well up his nose. It was Rags who had led his master over steep and smooth until they crossed the creek on the huge, slippery stepping stones that the boulders offered. It was Rags who now worked furtively into the brush.

The roan mare, Reata left behind him when the brush grew so thick that even she, trained although she was to move almost as silently as a mouse through thickets, was now apt to make a bit of a noise. Then he went on.

He could not see Rags now. The blackness under the trees was so profound he could hardly have seen his hand before his face. But the little dog knew how to lead his master in the dark, and waited, every moment or so, until the cautiously outstretched foot of Reata touched him. Then he went forward again, and, step by step, they proceeded in this fashion until the broken, golden rays of a fire pierced the undergrowth.

It was only a small fire, not big enough to throw a pronounced light above the tops of the trees, but it was a focus that brought Reata quickly to the verge of a small clearing. There was grass here for the horses, and there were rocks that had been piled up to screen the light cast by the fire.

But by the rays that escaped, Reata recognized the broad, rather good-natured face of Harry Quinn, the twisted, lean, half face of Dave Bates, and that beautiful and dangerous panther of a man, Gene Salvio.

Reata had thought that he knew them very well, until they had tricked and drawn him in on the matter of the Decker & Dillon golden treasure. Until that time he would have sworn that Harry Quinn was too devoted to him to betray him, and that there was too much fear in Dave Bates. As for Salvio, the man had the nature of a wild beast and never could be trusted — except to take chances. Every one of the three had owed his life to Reata — Salvio only indirectly, but nevertheless surely. Yet the three of them had combined to trap him.

Reata, leaning against a tree, found his wrath a little tempered. According to the brains of these fellows, they had not actually been trapping him. They had merely given him a chance to make a fortune. A fortune in which they could share. It was that thought which brought up his rage again.

They had let him go single-handedly to endure all the risks. They had reaped the profits. All the profits, when he washed his hands of the stolen money.

He stepped out from the trees. One of the horses threw up its head suddenly and snorted. All three heads turned, and Harry Quinn shouted: "Reata! Here's Reata!"

They laid friendly hands on him and dragged him forward.

"Hi! It's Reata!" cried Dave Bates. "I'm goin' to sleep sound tonight for the first time since we hit the trail. Reata, you know what we've got in those packs yonder?"

"Decker and Dillon gold, eh?" said Reata.

"Decker and Dillon nothing," said Salvio. "It's our stuff now. We sweated for it. So did you. The idea is, if you'll come back with us till we get the weight of it hidden out safely somewhere, you get your split, the same as you always were due to get, Reata."

"Is Pop Dickerman breaking up?" asked Reata.

"Him? They can't break him up," said Dave Bates. "But they've throwed the whip into him. Sheriff Lowell Mason ain't such a fool as we thought he was. He's searched that place from hide to hoof. He's been all though every junk heap. But he didn't find our stuff. Why? Because Pop had the idea a day before, and got us out with all the gold. *And* some other things. I tell you what we got in our hands, Reata. We got the whole savings of Pop Dickerman. We got 'em here. If you seen 'em. . . ."

"What that old gent had put away for the rainy season!" said Salvio. "Why, the gold's only a part of it all. It ain't the biggest part."

"How much is the old hound worth, anyway?" broke in Harry Quinn. "Everything that he's got ain't been kept around the house. You can bet on that. He's got accounts in a dozen banks. Why, he goes on peddling junk, but he's worth millions, Reata! Millions, or I eat my hat."

Reata said calmly: "Wonder to me that you fellows, now that you've got your hands on all that loot, don't put the whole of it into your pockets and let Pop Dickerman go hang."

"Would we be that much fools?" asked Dave Bates, shrugging his lean shoulders at the suggestion. "Him? With lines laid out all over the country like a spider with a web? Why, son, which way would a man run to get clear of Pop Dickerman? Like a damn' set of wasps rising and starting to fly and strings that they can't see catch hold of their wings, and the old spider comes out when it's good and ready and sucks the wasps dry.

No, no, Reata. You're damn' bright and mean, but you ain't bright and mean enough to talk turkey to Pop Dickerman!"

Reata, listening, felt a profound weight of truth in the words to which he had listened. There was no man in the world that he feared, hand to hand. Nature had given him a speed of hand that others could not match; training had equipped those hands with infinite cunning. But mere hands and ordinary wits were useless against Pop Dickerman. He was, in fact, like a spider couched in the center of a web, throwing out invisible meshes to entrap ordinary humanity. Nothing else that existed was worthy of being called evil. The whole realm of wickedness, it seemed to Reata, was embraced by the mere name of Pop Dickerman.

"All right, boys," said Reata, "you're done in to Dickerman, but I'm not."

Salvio laughed. "I thought that for a while. Lemme tell you a story. Go on with that cooking, Quinn. I'll tell you a yarn about what happened to me in the old days, before I found out where I left off and Dickerman began. I'd picked up a good cut of hard coin by sticking up a stage . . . Dickerman had planted the job for me . . . and I figgered that I'd take that coin and get away from Dickerman, so far that he couldn't ever put a hand on me. I headed off in a straight line. I rode out my hoss, gettin' to a railroad. I rode the beams on that railroad for fifteen hundred miles to New Orleans and stowed away on a ship for Cuba, and, when that ship pulled into Havana, there was a big, long, lean, thin-faced *hombre* that walks by me, amblin', and he says behind his hand . . . 'Better go back to Dickerman, kid.'

"I looked after that gent. The view of his back didn't do me no good. I wanted to ask him a flock of questions, but I seen that it was no good. I got the next boat out of Havana and went straight back to Dickerman.

"From that day to this, he's never mentioned it, and I've never mentioned it. But I know that there ain't miles in the country enough to get me away from the reach of Dickerman's rope!"

As Salvio ended, Quinn said: "Yeah. That's all straight, too."

Reata stepped back from them a little. "Boys," he said, "you're all mighty friendly to me, and I'm sorry to tell you what I've got in mind now. You think that I'm on your side, but I'm not. You think that I won't dare break with Dickerman, but I will. I was going straight, when you fellows roped me in on a crooked job. There's only one way for me to clean my hands. That's to get the gold you're carrying in those packs and bring it back to Decker and Dillon in Jumping Creek. I'm giving you a fair warning. We make an even start now. But, before I'm finished, I'm going to have that stuff in my hands. Watch yourselves!"

This speech had fairly stunned the three for an instant. It was Salvio who recovered first and shouted: "Take this where it'll do you the most good, then." He snatched out a gun as he spoke. In the frantic haste of his action the first bullet simply plowed up the ground at Reata's feet. The second one would have been through his heart, but he had leaped back behind a tree trunk into which the bullet spatted with a heavy impact.

"Get him!" yelled Salvio.

The three of them made a rush, but, after they had gone a stride or two into the outer darkness, away from the reach of the rays of the fire, they halted and bunched together.

"Get back to the light," said Dave Bates. "Reata can see like a cat in the dark. We got no chance in here among the trees. Get back into the clearing!"

They backed up slowly. They stood in the

clearing, each man facing out in a different direction, each with a gun in his hand. They looked like men making a desperate last stand against overwhelming numbers, resolved to sell their lives dearly. But their single enemy leaned against the side of a tree trunk and studied them casually, calmly.

They were dangerous fellows, all of them; he could hardly have picked out three worse enemies. Yet there was fear in them in spite of their numbers.

He heard Harry Quinn say: "He don't carry no gun, or he'd pick us all off, one by one."

"He'll get a posse on our trail," groaned Salvio.

But Dave Bates, wiser than the others, answered: "Reata works alone, mostly. He doesn't like the law any better than we do. We don't have to worry about him getting the sheriff after us. He'll give us enough trouble all by himself."

"We've got to keep a guard posted all night and every night," said Quinn.

"Sure," said Salvio. "Talk soft. The devil may be hearin' everything that we say, right now."

The devil was, in fact, overhearing every word, but his mind was empty of ideas as to how he might be able to attack them. He saw that he would have to wait for time and new chances before he struck.

IX

"CHESTER FALLS"

All the next day, the three fugitives moved slowly on, not directly to the north now, but diverging to the northwest over open, rolling hills, and Reata, as he followed them from a distance, made sure that they never approached even small clusters of shrubbery or patches of woodland. He could guess the reason. They were not intending to allow their enemy to come to grips with them. They preferred, therefore, to keep to the openest way, knowing that their guns could keep him off as long as they could see him.

He shook his head as he watched them, and began to respect the fair and open challenge that he had given to them. That would not have been their own course, for instance. He could still hear the bullet from the gun of Salvio, striking deep into the solid heart of the tree that had saved him. Trickery and murder were simply an ordinary part of the weapons of the men of Dickerman. Therefore, why should he have acted as though they were honorable enemies?

Finally, at the end of the day's march, he saw them journey down into the strange phenomenon known as the Chester Draw — that great dry, flat-bottomed valley that runs for many miles in a loose semicircle until it comes close to Chester Falls. The flat of it is hardly ever crossed by a run of water. The grass is very sparse and poor. There is practically no game to be found on foot in it. In every way, it is about as unpleasant a road as men could wish to travel.

This was the course that the three men had laid out for themselves, and Reata, setting his teeth grimly, could understand why. For, over the unbroken flat of the draw, even starlight would be sufficient to show the men the approaching of any dangerous figure. Even where, at the northern end, the bottom of the draw became very narrow, it was still wide enough and clear enough of all obstacles to be perfect for the intentions of Salvio and the rest. In this way they could safely complete their journey to Chester Falls, and, unless Reata found a way of rising out of the ground at their feet or falling from the sky over their heads, they would not be bothered by him.

All that he gained, as he watched the stream of six horses flow down the side of the draw into the bottom, was the definite knowledge that Chester Falls, or a place somewhere near Chester Falls, must be their ultimate goal. That was why he turned the head of the roan mare and struck straight out in the direction of Chester Falls. On the way there he might learn something, or in the town itself something must appear to give him a clue. Otherwise, he was beaten, and would have to admit it. It might be that he could pick up armed men enough to blot out even three such as Salvio and Quinn and Bates, but Bates knew that he would never adopt such tactics, and Bates was right. If he could regain the stolen gold from the trio, he would certainly do it only by some device, not by brutal murder.

That was the mind of Reata as he journeyed all that day back to the highway, and then down it toward the town of Chester Falls. He could see the town small in the distance, and it had grown to a good size when, at the end of the day, he came past a continual stir of dust that kept rising into the windless air from a wide flat of open ground where a herd of horses was being bedded down for the night.

There were hundreds and hundreds of the animals, guided by Mexicans. Even in the distance he could tell that the riders came from south of the Río Grande by the bigness of their hats and the thinness of their shoulders. He could tell, also, by something wonderfully light and graceful in the horsemanship of these men. Your cowpuncher may be as efficient as the *vaquero,* but he never has the same easy touch.

Reata rode by very slowly. A number of the mustangs broke loose and came pelting out of the herd, straight toward him. Two *vaqueros* went after them, helter-skelter, edging in on them little by little, little by little, gradually turning them into a circling flight that would bring them back to the herd they had just left. It was very neat work, perfectly done. Clumsy hands might have spurred wildly after those wild horses for a week, and never have brought them back.

As the mustangs came closer, Reata saw that they were the true product of the Mexican desert — little horses hardly bigger than mountain sheep, sometimes with rather lumpish heads and roached-up backs, and all of them famine thin, but one and all with four wonderful legs and with hoofs of iron. As they flashed by, he saw the brands in the velvet of the hides, big, scrawling brands, some of them still raw. He grinned, quick and small, as he made this out.

If these were not stolen horses from south of the Río Grande, he was a blind man, for certain. They were stolen, and these matchless riders, in their big sombreros and their gaudy outfits, were simply accomplished horse thieves. That was why Reata grinned without mirth. He saw the outbreak subdued, and the vagrant horses run back into the herd. Then he went on, jogging the roan mare, still looking toward the camp which the Mexicans were pitching. A winding of the road brought him close to it.

He saw three low wagons, a pair of old women working over a fire at the cooking of supper, a tall fellow with a handsome, savage, cruel face giving directions about everything, and a pretty Mexican girl, sulking as she waited in the saddle. She turned her head toward the passing stranger and gave him a smile that even to a witless ancient would have been a thing of danger. But Reata laughed as he went on. He had been in Mexico. He had been far and deep in it, and he had learned about the people a great many things that are not in books.

After he had left the stolen horse herd — he was certain that was what it was — he found the windows of the town of Chester Falls not far away, glimmering toward the west, and in a few minutes he was jogging through the town. He knew it as he knew most of these towns in his country — the memory of it needed a little refreshing, but on the whole the place was fairly familiar, and he knew that there was one place to put up the horse and one place to put up the man.

Over at the side of an alley that wound out of the main street there was a battered livery stable run by an old Negro who knew good hay and oats, and kept them. That was where Reata took the mare. The old man, with his moist eyes squinted, shook his head of white wool as he stared at the long, low lines of the mare.

"I recollect the last time you was here, mister," he said. "You had a mighty fine, upstandin' geldin' then, that must've cost you a whale of a lot or money, sir, but since that time I see you been spending *real* money on your horseflesh." He ran the tips of his fingers over the intertangling and flowing muscles of the shoulder of the roan.

He looked curiously, earnestly at Reata, and Reata stared back at him with interest. For he and the old Negro, as far as he knew, were the only men in the world who had been able to appreciate the lines of Sue at a glance. Yes, there was one other exception, and that was Dickerman, but he was more devil than man, of course.

"Say what you're thinking," urged Reata.

"I was thinkin'," said the old man, "God help gents that have *gotta* travel as fast and as far as this here mare would be takin' 'em. Because they wouldn't spend much time at home."

X
"OLD FORT CHESTER"

If that was the place for a horse to be put up in Chester Falls, the place for a man was in old Fort Chester. It had been a center for traders in the old days, one of those outposts where the pioneers dauntlessly defended the frontier. The fort was no longer a trading post, of course, but, since it had been built very solidly in order to make it defensible, it was still standing intact, with thick walls and small windows, a loosely grouped range of buildings around a central court. Owls and rattlesnakes lived in part of the old place. The rest had been cleared out a little and was used, without payment of rent, by a very knowing Portuguese who was called Manuel. He might have a second name, but no one west of the Mississippi knew about it or cared.

What was important was to sit down at one of the little tables that were placed under the interior arcade of the patio of the fort and get hold of a large portion of brown-roasted kid, fresh from the spit, and with it Mexican beans adorned by many mysteries of green and red and yellow peppers. The cookery of Mexico was not all Portuguese or all American or all Mexican. But everything that came out of his kitchen was delicious, and, afterward, one could spend the night sleeping on the mercurial softness of a deep feather bed.

So Reata went for this place of comfort as a cat goes for the coziest corner by the fire. He knew Manuel so well that the broad-faced old man, with a black, Mongolian mustache dripping down from the corners of his mouth, merely blinked and nodded imperceptibly by way of greeting. In the old days, he understood, most of the time Reata did not wish to be recognized or named. In the new days, also, it was much the same.

There was, in fact, roast kid that night, and the same beans which Reata could remember, and corn bread yellow as gold, and unsalted butter to soak it with, and wine, sweet and thin and clear, to drink with the meal. Reata got a table in a far corner and put out the lamp that lighted it. He preferred to dine in twilight which would leave him incognito while he used his own eyes. There was always something to see at Fort Chester, when one ate in Manuel's place. People of all sorts would be dropping in.

The townsmen came in, when they could afford it, and strangers were deflected a hundred miles from their proper course by the reputation of that strange little restaurant.

Before Reata had sat ten minutes in his obscure corner, he had something to see. That splendid *caballero* who was in command at the horse camp, outside of the town, appeared in much finery, with a cloak flooding down from his shoulders like a ghost of the 17th Century, and with him came the pouting little beauty of a Mexican girl. She was not pouting now. The pleasure of a new place kept her head turning and her eyes brightening until the *señor* spoke to her. After that, she checked the motions of her head, but her eyes were busier than ever. Reata, as he watched her, laughed to himself. There would be woman trouble on the hands of this proud Mexican before very many years were out.

There were perhaps a dozen other people at various tables, when a larger party entered, and the loud, dignified voice of Colonel Lester at once rang deep in the ear of Reata. There was the colonel with his famous, full-arm gestures, indicating where he would have a table placed and now admiring the antiquity of the old fort, and now directing his men to take their places at his table.

First and foremost of those men was Steve Balen, turning his grim face slowly and looking deep into the shadows, here and there. There was the fellow who had been on guard over Pie Phelps in the cellar of the colonel's house. Reata knew him well by his low and bulging forehead. There was a man of fifty, with all his years printed in his face. He had a battered and beaten look as though he had not slept well for many and many a night. And he had a way of opening his eyes very wide and rolling them to this side or to that when anything took his attention suddenly.

In two minutes, Reata understood that he was no other than Decker, of the Decker & Dillon Bank in Jumping Creek. How he had managed to join so quickly the party that was on the trail of Pie Phelps, Reata could not tell. The colonel seemed not only in charge of the party but particularly in charge of Decker, and, before the meal was five minutes old, he was reassuring the banker.

He said: "Time will have to help us, Mister Decker. But with time and strong efforts, we shall apprehend the rascals. Certainly we shall bring them to justice."

"For my part," said the banker, with a rather twisted smile, "I'd rather have the money back and let the justice go."

"A thing to say, but not to believe," answered the colonel. "I know, Mister Decker, that the upholding of law and of order comes with you before your personal affairs. For my part, I assure you that I've put my hand to this work, and that my hand shall not be taken away until the work is finished."

With this, the colonel struck the table lightly with his fist. It would be remarkable if the rest of those people at the table did not see that the colonel was a good deal of an ass. But pomposity is usually forgiven when there is money enough behind it, just as an overload of jewels will be forgiven a woman, if they are real.

The colonel went on talking. At every pause through the meal, it was his voice that dominated the conversation. But Reata would have given a hundredfold more to hear ten words out of the dry, stiff lips of Steve Balen than for the life works of Colonel Lester bound in vellum.

Decker said: "People think of a ruined bank without a great deal of sympathy. A bank is only a name. Hard-headed devils stand behind a steel fence and deal you out less money than you want. You go into the president's office, and he shakes his head at your security. Well, those are the things that make people hate banks. But behind every bank there are lives. When the bank goes smash, the people behind it go smash. Dillon's smashed. I don't know that he'll ever be a real man again, unless I manage to get my hands on some of that stuff that was stolen. I'm smashed, too. I can see it in myself."

"When a man's down," said the colonel, "it's the very time when he ought to look up . . . high."

This aphorism made Decker stare fixedly for a moment at the colonel, and then he said: "Well, Colonel Lester, that's something to hear, but it's a hard thing to do. Let me ask you. Were you ever down, really down, in your life? Do you know what it means to be worse than flat broke?"

The colonel waved a magnificent hand. "We all have our ups and downs, my dear fellow," he said. "But. . . . Hold on . . . here comes one of the ups, it looks to me."

For, at that moment, a pair of Queen Maggie's Gypsies, as gay as peacocks, came into the patio of the old fort with a flute and a violin and at once started rousing sweeter echoes than ever had flown from wall to wall of the court before. Right between them came Miriam, the bareback rider, and behind her rode not her companion artist, Anton — he was dead, and only Reata knew perfectly the manner of his death — but Georg, a slender nineteen-year-old whom Reata had seen long before among the Gypsies and never guessed at him as the understudy of the great Anton. Yet now, in his gaudy outfit, he stood up on the black stallion as well at ease, as commanding, as beautiful to see as ever Anton had been.

XI
"SUSPECTED"

Reata had seen the show a good many times before, but never when the riding was the only part of it given. They went at it by turns. Georg led off. His black horse was perfectly trained and went through the tricky evolutions at a swift but exactly controlled gait while the rider had the abandon of a Cossack. He got a good round of applause for that. Then Miriam came on with a few of her simplest tricks, and the colonel himself stood up and faced her and clapped his dignified palms loudly and for a long time.

"Gypsies?" Reata heard the colonel say. "Well, Gypsies or not, they're artists. What a world we have here in the West, my friends! What a world, indeed!"

Steve Balen, at this, gave the colonel a little side glance that might have caused his employer some uneasiness, but the colonel was flowing freely with good cheer by this time. Miriam, in crimson and blue, was standing on her horse in a corner of the patio, breathing hard from the work, and then Georg cut in with his second round.

He had his big, wide-blade saber out, and he turned it into glittering arcs of light as he slashed to this side and to that. He laughed with the joy of his work, as feline and beautiful a sight as ever a man could wish to see. He was under and over that horse like a trapeze performer, and finally, with his feet locked in the saddle, he made the black stallion race in such small, swift circles that the body of the Gypsy stretched straight out and, with his sword, he seemed reaching for the people at the tables. How was he to come back to the saddle without a terrible fall?

The Mexican girl stood up, gasping with admiration and terrified excitement. But for Reata, far more than the antics of Georg, was the picture of Miriam in the farther corner of the patio, standing on her horse like a slim, red candle flame that the wind blew and fluttered a bit from time to time.

Then, by a sudden miracle, Georg was again standing on the saddle and bowing right and left to the applause that came shouting to him. He dismounted, bringing the stallion to a sudden halt in the middle of the court, and, as he bowed, making a fine flourish with his saber, the stallion dropped to a knee, also, cunningly and invisibly compelled.

It was too much for the Mexican girl. She picked up a quantity of red wildflowers that Manuel had put in the center of her table, and then she ran out a step or two and threw them toward Georg with a little, musical cry.

Her escort, tall, forbidding, strode after her and drew her back — but there was Georg picking up the flowers as though each of them was a gold coin, and bowing with his cat-like, sinuous grace to the impulsive girl.

After that, he took an encore, as it were, making his horse go several times around the patio in various catchy steps that the flute and the violin artfully accompanied so that the rhythm of the stallion seemed to be following the rhythm of the music. It was a very pleasant and graceful bit, with Georg appearing astonished and delighted, as though he had never before seen the improvisations of his horse.

But, on every round, the eyes of the rider found the Mexican girl, and there was such an electric intensity in his glances, that Reata saw her tremble with excitement. She was so far carried away that she completely forgot the presence of her companion, it seemed. And the Mexican no longer made a protest of voice or of gesture. He simply sat erect, smiling, with a thousand cold devils in his face. The thunderhead was there above the horizon, plainly to be seen; the lightnings were gathering in it. Reata watched and slowly fingered the lean, hard coils of the lariat in his pocket.

As Georg came to the end of this encore, he stopped the stallion directly in front of the two Mexicans and, dismounting, made his bow and the curtsy of the horse at the same moment. It was a very pointed little compliment. The Mexican girl was out of her chair in a moment, clapping, crying out her appreciation. And Georg was only human. How could he help coming a little closer? How could he help forgetting that rigid, forbidding figure of the Mexican back there in the shadow? No, Georg was leaning over the girl, speaking, smiling, and what he said never came to the ears of Reata.

In fact, Reata was busily watching the tall Mexican. Little tremors had begun to run through the body of the man. His hand, on the table, opened and closed once convulsively. Suddenly the devil was up in him and away. He got out of his chair with a speed that almost forestalled the lightning hand of Reata.

Plenty of people saw that tigerish spring and the flash of the raised knife in the hand of the Mexican, but there was not time for anyone to cry out a warning. Certainly the blade would have been buried to the hilt in the back of Georg, except that Reata acted with the flicking speed of an uncoiling spring. Out of his hand, the noose of the lariat shot like a flat stone, cutting the air. It dropped over the shoulders and the two arms of the Mexican. The back pull jerked him down to a sitting position.

The scream of rage and surprise that came out of his throat half paralyzed even Reata. It made Georg and the girl jump into the air. The Mexican tried to cut at the thin rope with his knife, but in a moment three more loops of the lariat had showered down over him, and he sat helpless. Only his face was eloquent, and the flash of his teeth beneath his curling lip.

Reata, now that the thing had been prevented, rapidly freed his lariat from the prisoner, and, as the rope came free in his hand, he heard the sudden voice of the Gypsy girl crying to him: "Reata! Look out!"

Instinctively he turned around and found, confronting him, the long, stern face and the tall, lean body of Steve Balen, holding a gun in either hand.

"Stick 'em up, brother," said Balen. "Stick 'em up high."

"What's the matter?" said Reata. "Glad to see you, Balen. But what's the matter?"

"You ain't as glad to see me as I am to see you, old son," said Balen. "Drop that rope and stick those hands up . . . grab a star with each of 'em and then hang on. If you bat an eye, I'll drill you, Reata!"

Reata did not bat an eye. He raised his hands above the level of his head and stood perfectly still. He knew that death was the quiver of an eyelash away from him. He would rather have had against him an armed crowd than this single man with his pair of steady guns.

"Now tell us what it's all about?" asked Reata.

He could hear the Mexican girl chattering rapid Spanish, weeping over her man, Pedro. He could hear Pedro snarling, irreconcilable, and then the quiet voice of Georg saying: "Reata, say when. . . ."

"Don't budge. Don't lift a hand, Georg," said Reata. "Or I'm done for. This *hombre* likes to shoot, and he doesn't know how to shoot crooked. Just tell me what it's all about, will you, Balen?"

Colonel Lester had now appeared. There was a white spot in the center of either cheek, but he made his fine, full-arm gesture, pointing out Reata.

"There's the pickpocket of the Jumping Spring marsh, boys. Balen, good work that you spotted him. Very good work, indeed. Even if he did save the Gypsy's hide for him."

"I'm kinda thinkin'," said Steve Balen, "that this here is the gent that did more'n swing a hammer down there on the island in the marsh. I got an idea that this here is the one that tied up the guard that night, and got the gold, and walked it up the track on the handcar, and dropped it over the cliff, and climbed down after it where even a hawk would've got dizzy, and then bought the four hosses with one sack of the stuff, and then come along afterward and roped old Bill, yonder, and took Pie Phelps away safe and sound! I got an idea that this here is the *hombre* that we're looking for on account of a whole lot of good reasons, Colonel."

Lester, as he heard this speech, immediately struck his hands together and agreed.

"You're probably right. You're rarely wrong. Probably this is the ringleader of the three scoundrels who robbed the bank in Jumping Springs. Get him, and we'll get everything else!"

Steve Balen said: "No, he don't match up with what descriptions we got of the three of 'em. He don't match at all. Bill, would you do me a favor, and tie Reata's hands behind his back?"

Georg came forward and said: "This man is honest. You can't tie his hands."

Balen merely muttered: "Back up, brother!"

The colonel chuckled. "A Gypsy telling us what honesty is, eh? A fine judge. I don't doubt that from *your* point of view this man is honest enough. But the law may have something else to say to him. Bill, can you recognize this fellow as the man who roped you?"

Bill, picking up the thin line of the lariat that Reata had been forced to drop, fingered it for a moment, his rounded forehead puckered.

Then he said: "Well, gents, I've heard this here Reata speak, and I heard the voice of the gent that nabbed me back there in the cellar of the house. But voices is hard to swear by. And, when it comes to seein' other things, I was kind of dizzy, bein' grabbed and slammed down on my back, so hard."

"D'you mean to say that you didn't have a look at the man's face?" demanded the colonel angrily.

"Sure, I seen his face all right," said Bill. "But there was a bandanna drawed up over his nose, like a mask. Reata's got gray eyes, and those eyes that I seen was sort of yaller."

"Think, man, think!" said the colonel, urgently snapping his fingers, as though to urge on a child — or an animal. "You must have seen something else!"

"Sure I seen something else," said Bill very slowly. "I see Pie Phelps grab up one of my guns that had dropped to bash me over the head with it, so's I couldn't yell out and give the alarm while the pair of 'em was getting out. And I seen the gent in the mask knock that gun out of Pie's hand."

Bill rubbed his head softly, tenderly.

"The second gent, the one that roped me, he'd rather have took the chance that I wouldn't yell, anyway. He let me go, and ran on . . . and I yelled all right, and, because of my yellin', the pair of them was nearly caught." He added: "I can remember that, all right." Suddenly he looked straight into the eyes of Reata, and Reata knew that he had been recognized from the first, if not by face, then by voice, and by the thinness of that deadly little rope that Bill was fingering so thoughtfully.

"What do we come to?" exclaimed the colonel. "What have we here that we can use, my friends? What is there that the law can use against this rascal?"

Georg had drawn back. The girl, Miriam, was whispering to him. Now the two went quickly away. There was some purpose in the mind of Miriam, and Reata could guess very shrewdly that he would have the benefit of it before long.

All around him, a crowd was packed, and he looked constantly down to the ground. For it is hard to remember the face of a man who is constantly looking down, and one of the things that Reata knew best is that it is well to be unknown to crowds.

"We can close him up in one of the rooms here," said Balen. "While we got him there, maybe we can work up something ag'in' him. He's done some pretty fine things, but I reckon that the world would be a mighty sight quieter place, if Reata was kept out of it for a spell."

"You want law for that?" said Reata. For he thought of the three riders who were approaching Chester Falls by the long, roundabout way of the draw. If he were long detained, he would be helplessly out of the chase of them.

"Law?" said the colonel. "There's a higher law than law . . . there's the law of common sense!"

The sudden, yellow flare burned in the eyes of Reata. He stared at Balen and murmured: "This'll be a thing to remember, Balen!"

"Aye," said Balen, "I wouldn't want you to forget it." He allowed a smile to spread gradually over his hard face. That was the rashest thing that he ever did in a bold and active life.

XII
"A PRISONER"

Steve Balen did another thing which, although it was inspired by caution, turned out to be a bad device. He took the slender reata from the hands of Bill and laid it at a distance on a table. After that, they took Reata himself up the stairs into the second story of the fort and put him into a room with thick walls. It had a window more fitted for rifle shooting than for the giving of light and air. That window was hardly a foot high, and it certainly seemed less than two feet wide. It was placed, moreover, a good five feet from the floor, so that it would have needed a snake, and a long snake, to get out at that hole in the wall.

But, if one were actually through the window and in the deeps of the embrasure, the dull, rushing sound of the river that ran under the walls with a noise like that of a distant wind, or a coming storm, would have discouraged any but a winged thing.

When they got Reata up there in that room, with a bit of a wooden cot to serve him for a bed, and no bedding to put on it, they stood around for a time. There was the banker, Decker, and the colonel, and Bill, and Steve Balen.

Only two of them counted in the eyes of Reata. The first was Steve Balen, against whom he now had a grudge. The second was Decker, for whom he was genuinely sorry. As for Bill, he was a good fellow but he didn't matter. Reata only wanted to forget that Colonel Lester was the father of Agnes Lester.

Of course, the colonel did most of the talking. He said: "Reata . . . if that's the name . . . you see where you are. You see what happens to you when you stand out against the law. Now, then, be sensible and tell us everything that you know."

Reata looked up at him with a sidelong smile. "I know that Manuel is a good cook," he said.

Balen said, as the colonel exclaimed impatiently: "Look here. The only way to get anything out of him is to throw in the steel."

"Throw it into him, then," said the colonel. "For my own part, I think it is a crying pity that the whipping post has been abandoned. That would bring some of these young whippersnappers to time."

Balen stood a little closer to Reata. "We

330

can get enough things on you," he said, "to throw you into jail. And we're goin' to do it, Reata. It's too bad, because you've done some mighty good things. But we've got to find out what you know. Will you talk?"

"The fact is, Balen," said Reata, "that I like you so well that talking isn't enough for me. I'd have to take a lot of time to handle you the way I intend to handle you someday."

"The whole of it is that you won't talk, eh?" said Balen.

"Of course, I'll talk," said Reata.

"Very well, then. Where's Phelps?"

"Phelps? I've no idea where he is." For, in fact, he could not tell exactly where the Gypsies were camped this night.

"Look here, Reata. How did you find out where Phelps was kept in the house of Colonel Lester?"

"I've never been inside the colonel's house." That was true, also. Unless the cellar were accurately considered a part of the house.

"Let's go back to the night you stole the gold from the Jumping Creek marsh."

Again Reata smiled. "Balen," he said, "why do you think I'm such a fool? Even if I stole the stuff, would I be willing to tell you about it?"

"Reata," said Balen, "we sure can have you in jail, and we're goin' to do it."

"Balen," said Reata, "you mean well. But sometimes I think your hand is a great deal faster than your brain."

Balen colored with a sudden anger.

"There's no good talking to the insolent puppy!" exclaimed the colonel. "Let him go. We'll see what a competent judge can do about him in the morning. Is there any way he can get out that window? Or shall we tie him up?"

Balen said: "He might wriggle himself through that window. If he did, he'd have a hundred-foot drop down a sheer wall to the bottom of the creek. There's a ten-foot rise of wall above the window to the edge of the roof. He'd need to have a rope ladder lowered for him before he could get away. Close him up in this room, and I'll spend the rest of the night outside the locked door. If he comes out through that, he'll kind of wish that he hadn't."

There was about Balen the surety of a man who has had to trust himself through many a hard pinch, and who had rarely failed. But the eyes of Reata were glimmering with dangerous brightness as they searched the stern face of the foreman.

"That's all, then," said the colonel.

"We'll let him think things over till morning. If we can connect him with that bank robbery, it'll mean the best part of his life in prison, I hope."

The banker spoke for the first time, saying: "Well, to give pain to another man doesn't help an invalid."

After the others went out, Reata kept thinking about that last remark. To give pain was no help to a sufferer. There was nothing in revenge, therefore. Still, Reata wanted to get his hands on Steve Balen, particularly because Balen was the only man of the lot capable of really appreciating him. To be attacked by Balen with this persistence was a sort of treason.

Reata stretched himself on the cot. A cold wind struck in through the window and began to chill him, but if he were cold now, he would be far colder before the morning came, and the only thing for him to do was to harden himself against the discomfort and strive to forget his body. That could be done. He had done it before on long desert marches and in hurricanes above timberline. Now he made himself leave his body far behind while his mind dwelt on other things.

The Gypsy girl was the chief problem. It seemed to him that the greatest mystery in the world was what went on behind her eyes. If he could ever fathom that. . . .

Something tapped at the wall outside his window. He sat up and listened for a moment. Then there was a light hissing sound in the air and a light noise as of a falling rope on the floor of his room. He was off the cot in an instant, and his fingers touched the familiar hard, supple round of his own precious lariat! He gathered it rapidly, and found the weight on an end of it, by means of which it had been hurled through his window. With that slender bit of rope in his hands, he felt his strength renewed and remade.

There were only two ways out of the room. One was through the locked door — beyond which were Balen and his guns. The other way was through the narrows of the window, which would lead to the impossible situation which Balen had described.

Who could have thrown him the rope? Old Manuel was fairly friendly, but he would not have risked such an interference. There remained Georg — who might be very grateful — and Miriam. One of the two, or both of them, must have purloined the reata. It had been thrown in to him because they knew that with this for a weapon he had never failed to solve the most difficult problem that faced him.

He tapped on the door. Instantly the voice of Balen murmured: "Hello?"

"That you, Balen?" he asked.

"Aye, it's me."

"Why not come in and have a talk?"

"Are you ready to talk?" asked Balen eagerly.

"Why not?" said Reata. "Why should I stay in here and freeze?"

"I'll come in," said Balen. "But you back up across the room."

Reata obeyed.

"Sound off," said Balen.

"I'm here," said Reata.

"All right," said Balen, and, when the sound of Reata's voice had assured him that his prisoner was at a distance, Balen turned the key and pushed the door open. He was revealed, then, holding a lantern in one hand, and a six-gun in the other. The gun followed his eyes across the room until it found Reata and settled upon him. "There you are, eh?" said Balen. "Glad to see you, Reata. It's cold in here, all right."

"A little talk would warm us both up," said Reata. "Take that chair over in the corner." It was a little folding stool to which he pointed.

"All right," said Balen. "I wouldn't mind

a chat with you, Reata."

He still kept the revolver pointed at the prisoner, but he turned away a little to get to the stool. The instant his head had turned, Reata struck. It was, in fact, like the striking of a snake, that swift underhand flick of the forearm that shot the noose of the lariat at Balen.

The noose gripped his arms, paralyzed him, and the resultant powerful jerk staggered him off balance. The first loop of the thin rope gripped him about the throat, and Balen stood helpless to move or to yell. He could do nothing except pull the trigger of his Colt, but this was jammed right against his thigh by the grip of the lariat, and a bullet out of it would merely plow into his own leg.

"Any yelling?" asked Reata, as he twitched the gun away from those nerveless fingers.

Balen shook his head. He was rapidly being stifled.

"All right, then," answered Reata, and loosened the strangling pressure of the noose. "We'll tie you safe, Balen, and then we still might have a little talk together."

Balen said with some emotion: "Reata, I'd rather have ten bullets through me than be found inside this here room in the morning, tied up."

"Brother," answered Reata, as he made fast the arms of Balen behind his back, "there's nothing that I'd like better than to make you comfortable. But the fact is that you asked for trouble, and you're going to get it."

"If you're a wise man," answered Steve Balen, "you're goin' to cut my throat now. Because if I live, I'm goin' to spend my life trailing you, old son!"

"Lie face down on that cot," said Reata.

Balen obeyed, and he was tied hand and foot to the wooden frame of the cot. With his own handkerchief, Reata gagged his victim. Then he paused to make and light a cigarette. He smoked it out, sitting at the side of Balen, listening to his breathing to make sure that the gag would not stifle him. It was not the habit of Reata to hurry, when speed was not absolutely indicated. He was sitting beside his captive, when he heard a man's voice call from down the hall: "Ho, Steve! Oh, Balen!"

XIII
"THROUGH THE WINDOW"

Reata ran to the door noiselessly. Already the outer hall was awash with swinging light and shadow as someone came down the corridor with a lantern. Reata took the key from the outside of the door, closed it gently, and locked it from the inside. He gritted his teeth with angry impatience, realizing that he had paused there in the room thirty seconds too long. Then he blew out the lantern and waited in the darkness. He heard the footfall pause at the door.

"Hey, Steve!" called the other voice, which was that of Bill.

Of course, there was no answer, and presently a hand rapped on the door.

"Well?" called Reata.

"You ain't got Steve in there, have you?" asked Bill.

"Look in and see for yourself," said Reata.

"Not me," said Bill. "I wouldn't trust myself that much. But I thought that I'd find Balen here. It ain't like him to sneak away from his place."

"He thought that door was strong enough to hold me, maybe," said Reata.

"It's a queer thing," said Bill. "Steve Balen, I'd swear, wouldn't budge from his post."

"Likely he's somewhere stretched out, and having a good rest," said Reata.

"That ain't like him, either. I'll wait here and see when he shows up."

The feet of a chair grated on the stone flooring, as Bill sat down to take up his part of the vigil.

"Hey, Reata!" he called presently.

"Leave me alone, will you?" said Reata. "It's time for me to get some sleep."

"Aye, and that's fair enough," answered Bill.

When his silence was assured, Reata tried the window. If he had a fair level from which to approach it, the window might not have been so difficult. As it was, by standing on the cot, which was exactly under the embrasure, he was able to wriggle his head and one shoulder through. Gradually he worked his body deeper. He could not yet reach the outside edge of the wall, but he managed to get a deep finger hold on a projecting edge of stone, and, with this to pull on, he quickly wriggled his left shoulder through the opening.

He was now half through, and the hardest half, at that. Also, he was thoroughly wedged in his place. But little by little, expelling all the breath from his body and slowly, patiently contorting his muscles, he managed to get through to the hips. These followed, and now he was coiled up on the outer lip of the casement.

He sat on a deeply slanting shelf, which was canting down toward the darkness of the creek cañon. Soon his eyes were familiar with the starlight, until he was able to see the depth of the gorge, which was cut away far below the foundations of the fort. The opposite bank of the narrow ravine was higher than that on which the fort had been built, and there, under a tree, he made out two dim figures.

He waved his hand. After a moment, he made out that they were waving in return, and his surety increased that these must be Georg and the girl. If so, well, Steve Balen owed them something other than gratitude.

An occasional roughness of the stonework gave him foot and handhold so that he ventured to stand on the outer lip of the casement and look up. He could see, now, the edge of the roof above him, and a projecting drain a few feet to the side.

At the same time, danger exploded behind him in the room that he had just left. There was first a gasping sound, and then the voice of Balen, who must have worked the gag from between his teeth.

"Help, Bill! Help here! Reata's getting away!"

Reata, groaning, made a cast upward with his doubled lariat. It barely missed the projecting drain.

"Hey, what you mean?" sounded the dim voice of Bill beyond the door.

"Break down the door, you fool!" yelled Balen. "Raise the place! Call the rest of the men. Reata . . . he's getting away, and I'm tied here hand and foot!"

Reata, making his second cast, dropped the end of his loop securely over the drain. Would it hold him? He heard a great clamor from Bill, who was shouting at the top of his lungs in the outer hall. He heard Bill dashing his weight against that door. Well, it was oak and ought to hold out for a few moments!

Gradually, increasing the pressure on the lariat, Reata finally swung free from the ledge of the casement. He was dangling now, straight over that hundred feet of nothingness that extended between him and the bottom of the creek, and, as he swung there, pendulous, he heard a faint cry from a girl's voice beyond the stream.

After that, he handed himself up cautiously, for the least jar or jerk might cause the lariat to slip from its precarious hold on the drain. Now one more arm haul, and he would have his hold on the drain itself.

In the interior of the fort he could hear the rumbling of footfalls and the crashing of doors, as they were slammed by running men, and he heard the calling of voices, here and there, dimly behind walls. Far louder and closer at hand, he heard the door of the prison room crash down as Bill forced his entrance at last. That meant that Steve Balen, worth any three of the others at such a time, would soon be free. But Reata now had his grip on the drain and was swinging the weight of his body up onto the roof. The slant of it was very mild, and it was covered with strong new shakes. Therefore, he stood up and ran to the roof edge and then down the farther side.

But there was no hope of getting down into the inner court. Already it was full of swinging lights and men who ran here and there. Instead, coiling his lariat as he ran, Reata sped down the side of the roof and crossed the ridge again to the outer side, and there he saw his chance. The watchers had not yet come out to the open. There was a forty-foot drop, to be sure, but he had the length of the rope and a conveniently projecting drain, again, to fasten it to. He made the noose fast here, and was instantly on his way down. Two or three quick shakes and jerks, after his feet were on solid ground, served to free the noose from its grip above, and now, as he leaped back among some trees, he saw a quick current of men flow around the corner of the building.

The voice of Steve Balen led them on. His angry, snapping directions scattered them. Some he sent down the side of the wall. Others he told to fall back and scan the roof.

"He's somewhere not far off!" declared Balen. "He's most likely up there on that roof. And we want him, boys! I'm goin' to have the hide off of him for what he done to me this here night, and I'm goin' to have the hide off of them that got the reata back to him! Scatter . . . and use your eyes!"

They used their eyes well on the old fort, but Reata was stepping without haste toward the old livery stable where the roan mare and Rags waited for him.

XIV
"THE HORSE HERD"

When he got to the little livery stable, he found things in a bustle and a flurry, so that he almost thought, for a moment, that he would have to give up trying to go in and take Sue away with him tonight. He took refuge at the corner of the big-mouthed entrance until he made out the step and the face of Georg and the voice of Miriam somewhere in the shadows.

Then he saw her coming toward the door, leading Sue, with Rags posted as usual in his special place in front of the saddle. Miriam had arranged the entire thing, Reata could be sure. It was like her to be so forehanded as to think of getting the mare ready for him the instant that he was able to escape from the fort.

When he went up to her, she gave him hardly a word, except an injunction to hurry. It was Georg who gripped his hand so warmly and said: "You see, Reata! Day or night, while I live, if you call me, I shall be ready. But . . . death of my heart! . . . when I saw you dangling over the creek, I thought you were gone. Then Miriam dragged me and reminded me, and we came galloping here as fast as we could."

The girl stood a little back, smiling somewhat, nodding at Reata. She had not had time to change from the circus clothes that she had worn at the fort. She had over them a long, open-faced cloak, and Reata could see the dim shimmer and life of the crimson silk beneath. She kept nodding a bit as though in approval. There was something matronly, or sisterly, in her attitude, and this troubled Reata.

He went up to her and took her hands. She let her head tilt back while she looked up at him with a surveying glance and a smile that seemed still full of a rather impersonal admiration, and also there was a brightness, a mere touch of amusement.

"What did you do in there? What did you do to Steve Balen?" she asked him.

He noticed that her hands were cool and limp in his grasp. Her attitude put all the danger in the past.

"Steve is behind me," he said. "I'm not thinking about him."

"If you don't think about him, he'll get ahead of you again," said the girl, "and he's a dangerous fellow."

"Listen!" said Reata.

Out of the distance there was a muffled chattering of guns.

"Steve and the others have found a shadow, I guess," said the Gypsy girl.

"I want to know what you're thinking of me just now," said Reata. "As a sort of distant cousin, or a brother, or a man who loves you?"

"I'm thinking of you as Reata," she answered.

"What shall I make of her, Georg?" asked Reata, for the Gypsy had come close to them, urging Reata to be gone.

"Who can make anything of her?" said Georg.

Reata, with an exclamation, turned suddenly to the roan mare. He overpaid the old Negro by several measures, and threw himself into the saddle. Only for an instant he paused to grip the hand of Georg in a last farewell.

"I'd still be there in the fort, waiting for the daylight and jail," said Reata. "They would have cooked up an excuse to keep me there. I'll never forget, Georg."

"Hi!" said Georg. "When it is I that must talk of never forgetting!" He added: "Besides, it was Miriam who stole back the reata from under their eyes. While she

smiled, she stole it. It was she who planned
everything. Now ride! Ride fast! I hear them
just like hornets in the air!"

One last glance Reata had of the girl, still
leaning a hand against the wall, aloof,
smiling as if at an active child. Then he rattled over the wooden floor, and the roan
mare went down the street with her long
and flowing stride.

So they came out of Chester Falls into the
open country. He should have asked them
about Pie Phelps, he thought. But if Pie
were not well, one of them would have remembered to tell him. Phelps would be all
right in the Gypsies' hands. If he had never
been well treated before, for the sake of
Georg's spared life and through the influence of the girl, they would be kind to big
Phelps. That was some consolation. Behind
him, he heard the sounds of confused riding
hither and yon, growing dimmer and
dimmer, which showed that the search was
continuing busily for him in the streets and
perhaps through all the rooms and damp
cellars of the fort. What a fury the colonel
would be in. What a hot and festering rage
would possess Balen!

To have been found locked and tied and
gagged inside the room over the door of
which he had been set to guard a prisoner —

could there be a greater humiliation than this? Thereafter, some men would venture a ghost of a smile, when the name of Steve Balen was mentioned, and they would smile a little when they heard the tale repeated. It would grow in the telling; stories always do on the range. Reata felt that his revenge on Balen was complete enough. As the lights of the town died down and drew together behind him, Reata could turn his mind to another subject.

There was a moon yonder behind a river of clouds that seemed to be flowing up the long hill of heaven. Sometimes it whitened the high mists like flying spume, and again it was a vague light that showed mere rivulets of brightness coursing through a black continent by many meanderings. That same light, perhaps, was being watched by three riders, each with a loaded horse in tow, as they journeyed up the Chester Draw.

They could not have journeyed so rapidly as he had ridden that day. And they were coming almost twice as far by having to cover the long windings of the strange, flat valley, between its cliffs. But, by this time, they must have come fairly close to the end of the draw. It might be, now, that he had in mind the very agent that would blast them free from their loaded treasure horses. It might be that the thought which had come to him, while he watched the glimmering ranks and living coils of the horse herd of the Mexicans, would be sufficient for the purpose which he had in mind.

At any rate, when he came close to the ground where the horses were under guard, he went more slowly, and found by a detour a place where he could come very close, through brush high enough to hide horse and rider. From the verge of it, he looked out on a strange and peaceful scene. That herd had been long enough on the road to learn road manners. It was lying down. There was not a horse up grazing. The area was a good bit larger than that which a cattle herd would have covered, and still the space was not big. It was possible to consider the herd almost as a solid mass. When the moon brightened through a gap in the clouds, it gave a blink and a dull glimmering across the confused bodies.

They seemed too small to be real horses. Seals on a rock might have looked something like this. Around and around and around them rode a single man on the night watch, a lone rider who, as he journeyed endlessly, kept singing a quiet, droning Mexican song. To be sure, that herd must be well broken in, by this time, if the herders felt that they could trust all this mustang wildfire in the hands of a single guard.

Perhaps Reata could surprise them a little. He dismounted and, on foot, left the brush, when the guard was on the farthest side of the great circle. Little Rags went before him, and the roan mare trod stealthily behind.

XV
"STAMPEDE"

At the edge of the herd Reata, with a single
word, brought Sue to her knees, and then she
lopped over silently on her side, thereby
melting into the fringe of the sleeping horses.
To Rags, his master made a few quick gestures and whispered: "Get 'em, boy. Drive
'em. Drive 'em."

Rags pranced ahead, looking gaily, fear-
lessly from the sleeping monsters toward his
master. A final gesture of command started
him going, and he flew in like a fury, running back and forth and in and out, and
every horse he passed received a cut from
those needle-sharp teeth. A dozen horses
were instantly on their feet, snorting. The
noise of their commotion started another
and a longer wave of horses rising before
them. In an instant all the air was electric,
and then into the dim brains of those wild
beasts cut a hissing sound longer and more
deadly than had ever come from a snake.
They were frozen to deadly attention. The
entire herd was up in a flash.

Far away, Reata heard the Mexican guard lifting his voice and singing loudly, then calling: "Pedro! Pedro! The devil is loose in the air!"

At that moment, with another word, Reata made the roan mare spring to her feet, while he caught up Rags in his hand.

That was enough. The sight of horse and man rising suddenly out of the ground made the startled horses nearest at hand squeal with terror. A wild yell that burst out of the throat of Reata as he went in, waving his hat, was hardly needed. That whole herd sprang into movement, as if at a magic signal, and raced away like mad through the dimness of the night.

Out of the dark silhouette of the Mexican camp other human voices now were raised. Men were calling out for horses, but the hobbled saddle horses of the herders were making the best of their way after their wild cousins, and it would be some time before the high-heeled *vaqueros* would be able to overtake them.

Reata had on his hands a fair start, and a herd running in a blind panic; by the grace of good fortune and the point at which he had supplied the proper stimulus, the whole body of horses was headed in the right di-rection, where two hills, a little separated, marked the beginning of the low ranges that opened, funnel-like, into the head of the Chester Draw.

Off to his left, he heard the voice of the night herder, poor devil. He looked back and saw the rider already dropping behind. His horse had probably been wearied by hours of going the monotonous rounds. In any case, it would not be capable of carrying its rider along at a pace to match the un-weighted, panic-swift career of the bronchos. Farther and farther behind fell the rider, and swifter went the herd, until even Sue had to stretch her long legs to keep pace, and the wind of the gallop seemed capable of blowing little Rags off his perch in front of the saddle. How far would they go before they began to slacken?

Right and left, a few stragglers began to fall back, lamed horses or ones that were sore-footed from the long journey on the road. But the main body of the herd went at such a pace that rapidly the hills before them grew higher and blacker, and now the forefront of the mustang horde entered between the shoulders of the hills and beat up instantly a dull and rolling thunder.

It was music to the ears of Reata, who did not need to doubt that his horses would strike the mark now — if only Gene Salvio's impatient spirit had not urged on his companions to such a degree that already they were out of the draw and beyond the hills, somewhere on the plain and headed north. Perhaps, by a freak of chance, they were already in Chester Falls. A very neat freak of chance, if they appeared in that town and were recognized by Colonel Lester!

Now the whole front of the herd dipped down a shute that angled sharply away to the left, with high walls rising on either side of it. It was the beginning of the Chester Draw. Reata, laughing with a reckless happiness, pulled Sue well over past the left-hand wall, riding along the fringe of the top of it, and letting the mare speed with all of her might as the way grew level.

Even the speed of Sue, stretched and straining to her utmost, would never be able to bring her up to the head of that maddened herd before it was deep down the course of the draw. But it brought Reata far enough up to see, well ahead, the triple target at which he was striking. For yonder, in a brightening of the moonlight, he saw three riders coming at a walk, with three led horses behind them. Now they halted, for the thundering of the herd must be in their ears. Now they checked in and turned their animals. Now, as the forefront of the speeding mustangs swept around the nearest bend and poured in a frantic river down the draw, the three men were riding at full speed for the side of the ravine.

They had not a hope! Their leg-weary horses could hardly raise a gallop to compare with the arrow-like flight of that multitude. Through the high-flinging veil of dust that boiled up over the herd, Reata could see the three cutting loose their led horses. Aye, and with breaking hearts they might do that, but it was better so, than to be dragged back by the laggards and knocked down and beaten underfoot by the savage, living torrent. That was why Reata, as he galloped the mare along the edge of the draw, laughed long and loud.

As he came by, following dangerously close to the lip of the ravine, he saw the three barely rush to safety in a small indentation in the wall. Past them stormed the dusty herd, rearing, plunging, kicking like so many devils. Reata had one glimpse of them, and then swept on along the top of the cliff.

For a full hour, the good mare kept to her long-stroking gallop, and then Reata saw the speed of the mustang herd suddenly decrease. Far back among the lame and the halted stumbled the three loaded horses of

Gene Salvio and the others. As the herd slowed to a trot, then to a weary walk, Reata took Sue down the first easy slope that led to the bottom of the draw. There he caught the three burden-bearers of the gold easily, and tied them together by their own lead ropes, and then dragged them out of the Chester Draw and up to the ground above.

All of the four horses needed a rest by that time, so Reata tethered the pack horses to Sue and let them graze at a short distance from the cliff, while he sprawled at ease on the edge of it and smoked cigarettes, and finally, out of the moon haze up the valley, thickened by the still unsettled dust, he saw three men on three tired horses that were barely able to trot. They jogged on among the last of the herd. Gradually they pulled around the next wide-sweeping curve of the draw. So they passed away from the view of Reata.

He sat up, smiling. There was no great hurry. He had dodged Colonel Lester and Steve Balen; he had left Pie Phelps safely in the hands of the Gypsies; he had swept away from Gene Salvio and the others the stolen money of the Decker & Dillon Bank; and, in accomplishing all of these things, he had not shed a single drop of blood.

Before him opened the way back to

Jumping Creek. But it was more than an open way to a town. In restoring the money, he would wipe out the mark against his name. He would be able to hold up his head with the highest.

The thought of Pop Dickerman slid through his mind as a cloud's shadow slides over the face of a hill. But he set his teeth and smiled at the danger. The honest road is always uphill, but he was sure that he could make the grade. On the top — well, even the nature of the happiness that might wait for him there was vague as the moon mist. It might be that he would find Agnes Lester there. It might be that the Gypsy Miriam would be there, no longer smiling with amused, impersonal eyes.

IN MEDIAS RES

About the Author

Max Brand is the best-known pen name of Frederick Faust, creator of Dr. Kildare, Destry, and many other fictional characters popular with readers and viewers worldwide. Faust wrote for a variety of audiences in many genres. His enormous output, totaling approximately thirty million words or the equivalent of 530 ordinary books, covered nearly every field: crime, fantasy, historical romance, espionage, Westerns, science fiction, adventure, animal stories, love, war, and fashionable society, big business and big medicine. Eighty motion pictures have been based on his work along with many radio and television programs. For good measure he also published four volumes of poetry. Perhaps no other author has reached more people in more different ways.

Born in Seattle in 1892, orphaned early, Faust grew up in the rural San Joaquin Valley of California. At Berkeley he became a student rebel and one-man literary movement, contributing prodigiously to all campus publications. Denied a degree because of unconventional conduct, he embarked on a series of adventures culminating in New York City where, after a period of near starvation, he received simultaneous recognition as a serious poet and successful author of fiction. Later, he traveled widely, making his home in New York, then in Florence, and finally in Los Angeles.

Once the United States entered the Second World War, Faust abandoned his lucrative writing career and his work as a screenwriter to serve as a war correspondent with the infantry in Italy, despite his fifty-one years and a bad heart. He was killed during a night attack on a hilltop village held by the German army. New books based on magazine serials or unpublished manuscripts or restored versions continue to appear so that, alive or dead, he has averaged a new book every four months for seventy-five years. Beyond this, some work by him is newly reprinted every week of every year in one or another format somewhere in the world. A great deal more about this author and his work can be found in THE MAX BRAND COMPANION (Greenwood Press, 1997) edited by Jon Tuska and Vicki Piekarski.